*"You must let me go," Sandra said.
"I can't bear to be shut up in this heat.
Can't you see I'm ill?"*

He said that she would feel better if she ate her food.

"How can I eat, when you're keeping me prisoner? It's dreadful in here. You *must* let me go."

He said that he needed her. If he let her go he would lose her.

"But you can't keep me here indefinitely!"

He said that he had too much need of her to let her go.

"If you don't, I'll die," she sobbed.

He said that if only she would do as he asked, he would always take care of her. . . .

FATE WORSE THAN DEATH
by Sheila Radley

Bantam Books offers the finest in classic and modern English murder mysteries. Ask your bookseller for the books you have missed.

Agatha Christie

Death on the Nile
A Holiday for Murder
The Mousetrap and Other Plays
The Mysterious Affair at Styles
Poirot Investigates
Postern of Fate
The Secret Adversary
The Seven Dials Mystery
Sleeping Murder

Patricia Wentworth

The Ivory Dagger
Miss Silver Comes to Stay
Poison in the Pen

Margery Allingham

Black Plumes
Deadly Duo
Death of a Ghost
The Fashion in Shrouds
Pearls Before Swine

Dorothy Simpson

Last Seen Alive
The Night She Died
Puppet for a Corpse
Six Feet Under

Aaron J. Elkins

Murder in the Queen's Armes

P. C. Doherty

The Death of a King

Sheila Radley

Fate Worse Than Death

John Greenwood

The Missing Mr. Mosley
Mosley by Moonlight
Murder, Mr. Mosley

Catherine Aird

Harm's Way
Last Respects
Parting Breath
Slight Mourning

Elizabeth Daly

The Book of the Lion

Ruth Rendell

The Face of Trespass
The Lake of Darkness
No More Dying Then
One Across, Two Down
Shake Hands Forever
A Sleeping Life
A Dark-Adapted Eye
  (writing as Barbara Vine)
A Fatal Inversion
  (writing as Barbara Vine)

FATE
WORSE
THAN
DEATH

Sheila Radley

BANTAM BOOKS
TORONTO · NEW YORK · LONDON · SYDNEY · AUCKLAND

FATE WORSE THAN DEATH

*A Bantam Book / published by arrangement with
Charles Scribner's Sons*

PRINTING HISTORY
Charles Scribner's edition published April 1986
Bantam edition / July 1987

Bantam Books are published by Bantam Books, Inc. Its trademark,
consisting of the words "Bantam Books" and the portrayal of a
rooster, is Registered in U.S. Patent and Trademark Office and in
other countries. Marca Registrada. Bantam Books, Inc., 666 Fifth
Avenue, New York, New York 10103.

PRINTED IN THE UNITED STATES OF AMERICA

O   0 9 8 7 6 5 4 3 2 1

FOR KAY AND BARBARA CRISPIN

1

Waking again to stifling, shuttered darkness, she despaired. If she had to endure much longer, she knew that she would die.

Already she felt ill. After weeks—or was it only days?—of shouting and beating her fists on the door she was too exhausted to weep. Her chest was so tight that drawing breath was painful, her bruised hands throbbed, her head felt as light and inconsequential as a balloon. Her skin was clammy, crawled upon by flies. She kept shivering, despite the summer's heat, and her limbs seemed too heavy to be moved without conscious effort.

She could no longer eat. When food arrived, so too did her new room-mates, rustling and squeaking, their small eyes glowing at her in the dark. Fear and revulsion splattered out of her into the bucket in the corner, and the smell compounded her nausea. She would die if she stayed here. She was going to die.

But dear God, how long would it take?

2

In the hottest August for half a century, everyone wilted. So too did the old climbing roses, the yellow and apricot Gloire de Dijon, the fragrant pink Zephirine Drouhin, that clung to every wall in Fodderstone Green and gave the hamlet the reputation of being the prettiest in Suffolk.

It was also reputedly the smallest and most remote. Fodderstone Green had been purpose-built by an early nineteenth-century Earl of Brandon to house some of his estate workers. The estate was in Breckland, then a tract of heath and twisted pine trees and flinty sheep pasture, haunted by stone curlews

and the peewit cry of lapwings, that covered miles of sparsely
populated upland to the west of Breckham Market.

Although the estate had been broken up in the 1920s and
the Earl's great Hall demolished, the hamlet remained essen-
tially unchanged. Fodderstone Green was officially listed in
its entirety as being of Grade 1 architectural and historic
interest. No new building was permitted and no exteriors
could be altered, although planning restrictions were relaxed
sufficiently in the latter part of the twentieth century to allow
the inhabitants inconspicuous access to electricity, telephones,
and plumbing.

To outward appearance, Fodderstone Green remained a
perfect example of a hamlet in the Gothic Revival style,
designed for picturesque effect. It consisted of ten individual
cottages, bowered among lime trees and dispersed about a
village green. Each cottage was thatched, its roof steeply
pitched and hipped, its pointed windows filled with interlacing
lattices of lead, its arched front door sheltered by a thatched
porch supported on rustic poles. The result was slightly absurd but entirely charming: a setting for a fairy-tale, a city-
dwelling exile's dream of age-old rural England.

It was, of course, a sham. Age-old rural England had never
looked like that. Fodderstone village proper, situated at a
windswept Breckland crossroads a quarter of a mile from the
Arcadian green, was far older and more authentic. But
Fodderstone—a huddle of houses in different building-styles
and materials, together with a plain eighteenth-century pub
called the Flintknappers Arms and a church and a school,
both now redundant because the population had shrunk—was
not picturesque. No sightseers in search of Regency *cottages
ornés* gave Fodderstone a second glance. They lingered instead on Fodderstone Green exclaiming, "Isn't it delightful!"

But that was in summer. In winter, when sightseers no
longer came, the hamlet gave a different impression.

The cottages were built entirely of local material: Suffolk
reed for the thatch, Breckland flint for the walls. But Breckland
flint is not like the rounded cobblestone flints that were once
gathered from the shingle banks of the North Norfolk coast
and used for building in that area: there, the pale-skinned
stones, laid intact in regular rows, make cottage walls look as
warm and chunky as a fisherman's hand-knitted sweater.

Breckland flint is different. In the days when it was used
for building—or for making Neolithic axe-heads, or flintlocks

for eighteenth-century muskets—it had to be hewn out of the underlying chalk in large, irregular nodules. Before use the nodules had to be split into manageable halves or quarters, exposing the black flint inside the thin chalk crust. And when facing material was wanted, for a mediaeval church tower and porch or, as at Fodderstone Green, for early nineteenth-century domestic buildings, small slices of flint were chipped off—knapped—and then mortared together like pieces of a jigsaw puzzle. The resulting wall surfaces were hard and flat and black.

In summer, when the cottage walls were smothered by roses, little could be seen of the knapped flints except an occasional sparkle when the sunlight caught them. But the residents knew that when the roses were dead and the sun no longer shone, Fodderstone Green looked a cold, sombre place. Gloomy. Peculiar. Enough to give you the creeps.

In the month preceding the hottest August for half a century, someone kidnapped Beryl Websdell's gnome.

Garden gnomes are not indigenous to rural Suffolk. Mrs. Websdell's Willum, who had sat on a stone toadstool beside a lily pond in the front garden of her cottage on Fodderstone Green for more than twenty years, was a foreigner from Great Yarmouth. But Beryl was fond of him because her husband Geoff had won him at a fairground shooting-gallery while they were on their honeymoon, and so she gave the plaster gnome an annual spring clean, repairing his weather-beaten features with Polyfilla, repainting his hat green and his jacket red, and fixing an encouraging new string to his fishing-rod even though the goldfish in the lily pond had long since been eaten by a heron.

When the gnome disappeared, in mid-July, Beryl was upset. She didn't think it funny that a ransom note had been spiked on a rose bush by the garden gate, demanding a pound of jelly babies for his safe return. Her friends and neighbours didn't think it funny either; nor did the police. It seemed a particularly cruel trick for anyone to play on a woman whose only daughter had disappeared without explanation two days earlier, just before she was to have been married.

Geoff Websdell had called in the police as soon as the girl disappeared, but they had found no reason to fear for her safety. Her honeymoon clothes had gone with her, and everyone who knew her—with the exception of her understandably aggrieved fiancé—thought that Sandra had found that she couldn't face the marriage, and had cut and run.

Beryl, a joyful Christian ever since she had attended a Revivalist meeting on a more recent holiday in Great Yarmouth, was philosophical about the cancelled wedding. About her daughter she was entirely optimistic, convinced that Sandra would telephone or write just as soon as she had sorted herself out.

But the kidnapping of the gnome was a blow. Beryl's eyes, usually shining with born-again happiness, were temporarily dulled.

"It's only a silly joke," she said with forced brightness to her neighbours, Constance Schultz and Marjorie and Howard Braithwaite; but she and her husband couldn't help wondering whether it *might* have some connection with their daughter's disappearance.

The police wondered the same thing. But on the more probable assumption that it had been nothing more than a casual prank, they advised Beryl to buy the jelly babies and leave them on the stone toadstool on the appointed night. Geoff Websdell kept watch; but the ransom was not collected and Willum was never returned. The jelly babies were still there in their limp paper bag three weeks later, congealed by the heat into a mono-coloured gunge.

Ill as she felt, Sandra Websdell could not passively wait there to die.

She knew now that although he intended her no physical harm, he would never voluntarily let her go. She had of course refused to co-operate, but at the same time she had tried to reassure him by promising that if only he would let her go she would tell no one what had happened. She intended to leave Fodderstone anyway, she told him, and she would say nothing to anyone before she went. But he refused to listen to reason, and everything else she tried—pleading, cajoling, weeping, screaming—all had the same negative result.

She hadn't attempted violence, but a direct attack on him was out of the question. The room, sparsely furnished for her captivity, contained nothing that she could use as a weapon. Besides, he was much too strong for her, even if she still had her health. But her weakness had given her one major advantage: he no longer kept her tethered to prevent her from trying to escape when he came to bring her food and change the buckets.

If she pretended to be amenable, ate enough to build up her strength, she might one day be able to dodge him and make a run for the door.

And then what?

She had no way of knowing exactly where she was. She could make guesses, based on distant and infrequent sounds of vehicles, but she couldn't be sure. She had heard no voices outside, but that didn't necessarily mean that there was no nearby habitation. If only she could get out of this building, she might find help before he caught up with her. It was worth trying, anyway. Anything was better than staying here to rot.

But if she took a chance and ran, she had to be prepared for the fact that he would do everything he could to stop her. He might even lose his head and use force.

She could be hurt. Or worse. Supposing that, in trying to stop her, he panicked and used too much force: supposing he killed her?

It was a hideous risk for her to take. But she felt so ill . . .
Better a quick death, she thought, than this protracted dying.

Confident of her daughter's safety and eventual return, Beryl Websdell got over the loss of her gnome by the end of the following week.

"Oh well, it was just a piece of foolishness," she said, thinking of the kidnapper's potential for salvation. "I expect Willum's been put in someone else's garden for a joke. He's probably in another village, enjoying a change of scene," she concluded, happily unaware that the gnome was no further away than the outskirts of Fodderstone, lying irretrievably damaged in a roadside ditch.

3

Somewhere above the remote corner of East Anglia where the counties of Suffolk, Norfolk and Cambridgeshire meet, a light aircraft buzzed across the cloudless sky.

From the ground, it looked a beautiful day for flying. From 2,000 feet, it was not. The horizon was obscured by a heat haze, and visibility was also hampered by rising smoke from harvested cornfields, where farmers were burning surplus straw. The pilot, a fair sharp-featured man in his middle twenties, shirt-sleeved and wearing sun-glasses, silently cursed the farmers as he searched for the landmarks he needed. With an impressionable passenger beside him in the tiny cockpit, this was no time to be lost.

He checked his heading again, and looked out to the side. Below him was the unmistakable Breckland landscape of Forestry Commission plantations interspersed with large arable fields, grassy heath and older private woodlands. And yes, there was the railway line he was searching for . . . and there was the busy A11 road . . . and there was the bridge carrying the road over the railway. His airfield—the flying club's grass airfield at Horkey—ought to be visible now, south-east of the bridge. It must be there. He'd taken off from it only forty minutes ago.

He banked, and immediately saw the airfield just where it should be on the heading he was flying. His navigation was so exact that the field had been temporarily blocked from his view by the nose of the Cessna. Not bad, not bad at all . . .

He pressed a button on the control yoke and spoke into his headset microphone: "Horkey, this is Golf India Romeo Sierra Romeo, Cessna 152, inbound. Heading 350 at 2,000 feet on QNH 1015, estimating overhead at 20, over."

The reply from the control tower came crackling over the radio. Alison Quantrill, the passenger, taking her first trip in a light aeroplane, marvelled that her pilot found the crackles intelligible. She knew that he wanted her to be impressed, and she was. There had been times in the past when she had found his self-assurance repulsive, but the thoroughness of

6

his pre-flight checks and the quiet confidence with which he handled the aircraft filled her with admiration. Her father had often said, irritably, that the most maddening thing about Martin Tait was that he really was as good a detective as he thought he was. And as good a pilot, too, Alison intended to tell her father. Flying with Martin was exhilarating, the most exciting thing she'd done for years.

He repeated the runway and QFE instruction, reset his altimeter and then turned his head to glance at her, enjoying the sparkle in her eyes. Pity she looked so much like the old man, his former boss: same green eyes, same dark hair, except of course that Doug Quantrill's was now streaked with grey. But there the resemblance ended, thank God. Alison was lovely . . .

There was no need for him to touch her in order to draw her attention. He had given her a headset to wear so that they could speak through the intercom instead of having to pitch their voices against the throb of the engine. But she was wearing a sleeveless dress and he wanted to feel her cool bare arm under his fingers.

"There's the airfield," he told her. "When we're over it, we descend to 800 feet and then make a circuit before landing. And look, there's Fodderstone, the village where my aunt lives. You see how near it is to the aero club—less than ten minutes by car. An ideal place to come and spend a flying holiday."

Martin Tait was looking forward to his leave. It had already been postponed twice on account of the demands of his job as a member of the Regional Crime Squad. An undisguisedly ambitious man, he was always ready to put work before pleasure; but this particular leave would have a special flavour. Although his current car was a used Alfa Romeo Alfasud 1.5 rather than the new 2000 CTV coupé he aspired to (on his way to the bachelor's dream, a Porsche 944) he had just acquired a more distinctive possession. Having recently qualified as a private pilot, he knew that he was the only police inspector in the county force to be part-owner—although his share was, admittedly, only a twentieth—of a two-seater aeroplane.

Not surprisingly, since his only income was his salary, he had no plans to marry in the near future. Time enough for that when he was thirty or a Chief Superintendent, whichever came sooner. It would be important to choose his future

wife carefully, because he intended to be a man in the public
eye: the youngest-ever Chief Constable in the country. After
that, in due course, Her Majesty's Chief Inspector of Con-
stabulary; or else Chief Commissioner of the Metropolitan
Police. Either job would earn him a knighthood. By the time
he was ready to retire from the force, in his middle fifties, he
and his wife would be Sir Martin and Lady Tait.

And by then, in thirty years' time—hopefully much sooner,
within the next ten years, but it seemed indecent to anticipate the death of a member of his family of whom he was
quite fond—he would have inherited a sizeable legacy. He
wasn't sure what it would amount to, but at a guess at least a
hundred thousand. Certainly enough to put him in the BMW
bracket. Perhaps he'd even be able to afford to buy a Cessna
of his own . . .

The airfield was directly below him. He called the control
tower: "Horkey—Sierra Romeo overhead."

"*Sierra Romeo, roger,*" crackled the radio. "*Call downwind.*"

The aircraft bucked a bit as Tait descended through the
thermals to circuit height. "You'll get a very good view of
Fodderstone as we fly the downwind leg," he said to Alison.
"My workload will be heavy at that stage so I shan't have
time to point out Aunt Con's cottage, but it's one of a small
group round a green just to the north of the village. Hers is
the one with the row of beehives in the back garden. I told
her that I'd be giving you a flight before presenting myself on
her doorstep, so if you see her down there you might wave to
her for me."

Alison nodded, too eagerly intent on absorbing new experi-
ences to reply.

Tait smiled to himself as he levelled at 800 feet and turned
on to the crosswind leg. He liked the way Alison had matured
since he'd first met her, two years before; but he loved the
fact that maturity didn't inhibit her from showing her excitement over this flight. She really was an attractive girl. For
the dozenth time in the past few weeks, ever since she'd
returned from London to live and work in Yarchester and
they had begun to see each other regularly, he wondered
whether she would eventually make the right wife for him.
Was she suitable material for the future Lady Tait?

If he had the money to marry now, instead of having to
wait until he reached an adequately salaried rank, he might
well be tempted to take a chance on her. With no money,

marriage was out of the question; but he was coming to the conclusion that unless he put in some kind of claim, he would run the risk of losing her.

His immediate problem, though, was to get her safely to the ground. He turned the aircraft again. "Sierra Romeo downwind," he radioed, before making routine checks on the Cessna's fuel supply and carburettor heat, and the security of his own and his passenger's harness.

He blew her a kiss as he tested the fastening of her seat belt. "Happy landing," he said. "And many more to come."

"Hope so!" Alison agreed.

She gazed down at Fodderstone, fascinated by the unusual intimacy that the low-level overhead view provided. There was the main street, the crossroads, the church; a farm and its outbuildings; a pub and its car park. She could see how isolated the village was, miles from any other community, surrounded by large pale harvested fields, scattered copses and belts of woodland. But what intrigued her most was the detail that could never be seen from ground level: the layout of everyone's garden, and the pattern of unmetalled tracks and paths that linked the more isolated houses with the village and its adjoining hamlet.

Fodderstone Green, where Martin's Aunt Con lived, was unmistakable. But although Alison looked down into the back garden of every cottage, she could see no beehives, and no one stood there waving.

4

Lois Goodwin, wife of the landlord of the Flintknappers Arms at Fodderstone, hated serving behind the bar.

She didn't mind the hard work involved in running the pub, although she hadn't realized before she started how much sheer drudgery would be needed to keep the inconvenient old premises clean. Nor had she bargained for the permanent tiredness that would set in after she and her husband had worked sixteen hours a day, seven days a week, for over a year without a break.

But Phil, who had worked as a salesman for a kitchen-unit

manufacturer, had lost his job. His company had been taken
over by a German firm with an unpronounceable name, and
Phil had had a difference of opinion with the management in
Mannheim. Using his severance pay to buy the tenancy of a
country pub and work for himself had seemed to him a great
idea; Lois had been reluctant, suspecting that it would be less
idyllic than it sounded. But she had agreed, and so she saw
no point in moaning about it now.

What she had come to dread, though, was being left alone
behind the bar. She knew she wasn't good at being jolly with
people. She'd never enjoyed going to pubs, and the prospect
of standing behind the bar chatting to strangers for hours at a
time alarmed her. She had told her husband so when he first
began enthusing.

"Don't worry about that, love!" Phil had exclaimed. "I'll
serve the drinks. You concentrate on doing the food, and
leave the talking to me!"

That was typical of him. All talk. He'd once been his
company's Salesman of the Year. True, he always served
behind the bar when it was mildly busy, in the evenings and
at weekends; but he disliked the lunch-time regulars just as
much as Lois did—although for a different reason—and so he
had taken to rushing off in the middle of the day and leaving
her on her own.

"Must go to the bank!" he'd exclaim through his catfish
moustache. Phil Goodwin still retained the facial hair and the
tinted spectacles that had been fashionable among young
executives when he'd won his award. He also retained the
sense of urgency that had enabled him to outsell his colleagues. Staying in one place and waiting for customers to
come to him was, as he quickly discovered once he became
landlord of the Flintknappers, sheer frustration.

When he couldn't escape from his duties, he shed his
surplus energy by hustling about the pub emitting noise. He
never merely spoke. Verbalizing his natural aggressiveness,
he chaffed the customers loudly, roared with laughter, cursed
the brewery, hollered at the draymen, bawled out his children, shouted at or for his wife.

"Just going to get some change for the till!" he'd yell to her
as he took off in mid-morning, as though the bank were
round the corner instead of fifteen miles away in Breckham
Market. Or, "Just going to the cash-and-carry, must get another case of potato crisps!" Or, "Just going to get a haircut!"

Useless for Lois to remind him that a local man did part-time barbering in a back room of the Flintknappers Arms every Friday night; Phil was very particular about the cut of his thinning hair.

"You'll be all right on your own!" he would cry encouragingly, lifting his moustache in the shape of a smile although his eyes usually slid guiltily away from hers. "Bound to be quiet at lunch-time. Love you!" he would call over his shoulder as he fled, by way of acknowledgement that whatever he might be after in Breckham Market, he couldn't do without his wife.

He was right about the quietness of the pub at midday. It wasn't the unlikely prospect of busy-ness that alarmed Lois; if new customers were suddenly to flock in, clamouring for beer and bar snacks, she would rush about to serve them, flustered but willing to work. What bothered her was the quietness itself, the fact that there were usually no more than four or five customers who had all the time in the world.

In the evenings and at weekends the pub attracted what Lois thought of as normal people: those inhabitants of the village who went out to work during the day, whose horizons—and therefore whose conversation—extended far beyond Fodderstone. But it seemed to her that the only customers who came in at lunch-time were eccentric, or idle, or both. She found them difficult to understand, and their attitude towards her was irritating and, ultimately, alarming.

When she faced them on her own Lois felt trapped, a prisoner behind the bar. She was a neatly attractive woman in her mid-thirties, her figure still good, her smooth fair hair held back from her round face by a band of ribbon, her twice-daily fresh blouse either pie-frilled or tied at the neck in a bow. But her anxious brown eyes and full, slightly drooping cheeks gave her the look of a worried hamster, and it was this obvious vulnerability that was the attraction for the lunch-time regulars. Realizing that she disliked being teased, some of them liked nothing better than to tease her.

One of their favourite pastimes was to engage her in discussion of the food. Lois was a good cook, and she and Phil had taken over the pub with the intention of building up a trade in hot and cold bar snacks. This was an innovation at the Flintknappers Arms, and the more vocal of the regulars found Lois's chalked-up menus an inexhaustible source of entertainment. They would read them aloud, haltingly, like great stubble-chinned backward boys, solemnly enquiring about the ingredients of each dish; and Lois, hopeful of their custom, had at first explained and described with kindly patience.

But there seemed to be nothing on the menu that they ever fancied. What they would *really* like, they finally said in answer to her desperate enquiry, was a juicy rabbit pie, well flavoured with onions, such as they remembered from their youth.

Anxious to please, Lois went out of her way to procure a rabbit and made them their pie. She chalked it up on the blackboard with pride. Ah, said the regulars, nudging each other, but was it a *fresh wild* rabbit? They knew perfectly well that a lingering strain of the myxomatosis that had decimated the Breckland rabbits in the 1950s had effectively stopped any trade in the creatures.

Lois had no sense of self-preservation. Unwilling to lie, she admitted that the only rabbit she had been able to find was in a deepfreeze cabinet in the International stores at Breckham Market.

Frozen rabbit? said the regulars, scandalized. No, no, that weren't no good. 'Tweren't no use offering them rabbit unless it was fresh from the warren. They couldn't stomach aught else, they said, sniggering surreptitiously. It wasn't until they had gone through a similar routine with their next request, for steak and mushroom pie (*bought* mushrooms? No, no, mushrooms had to be fresh-picked from what used to be the paddock at the old Hall. Hoss muck, that was what mushrooms needed—why, you used to be able to gather great ol' things as big as saucers, nothing to beat 'em for flavour. They couldn't fancy *bought* mushrooms) that Lois realized it was all a tease. With the exception of Howard Braithwaite and Desmond Flood, not one of the regulars had any intention of spending money at the Flintknappers on food.

Lois was vexed. She thought their joke stupid and inconsiderate, and she allowed her hurt feelings to show. The men loved it, watching with coarse-featured, gap-toothed glee as her cheeks reddened and her breasts heaved with suppressed indignation. They felt no malice towards her, but they shared a streak of ancient rural barbarism that led them in instinctive pursuit of anything defenceless. Sensing her growing fear of them, they never tired of tormenting her.

It was so easy to fluster Lois. They soon found that they could take it in turns to get her in a tizzy by calling out an order while she was serving someone else and then claiming, when she had pulled their beer, that they had ordered something different.

And then there was the money game. "You've given me the wrong change!" one of them would protest. The others would support him, staging loud and inaccurate reconstructions of the transaction and confusing Lois completely. It was not their intention to rob her, but they always carried the joke and its many variations to the brink, harrying her until she was prepared to placate them with money. Only then, when she stood at bay beside the open till, would the originator relax and look again at the change she had given him and say with a smirk, "Ah, no—hold you hard. I do b'lieve you're right, my dear. My mistake."

Lois grew to hate the lot of them. But as long as she was left in sole charge of the bar only on the odd occasion, she was prepared to endure. What finally drove her to protest to her husband was the unusually hot weather that occurred during their second summer at the pub; the low-ceilinged bar room became unbearably stuffy, and the mingled smells of the customers' beer and sweat sickened her. And now she was forced in there much more often, because Phil had taken to disappearing almost every day.

When she complained one morning, her husband was noisily incredulous.

"Oh come *on*, Lois—don't try to tell me you're run off your feet, I can see from the takings that you aren't. Surely you can give me a break at lunch-time, considering that I'm stuck behind the bar every single night of the year!"

Lois explained why she found the regulars unpleasant. She longed to tell them to take their custom elsewhere, she said, but she was afraid to do so because trade was so slack.

Phil Goodwin shouted in alarm. "Don't do anything to turn them away, for God's sake! The takings are too low as it is, we need every penny we can make. And don't be so sensitive—if they try to tease you, just laugh it off. They're all trogs," he added with contempt; he avoided his midday customers because he despised them. "They must be direct descendants of the Neolithic flint-miners!"

"Not all of them. You can hardly call Howard Braithwaite a trog, or Desmond Flood. They don't belong to this part of the country any more than we do. But that doesn't make them any easier to deal with. I feel sorry for Desmond—it's humili-

ating for him that Sandra went off just before they were going
to be married—but I'm glad he's stopped lunching here now.
He was always such a misery. As for Howard, he's bad-
tempered and picky with his food. From the way he barks
and complains you'd think he couldn't stand the sight of me,
and hated coming here. But he hides behind the *Financial
Times* so that he doesn't have to talk to the other customers,
and sometimes he holds the paper upside down. Whenever I
happen to look in his direction I can see him peering at me
over his half-moon glasses . . . I don't like him. He's creepy."

Her husband dismissed her unease. "An old fool having
harmless fantasies. Ignore him."

"And Charley Horrocks isn't a trog either, not with that
upper-crust accent. But he's the most difficult of the lot."

"Charley Horrocks is a nutter!" Goodwin exclaimed. "If
you can get rid of him, do. He'll be no loss!"

"Don't think I haven't tried. But I can't deal with him,
Phil—he's impossible to communicate with. I'm sure he's
been getting worse lately, the heat must have gone to his
head. Couldn't you make a point of staying here today and
getting rid of him yourself?"

"Ah, well, yes, I'd stay if I could, love. But I have to go
and see the accountant. My appointment's at twelve—God, is
that the time, I'll have to rush!"

Lois wasn't surprised by his reaction. She knew her husband too well. For one thing, he wasn't really any better at
coping with the regulars—and with Charley Horrocks in
particular—than she was. For another, he was obviously up
to something.

The pub closed, as the licensing laws demanded, from
two-thirty in the afternoon until six in the evening. The
Goodwins had those few hours to themselves each day, and it
would have been more practical for Phil to see his accountant
then. It would also be a useful saving of petrol if Lois could
take the opportunity to go to Breckham Market with him and
do the shopping. So if Phil deliberately made his appointment at a time when she couldn't accompany him, it must be
because he had some good reason for wanting to shake her
off. Probably he wasn't going to see the accountant at all;
perhaps he wasn't even going to Breckham Market . . .

"You've plenty of time," she suggested brightly. "You needn't
leave for at least half an hour. I've been thinking—if you
really must go into town today, why not take the children to

the swimming-pool? They'd love that. I'll see if I can find them."

"No!" Phil used the second finger of his right hand to make a characteristically nervy tour of his three-sided moustache, as though to make sure that it was still there. "No point in trying to find them, they'll be in the forest with their friends. Anyway, I can't hang about, you know how difficult it is to park in Breckham. I'd better leave now. Listen, don't worry about Charley Horrocks, everybody knows he's harmless. Just don't let him con you, that's all. The trogs are honest, I'll say that for them, but Horrocks will do us down if he can. Don't for God's sake give him any credit! All right? Good girl—"

As a parting gesture, he patted her bottom. It was not a form of caress that Lois greatly cared for at the best of times and she particularly disliked it when, as then, it was done absent-mindedly. But she took it as conclusive proof of what he was up to.

She recognized all the symptoms. He was on the prowl again. Whenever he was dissatisfied and restless, he went looking for excitement with another woman. She minded, of course; but she knew better than to take any of his affairs seriously. Phil was always full of talk, but not much use when it came to action.

5

The Flintknappers Arms opened at ten-thirty in the morning, every day of the week, and closed finally at eleven at night. The Goodwins did all the work themselves, except on Saturday mornings when they employed Beryl Websdell to give the bar room a thorough cleaning.

They rarely got to bed until well after midnight, and were always up again before seven each morning. There was always so much for both of them to do: last night's final glasses and dirty ashtrays to be washed, the bar towels to be laundered, the ladies' and men's lavatories to be swabbed out, everywhere to be cleaned and polished; hot and cold food to be prepared, the bar to be checked and restocked, the till to be cashed up, crates of empty bottles to be heaved out, crates of full bottles to be heaved in. The cellar work alone—disconnecting empty beer casks, cleaning the pipes, connecting full casks—took Phil Goodwin anything up to two hours a day.

Lois had to fit in her ordinary domestic work in their private quarters as and when she could. One of her grievances about being tied to the bar from ten-thirty to two-thirty was that it was such a waste of her time when she had so much to do elsewhere. In a smaller, more compact building, it might have been possible for her to keep an eye on the bar from her kitchen; at the Flintknappers the two were separated by a lobby, a long passage and four doors. In a more civilized community, the regulars might postpone their visit to the pub until at least noon; in Fodderstone, Charley Horrocks was invariably on the doorstep at opening time every day of the week, every week of the year.

"Hottest August for half a century or I'll eat m'hat!" he boomed as he shambled past Lois on his way to his favourite bar stool. His massive body was clothed in a government-surplus khaki shirt and trousers of voluminous World War II cut, and his features were overshadowed by a solar topee as worn in India in the days of the British Raj. He frequently asserted that the hat had been bequeathed to him by his grandfather, the third Earl of Brandon; but everyone in Fodderstone knew perfectly well that Charley had bought it for fifty pence at a village jumble sale.

"Hottest, or I'll eat m'hat," he repeated as he sank panting on to the stool. His beetroot complexion was glazed with sweat. "Eat m'hat," he concluded, taking it off to reveal sparse grey hair hanging limp about his ears. He wiped his forehead with his sleeve. Lois was still at the double doors, fastening them back so as to let in as much air as possible, and having recovered his breath he summoned her by slapping his hand on the counter. "Service! Let's have some service here!"

Lois should have taken a firm line with him from the first, but she had been over-anxious to please every customer. Now it was too late for her to try to insist on courtesy. She glared at his back, pursed her lips above the pie-frill of her collar, and went round to her side of the bar, silent with a disapproval that Charley failed to notice.

" 'Mornin', m'deah," he boomed with lordly affability, as

though he had only just seen her. Unlike her husband, he never shouted. He had no need to. He possessed the naturally penetrating voice of the horsey upper classes, having been bred to make himself heard above the noise of pounding hooves. "I'll have a pint of your best."

Lois closed her eyes and drew a deep breath. She knew by heart how the conversation would proceed. It was always the same, every day of the week, every week of the interminable year.

"Only if you pay cash."

He affected not to hear. When she repeated it he blustered, "Haven't been to the bank today. Just put it on the slate."

His tone of command never failed to infuriate her, but she kept her dignity. "You know perfectly well that we don't give credit."

"And why not, hey? Are you implyin' that my credit isn't good? Now see here, m'family used to own this village, and most of Breckland as well. My credit's good throughout Suffolk. Just you pull me a pint, and let's have no more of this bloody nonsense."

"Not until you pay for it in cash."

"For God's sake . . ." He tugged a chequebook from the pocket on his bulging hip. "Change one of these for me, then. Twenty pounds'll do to be going on with."

Lois took a second deep breath. Charley Horrocks had owed them money for over a year. Phil frequently demanded repayment, and every so often Charley would condescend to write him a cheque; but the cheques always bounced.

"You know we don't change cheques without a bank guarantee card," she said.

Charley huffed and puffed, attempting to blow down her defences. No gentleman, he asserted, could be expected to carry pieces of plastic about his person. "Fetch me your employer, m' good woman," he commanded, waving his chequebook. Lois's hamster cheeks quivered but she said nothing, knowing that he would eventually discover that he had just enough cash in his pockets for his immediate needs.

When credit was refused him Charley Horrocks could always produce a small amount of cash, although never enough to pay his debts. His demand for credit was a daily routine, no longer a serious try-on but a form of conversation. He never allowed silence to fall. When he wasn't giving com-

mands and making assertions ("This beer's orf," was one of
his favourites, though he never hesitated to drain his glass),
he reminisced to her about "M' grandfather the third Earl."

Initially, Lois had felt some sympathy for Charley Horrocks.
She had seen him as a mountainous toddler, abandoned in
Fodderstone by his family and making infantile demands for
attention. No one seemed to know or care about him: he
lived alone, did no work, had no friends. Lois was a good
listener and would at first have been prepared to lend him an
ear, but now that she had been forced into his company more
often she had changed her mind. She found him highly
objectionable, not merely an ill-mannered snob but a thorough-
going pig.

Charley always took to the pub his favourite newspaper,
the *Sun*. As soon as the other regulars—the ones Phil Goodwin referred to as "the trogs" —came in, Charley would open
the paper at the page 3 nude photograph, lay it flat on the bar
under Lois's eye and discuss the merits of the girl of the day
in loud agricultural terms.

Then he would comb through the newspaper and read out
any items that he could relate in a derogatory way to women.
All women who had been murdered, raped or battered had,
according to Charley, "arsked for it." Any women who spoke
out in public, for whatever cause and however reasonably, in
his opinion deserved "a good thrashin'."

"A *bloody* good thrashin'," he would add with relish, and
the trogs would snigger their support, glancing sideways at
Lois to see how she was reacting. She hated them all for it.
Separately, Charley and the trogs were disagreeable enough;
together, egging each other on, they were abominable.

The doorway darkened as two of his drinking companions
slouched in, hot and permanently grimy. Both self-employed
agricultural contractors, they brought with them smells of
sweat and smoke, and a considerable thirst. Charley stopped
boring on about his grandfather and reached happily for the
Sun. Lois braced herself to cope with routine unpleasantness.

But today, something was different. The newcomers, Stan
Bolderow and Reg Osler, thick-set men of the string-vest
generation, were snuffling with laughter. Stan, the shorter of
the two, whose baldness was compensated for by a thick
growth of greying chest hair that frizzed out through the
trellis of his vest, was carrying something behind his back.

"'Morning, Lois," they chorused, their stubble split by gappy grins. "How do, Charley."

They paused expectantly. "Two pints?" Lois enquired, forcing a professional smile.

"Ar," said Reg. His head was well thatched and his face was framed by sideburns, but his oil-stained vest hadn't a single protruding hair. "Two pints o' bitter for us—and a half for Stan's new friend."

Lois was puzzled and cross, as they intended that she should be. "Who do you mean?"

They nudged each other. "Him, o' course," Reg snickered. "Gent with the beard, on the stool here."

Lois looked where he was pointing. At first she could see nothing, but then she stood on her toes and peered across the top of the bar counter.

"What on earth—? Good heavens, it's a—oh, it's absolutely filthy! Take it outside, for goodness' sake!"

Reg and Stan lurched about with laughter. Charley Horrocks rumbled an accompaniment, his great shoulders heaving.

"Take it out!" Lois repeated shrilly. Then, "No, wait a minute." She hurried round to the customers' side of the bar and looked more closely. The object squatting at the stool, two feet high, battered and dirty, was a plaster garden gnome. "Is it Beryl Websdell's?" she asked.

Stan wiped tears of amusement from his eyes with the back of his smoke-grimed hand. "Reckon it must be Beryl's. P'r'aps she'll give me a reward!"

"Bag o' jelly babies, I shouldn't wonder," said Reg. They doubled up again.

"Poor Beryl," said Lois, "she'd be quite upset to see it like this. I'd better give it a scrub before she comes again. Where did you find it?"

The bald-headed man sobered and shrugged. "In a ditch, 'longside the Horkey road."

"How on earth did it get there?"

"Hanged if I know." He became irritable. "What about that beer? We've been burning straw all morning an' I'm wholly dry."

"What were you doin' on the Horkey road?" asked Charley.

Stan took the pint from Lois, and gave him a quick, disagreeable stare. "Minding me own business, bor," he said. The deference that former inhabitants of Fodderstone had

shown towards the family of the Earls of Brandon was not
extended by present-day villagers to the third Earl's grandson.

Charley Horrocks glowered. He found it impossible to
believe that he had no status. "Horkey road be damned," he
sulked. "Those fields were burned orf a week ago. Shouldn't
be surprised if you've been hidin' the stupid gnome yourself."

"Are you calling me a liar?" demanded Stan, his eyes and
biceps bulging. "Why you great bag o' guts, I'll—"

"Leave it," advised his friend with the sideburns. "What's
the betting Charley took the gnome himself, eh?" He gave
Stan a nudge; where the bald man was aggressive, Reg was
sly. "Wanted a bit o' company at nights, did you, Charley?"
he jeered.

"To hell with the pair of you," growled Horrocks. He
turned on Lois. "This beer's orf!" he proclaimed.

Her respite had been brief. The regulars never disagreed
for long when they could unite in teasing her. They began to
comment on the photographic model in Charley's copy of the
Sun, but were almost immediately diverted by the entrance
of a villager who rarely visited the Flintknappers Arms from
one year to the next.

"Well, if it isn't young Christopher!" said Reg, amused.
"How are you, boy?"

The newcomer's youth was relative. Christopher Thorold
was a solid man in early middle-age. But he had such an aura
of shy, clean-shaven innocence that most of his fellow villagers found it impossible to treat him as anything other than a
slow-witted adolescent. His greying fair hair stood up in
unbrushed tufts. He wore a striped flannel shirt, tieless but
buttoned at the neck and wrists despite the heat of the day,
and a pair of old grey trousers that had been torn at the knee
and mended with large uneven stitches of green thread.

"N-nicely, thank you," he replied to Reg's question. He
had no speech impediment, but shyness usually brought his
first words out in a stammer. He stood uneasily just inside
the door of the pub, shuffling his heavy boots and blinking
eyelashes that were as thick and pale as a bullock's. "Er—
'scuse me, Mrs. Goodwin—will you be wanting a load of
firewood?"

The other men shouted with laughter. "Hottest August for
half a century, and he's talkin' about fires!" boomed Charley
Horrocks, slapping his meaty thigh.

Christopher Thorold blinked unhappily. "I can let you

have it a bit cheaper, you see, if you order it now," he appealed to Lois. He was another self-employed man, buying unusable wood from the Forestry Commission and hawking it from door to door.

"You'll have to buy a drink now you're here, Chris," said Reg. "Can't come into a pub without. Me an' Stan are drinking pints—"

"And the same for me," rumbled Charley.

Lois, who was temperamentally incapable of thinking in terms of profit, glared at the regulars. Recognizing Christopher as a fellow victim, she ordered a load of firewood from him and offered him a drink on the house. He refused; but nervously anxious to do the right thing, he took out his purse and insisted on buying a round.

"An' don't forget my friend here," said Stan, pointing to the gnome. "He drinks halves."

Christopher stared, bewildered. "I thought that belonged to Beryl Websdell," he ventured.

Lois had forgotten about it. She went round the counter, picked the gnome up—gingerly, because of its coating of dirt—and put it on the floor at the back of the bar, intending to clean it and return it to its owner. Meanwhile, Stan had seen an opening for some fun at Christopher's expense.

"How come you know that gnome belongs to Beryl?" he wheezed with mock ferocity.

Alarmed by Stan's aggressiveness, Christopher explained uneasily that he recognized the gnome. He'd often seen it in Beryl's garden when he went to deliver wood.

"Oh yes? Well, that's now stolen property, that is. Somebody nicked it, and threw it in a ditch. The police have been enquiring about it."

Christopher's eyelids opened wide for a moment, and then began to blink rapidly over his pale-blue eyes. "I didn't know that . . ."

"They must have overlooked you, then, because they've been trying to find out who knew that Beryl had a gnome. I reckon you could be just the feller they want to talk to!"

"Very likely," agreed Charley, wiping away from his puffy lips the foam from the beer that Christopher had bought him.

"Definitely," confirmed Reg. "When you come to think about it, Stan, young Chris is the obvious suspect. Goes in an' out of everybody's garden, so he can take whatever he likes. Fancied a little bit o' gnome comfort, did you, Chris boy?"

The hot stale air of the bar thickened with the laughter of the three regulars. Christopher Thorold stood among them like a baited bullock, swinging his head, shifting his feet, and blinking in bewildered alarm.

Pitying him, but thankful that she herself was for once not their victim, Lois slipped away from the bar for a few minutes. She took with her Beryl Websdell's Willum, and put him under the scullery tap.

The dirt came off easily enough. But whether, clean, he was in a fit state to be returned to his owner was a different matter. If Lois herself were in Beryl's position, the mother of a daughter who had disappeared, she felt that she would rather not have her missing garden gnome returned to her with the lower half of its body smashed out of recognition.

6

For half an hour after they landed, Martin Tait and Alison Quantrill were still flying.

Exhilarated, happily aware that they were on the way to being seriously in love, they hardly touched the ground as they went from the Cessna to the flying club headquarters. Tait relinquished Alison's hand for long enough to buy cold drinks from the bar, and then carried the glasses out to where she sat in the sun. He lowered himself on to the grass beside her, close enough to touch but not touching. Gradually they fell silent.

Mechanics were at work on aircraft in the hangar some distance away but, apart from a student pilot being debriefed by his instructor in the clubroom, and another instructor on duty in the control tower, the hutted premises were deserted. So were the acres of grass airfield. Hot air shimmered above the empty tarmac of the perimeter track. There was aerial activity at various heights—a jet aircraft leaving its silent contrail at 30,000 feet, a club Cessna climbing to 2,000, another puttering round the circuit at 800, a lark singing as it hovered at 20—but Martin and Alison were conscious only of

their immediate surroundings. Their view had contracted to
the patch of clover-filled grass where they sat, their hearing
was attuned to nothing but each other's breathing.

He gazed at her from behind his sun-glasses, planning an
approach that would secure her as a possible future wife
without at this stage going to the extent of proposing marriage. Alison didn't look at him at all. She had taken the
opportunity to do that while he was preoccupied with the
aeroplane, and she knew well enough the sharply intelligent
contours of his face and the good shape of his fair head. She
had also taken stock of what he was wearing, and she approved of it.

When she first met him, Martin Tait had been a trendy
dresser. She recalled with amusement Cuban heels, a pink
summer suit with flared trousers, perpetually open-necked
shirts, a silver neck chain. He had liked himself so much, in
those days, that she had found it difficult to like anything
about him.

But promotion to inspector eighteen months ago had encouraged him to alter his appearance and wear formal, well-cut
suits and good shoes. His casual clothes, too, had acquired an
expensive air. Today he stayed cool in the heat in a blue
shirt, white trousers, and shoes that looked like Guccis even
if they were not. He had told Alison that he expected promotion to her father's rank by the end of the year, and it was
clear that he intended to be the best dressed as well as the
youngest detective chief inspector in the county force.

Alison welcomed the improvement in his wardrobe as a
sign of maturity. It certainly made him a great deal more
attractive. He was, too, far less brash. She liked him, now . . .
was excited by his confidence, his abilities . . . found him
really rather amazing.

But she was cautious. Her father had once said scathingly
that Martin Tait seemed to think he was irresistible to women.
She had found no difficulty in resisting him two years ago,
partly because of instinctive antipathy and partly because,
having lived with a lover who had made use of her and then
moved on, she had at the time gone off men. She now felt
better disposed towards the male sex in general and Martin
Tait in particular, but she was in no hurry to embark on a
relationship with him or anyone else.

It was undeniable, though, that the sun had shone on her
more brightly in these past few weeks. She lifted her face to

it, listened to the lark, watched the invisible jet spilling trails of salt across the blue cloth of the sky. "Isn't this a brilliant summer?" she said.

"The best I can remember. Glad you came back to Suffolk?"

"Of course. In London I was just a secretary at the BBC, and I love working here in local radio as a presenter. A proper career at last. And there was no point in my having a car in London, with all the parking hassle there, but now I've got wheels of my own . . ."

"I didn't mean that."

He had taken off his sun-glasses and she looked at him for the first time since they had landed. His eyes were an uncomfortably piercing blue: a detective's eyes, seeing through evasions, noticing too much. She looked away again, blushing.

"I know you didn't," she said. "Yes, I'm glad I'm back."

Their hands moved together, fingers entwining. They began to speak tenderly, exchanging guarded expressions of affection; taking care not to expose their emotions completely, but for the first time trying words like "we" and "us" for size.

Then Martin steered towards the subject of accommodation. He suggested that sharing a house in Yarchester with a mixed group, as Alison did, was thoroughly unsatisfactory. She agreed, saying that she was looking for a place of her own. He said that he was planning to move, having found a better flat: "A bigger one. Large sitting-room with balcony, one large bedroom, good kitchen and bathroom—"

"Very nice."

"Yes. But very much nicer if we were to share it."

Alison went quite still. Then she said evenly, "It's a place of my own that I'm after. I don't think cohabitation is a good idea. I tried it, once."

"I know you did."

She took her hand away from his. "I might have known you'd know," she said, her voice edged with remembered dislike. "You're a detective, after all."

He cursed himself silently for reminding her of it. Two years before, misinterpreting his single-mindedness in pursuit of villainy, Alison had called him an unprincipled liar. He had hoped she'd forgotten that incident.

"Finding out about you, when we first met, was nothing to do with my being a detective," he said quickly. "It was my natural reaction because you're such a very attractive girl. And your father told me more about you than he might normally have done because you worried us sick by disappearing . . . remember? From what he told me, the man you had been living with gave you a very raw deal."

Alison shrugged. "I was young and silly, and Gavin was a pig. I lived with him because I loved him. He lived with me because I was fool enough to wash his dirty socks and cook for him. I'm not walking into that trap again."

"You wouldn't, with me. I'm not that kind of man. I'm an excellent cook, and I send all my dirty clothes to a laundry. I want to live with you because it's the natural extension of our relationship."

She looked at him coolly. "Well, yours is a different approach, I'll say that. Gavin Jackson talked me into living with him by swearing that he loved me. At least you're being more honest than he was."

Tait opened his mouth and closed it again, alarmed by the verbal minefield that lay ahead. He suspected that he did indeed love her; certainly he'd never before in the whole of his life felt about any girl the way he felt about Alison. He loved her and he was almost sure that he wanted to marry her: *but not yet*. If he talked of love, how could he avoid the subject of marriage? But if he didn't mention love, how could he contrive to keep her in reserve for the next four or five years?

"I tried to tell you how I felt about you two years ago," he reproached her, "but you wouldn't listen. You didn't want to know. Don't you realise how humiliating that was? Can't you see that I'm wary of expressing myself, this time, because I'm trying to keep a little pride . . .?"

It was the corniest of tactics, he knew; but it worked. Alison was remorseful. She put her hand on his, and they moved closer. With the minefield safely negotiated, he began to talk again about the advantages—the desirability—of living together. Alison seemed to concur, though the memory of Gavin Jackson's behaviour made her understandably hesitant.

"I'm talking about a serious long-term commitment," Tait said, seeking to reassure her. "That's what it would be on my side, anyway. On yours too, I hope?"

She frowned. "Commitment? That's not a word I expected you to use. I'd want you to be serious about it, yes, because I'd only consider living with you if I thought it would work as a long-term relationship. But living together can't ever be any kind of *commitment*. If it's commitment you're after—and

don't mistake me; I'm not proposing to you, just trying to
understand your motives—why aren't we discussing the pros
and cons of marriage?"

God, she was like her father! That same down-to-earth attitude, that same clear insight, bluntly put. But Alison was
beautiful with it. Whereas Doug Quantrill's eyes were the
sour green of little apples, his daughter's had the soft translu-
cence of peeled grapes. She was honest, generous, intelligent, shyly sensual—a lovely girl. And yes, Tait definitely did
want to marry her. Eventually.

He held both her hands and told her so, explaining about
the problem of money. So many men, he said, married too
early in their careers. He'd seen it happen to most of his
friends from school and university. As long as the couple
remained childless, they could live well on their combined
salaries; but as soon as they started a family, the husband's
income was inadequate to maintain their standard of living,
and the wife and children suffered. And he, Martin Tait, was
determined not to marry until he had an income large enough
to support his family in considerable comfort.

That was what he told Alison. So far as it went, it was true.
What he didn't add was that he'd seen too many good men's
lives spoiled: all the pleasures of their young manhood, their
interests, their ambitions, subordinated to mortgage repay-
ments, pregnant wives and sticky-fingered brats. In his private opinion, that was one good reason why a lot of men tried
to opt out of their marriages in middle age. Not because they
were seeking to recapture their lost youth, but because they'd
never given themselves the chance to enjoy it in the first
place. And he intended to enjoy his youth to the full.

"You do see what I mean?" he said, deploying his argu-
ments. "I very much want to settle down and have children.
That's what marriage is about, ultimately, isn't it? But you've
only just started your career in radio. You told me a few
minutes ago how much you're enjoying it. So what kind of a
pig would you think me if I were to say, 'Scrap all that,
Alison. Marry me and start a family instead'? You'd tell me to
shove off, wouldn't you?"

She retrieved her hand, pulled a blade of grass and looked
at it intently. "I'm not sure what I'd say . . . I can tell you
now that I wouldn't dream of scrapping my career and start-

ing a family immediately. But I suppose I might be prepared to discuss options . . . if I definitely decided to marry you, that is. And I don't know about that. I'd need time to think it over."

"Of course you would," he said, breathing more freely. "This is what I mean about living together—it'll give us the time we need to be sure about each other. And it'll save money, too. We'll both be in a much better financial position when we do begin discussing marriage."

She gave him another of her devastatingly level looks. "*I* shall be in a better financial position, yes. But then, I try to save something, even if it's only a little, every month. My parents had to bring three of us up on a police constable's pay, so I know all about being careful with money. You don't, though, do you, Martin? I imagine you spend every penny you earn. Dad told me—all right, I admit I've been asking about you—that it cost you over a thousand pounds to learn to fly. And now you actually own a share in an aeroplane—"

"Only a twentieth!" he revealed.

"Oh. I had the impression it was more . . . Still, flying must be the most expensive hobby you could possibly have chosen. I know you're getting accelerated promotion, and in a year or two you'll outrank Dad, but if you're not prepared to drop your standard of living I don't see that you'll ever be able to afford to raise a family."

"Your father may know a lot about me," Tait retorted, "but he doesn't know everything. As a matter of fact, I have money coming to me. A family legacy. A large one. So I don't anticipate that money will be any problem at all, in a few years' time."

Alison was taken aback. "Sorry . . . I had no idea. That does make things different for you, of course. I thought you were being irresponsible, you see, and ever since Gavin I've tried to keep away from irresponsible men."

"Very wise of you." Tait gave her a forgiving kiss on the cheek. "I don't usually talk about the legacy, but now we're thinking in terms of eventual marriage it's only right that you should know it's there."

"Well . . . it's rather a shattering thought. There's never been enough money in my family for any legacies. I don't even know how they work. Is it a lump sum that's waiting for you when you reach a certain age?"

He hesitated. "It's not really as definite as that. There's no

way of knowing when I shall actually get it. It's my Aunt
Con's money, you see. My father's elder sister. She was lucky
enough to have a rich godmother who left her a packet. Aunt
Con has no children and I'm lucky enough to be her only
nephew. We've always got along very well, and she's gener-
ously left me everything in her will."

Alison frowned at him. "Your Aunt Con? The one you're
going to stay with in Fodderstone?"

"That's right. Mrs. Constance Schultz. She sounds like a
comfortably rounded middle-European, doesn't she? In fact
she's tall and thin and unmistakably English—slightly eccentric, in a genteel sort of way. I'm very fond of her. She's
always interested me because she was the black sheep of the
family.

"Her father—my grandfather Tait—was a respectable solicitor with a practice in Woodbridge. It seems that Aunt Con
lived at home, leading a quiet dull life, until the 1940s. Then
she suddenly discovered the opposite sex. Apparently the
countryside was swarming with lonely servicemen of various
nationalities, and Aunt Con befriended them with a bit too
much enthusiasm. Woodbridge was scandalized, and the rest
of the family didn't know which way to look.

"Aunt Con must have got married at some stage, but her
husband disappeared years before I was born. He was never
mentioned in my hearing, and I don't know whether she's
now divorced or widowed or separated. Or whether Schultz
was an American airman or a German ex-prisoner of war. The
story has always intrigued me, because it seems so totally
unlikely when you meet her. And I hope you will meet her,
because I'm sure you'll—"

"Hold on a minute." Alison's frown deepened. "How old is
your aunt?"

"Just turned seventy. She must have been pushing thirty
during the war, so I suppose she was trying to make up for
lost time."

"Seventy's not all that old, these days. Your aunt could
easily live for another fifteen years. Twenty, perhaps."

"Have a heart!" Martin grinned. "It'll be nowhere near as
long as that, with any luck."

Alison stiffened. Strongly as she was drawn to him, she
found his preoccupation with money alien and repellent. She
hadn't realized how *very* much material things mattered to

him, and how casually he could anticipate the early death of a relative from whom he had expectations.

"*With any luck?*" she protested. "And you claim to be fond of her—"

"Who wants to live to be ninety? I'm sure Aunt Con doesn't. I don't wish a long and infirm old age on her—but that doesn't mean I'm not fond of her."

"Like hell you are, Martin!" Alison sprang to her feet, her hair swinging with vigorous indignation, her cheeks pink, the green of her eyes sharpening to emerald. "How can you say you're fond of your aunt, when you're basing your entire lifestyle on the money you anticipate getting when the poor old lady's dead! I think that's disgusting. No doubt you'll make a great fuss of her while you're staying with her, but all the time you'll be hoping that she'll conveniently drop dead within the next four or five years, so that you can afford to get married without giving up any of your pleasures. Well, you can leave me out of your calculations! Of all the rotten, scheming—"

Alison stopped to draw breath. She was trembling with fury. Martin Tait stood beside her wondering what had hit him. He tried to touch her, to soothe her, to explain, to change the subject, but she was beyond reason. Two years ago she had called him an unprincipled liar; this time she called him a selfish hypocrite. Now, as then, she told him that she never wanted to see him again.

7

For the first time since her incarceration, Sandra Websdell had spoken kindly to her captor when he came to bring her breakfast. For the first time for days she had forced herself to eat.

Already, buoyed up by the thought of attempting to escape, she felt a little better. To have a purpose was, in itself, she discovered, a kind of freedom.

But she couldn't hope to get away simply by rushing for the door when his back was turned. Unless she could disable him in some way, at least temporarily, she would have no chance of breaking free.

She took no pleasure in the thought of causing him physical pain. She didn't hate him, she pitied him. But that wouldn't stop her from damaging him—if only she could think of a way to do it without using up the strength she would need for running.

If only she could think . . . Her head seemed to be filled with foam rubber. She couldn't see clearly, either. The air in the room was so hot and stale that sweat stood on her forehead and trickled down into her eyes, stinging and blinding her. And if her sight wasn't clear, how could she hope to—?

Eyes . . .

That was it. She must blind him temporarily, go for his eyes.

An atomizer would be just the thing to use. If only she had put a spray—hair spray, toilet-water spray—in one of her honeymoon suitcases. She rummaged in them just to make sure, but she knew she hadn't. She had packed the cases with nothing but clothes, and had left them in advance in the rented cottage where she had intended to begin her married life. After changing her mind about getting married she had gone to the cottage to pick up the clothes; and it was then that he had come for her, tricked her, blindfolded her and brought her here, suitcases and all.

She had no spray, then. But that was the kind of thing she needed, something that would prevent him from seeing for long enough to allow her to escape. What could she use? If only she could concentrate, if only she didn't feel so light-headed . . .

And then the answer came to her, such a simple one that she laughed aloud with relief. She could hear her own laughter, so high and cracked that she imagined for a moment that it must come from someone else.

Of course! Why hadn't she thought of it before? He would bring her the weapon she needed—he would literally hand it to her on a plate. Breakfast wouldn't do, because that was invariably a sandwich. But in the early evening, just before six o'clock, he brought her a main meal of cold meat with lettuce and a tomato. And with the meal he always brought a dish of stewed plums covered by a thick yellow blanket of cold custard—a gooey, throwable custard pie . . .

She imagined herself talking to him to distract his attention as she balanced the pudding dish in her hand and took aim. The ruse would work, she felt sure. As long as she flung the contents squarely in his face, she could be well away before he finished wiping the mess out of his eyes.

In health she could run much faster than he could, she had no doubt about that. It was not knowing which way to run that bothered her—that, and the possibility that in her weakened state she might stumble or trip. She dare not dwell on what he might do if she fell and he caught up with her. He kept protesting that he would never harm her, but by abducting her he had already forfeited her trust. He was odd, unpredictable. He might do anything . . .

Despite the heat Sandra felt a momentary shrinking of her flesh, a goose-pimpling presentiment that someone was walking over her grave.

8

In the kitchen of her Regency Gothic cottage on Fodderstone Green, Constance Schultz—*née* Tait, and known to her relatives and friends as Con—was making preparations for her nephew's visit.

Most of the ten cottages on the Green were owned by the Forestry Commission and occupied by its employees or pensioners. Geoff Websdell, who lived with his wife Beryl at number 8, worked as a forester. But two of the cottages were in private ownership.

Numbers 9 and 10 had changed hands many times since the third Earl of Brandon's estate had been broken up in the 1920s. Middle-aged summer visitors fell in love with the cottages and bought them for holidays and eventual retirement, without taking into account the hard work that would be involved in keeping up the large gardens, and without realizing what a bleak, isolated place Fodderstone Green was in the winter. Con Schultz had stuck it for longer than most—for ten years, ever since she had retired from her job as an assistant public librarian in Ipswich—but she was by preference a solitary person. She was also an enthusiastic

gardener, and she had always wanted to live somewhere
where she could keep bees.

Her neighbours at number 10, Marjorie and Howard Braithwaite, had been in residence for two years. Howard, formerly
the managing director of a light engineering firm in Chelms-
ford, spent his retirement fishing; he set off with pike rod and
tackle every morning of the season for the lake in what had
once been the grounds of the Hall. His wife, like Con, was a
keen gardener.

Their love of gardens was the only thing the two women
had in common. Even in this, they differed. Con's gardening
was a random activity, her pretty garden not so much a
creation as an assisted happening. Marjorie on the other
hand, a born organizer, liked to keep everything about her
well under control. The climbing roses on her walls were
orderly, her lawns were frequently shaved, her borders were
stiff with hotly coloured municipal bedding-plants. Any flowers that had the temerity to put in an appearance where she
had not planned they should grow were ruthlessly given the
chop.

So efficient was Marjorie's gardening that she still had
plenty of energy for other projects. She had taken charge of
every community activity in Fodderstone, but there were too
few of them to provide sufficient scope for her abilities. With
time to spare, she had turned her attention to her disorga-
nized neighbour.

"What on earth are you *doing*, Constance?" she demanded,
marching into the kitchen of number 9 without so much as a
token knock.

Con flinched. It was, she knew, ungrateful of her to do so;
her neighbour was generous and usually brought with her
some small gift. The gifts were often edible, presumably
because Marjorie thought that Con, who was built in the
classic English gentlewoman shape with a long narrow face,
long narrow hands and feet, and a body as flat as a plank,
needed feeding up. This morning's gift was a bowl of home-
made muesli. Marjorie lectured both publicly and privately
on the importance of dietary fibre, especially for the over-
fifties, and the principal constituent of her muesli was bran.

"What are you up to?" repeated Marjorie. Con often thought
that her neighbour's frequent visits were made for the purpose of finding out what she was doing and telling her either
to stop it or to do it some other way. Marjorie was not a

particularly large woman, but everything about her—firm features, greying hair worn straight with a fringe, spectacles worn with a retaining chain that hung in loops on either side of her cheeks, home-made summer tent-dress, strong flat sandals—proclaimed a formidable practicality. Con found her overpowering: too loud, too inquisitive, too personal, too interfering. She wished Marjorie would leave her alone, but she was too polite to say so.

"I'm making a casserole for supper," she replied patiently. It was an unwelcome job on such a hot day. She knew that her face must be shining, and she hoped that Marjorie would not comment on it. "I'm not sure when my nephew will be arriving, so I thought I'd make something now and heat it up this evening."

Con ate little and cooked less. During the last few years of her working life she had cared for her aged mother, and after the old lady was removed to a nursing-home Con had thankfully given up the practice of cookery. Her favourite meal was bread and honey, or a piece of cheese and an apple, eaten absent-mindedly while she read a book.

Having got out of the way of cooking, she found it difficult to do so while anyone watched her. That was why she had decided against giving Martin a steak, because he would be sure to come into the kitchen to talk to her while she grilled it. She was becoming so forgetful, so easily confused . . . as she was now, under Marjorie's disapproving eye.

"A *casserole*, in this weather?" her neighbour hooted. "No wonder you're sweating—what an idiotic thing to do! Why on earth aren't you giving your nephew a cold meal?"

"Er . . ." Con tried to remember whether she had seasoned the neck of lamb before browning it. At the moment she was frying chopped onion—and gosh, it was so hot, standing over the cooker. If only Marjorie would go away instead of watching and criticizing . . .

Despite her lined face and grey head, there was something almost coltish about Con Schultz. Her hair was cropped, her movements were nervous and awkward, her manner gauche. It was impossible to imagine her as a 1940s good-time girl, but not at all difficult to see what she must have been like in her last year at school. Her clothes—she always wore plain skirts and blouses—were a kind of uniform, and her favourite expletives came straight from the pre-war *School Friend* magazine.

Marjorie, who never took silence for an answer, was still
waiting to hear why she wasn't giving Martin a cold meal.
Con tried to remember why not, as she pushed sizzling
onions about the pan and suffered in the heat. Eventually,
dragging up some recollection of the long-departed Mr. Schultz,
she suggested that men preferred hot food.

"Rubbish!" declared Marjorie. "A complete fallacy. Men
think they prefer hot food, but that's because they haven't
been properly trained. Take Howard: when he was at work
he always ate a hot lunch in the directors' dining room, out
of habit. But now that he spends all day fishing he's perfectly
happy with the wholemeal bread sandwich I make him for
lunch, and a vegetable salad in the evenings. It's far more
nutritious, and so much better for his bowels. He agrees that
he feels healthier for it, and so would your nephew. You'll be
doing the boy a great disservice if you don't take the opportunity to restructure his diet while he's here."

Con sighed, and fried on, and said nothing. Marjorie might
well be right about the importance of dietary fibre, but for
herself Con was past caring; and she had never thought it her
mission in life to reorganize anyone else's. Besides, she knew
that Marjorie was wrong about her husband. Her other neighbour, Beryl Websdell, had recently happened to mention
that Howard Braithwaite bought himself a cooked lunch every day at the Flintknappers Arms.

Con kept the knowledge to herself, of course. The Braithwaites' domestic arrangements were no concern of hers. She
might have felt sorry for Howard, knowing that he had to
resort to subterfuge to provide himself with a square meal, if
it weren't for the fact that he was such a cross, impatient
man.

Village life carried with it, Con believed, an obligation to
speak to one's neighbours. Not to buttonhole them or bore
them, but never to pass them by without a greeting and some
observation about the weather, or an enquiry about the health
of anyone known to be ill. But Howard Braithwaite preferred
to ignore everyone unless he was spoken to directly, when he
answered with a bark.

Probably, mused Con, he'd found barking the best way of
dealing with his wife. She ought to try it on Marjorie herself—
except that it was now too late to bother; her neighbour's
tiresomeness didn't matter any more, she'd soon be out of it,
thank God . . .

"Constance!" The chains on either side of Marjorie's cheeks swayed and clashed with irritation. "You're burning those onions! Stir in the flour, quickly, and add some hot water—really, you are absolutely hopeless. Now, do try to concentrate for a moment because I can't stay long, I'm going to Ashthorpe this afternoon to give a talk on nutrition to the Evergreen Club. What I want to know is whether you've finished preparing the schedules for the honey section at next month's garden produce show? I know what you're like. If I don't keep an eye on you—"

"Crikey!" Con stood still, one hand holding a wooden spoon that immediately dripped gravy over the cooker, the other clapped guiltily to her mouth. "The produce show? But I thought we'd agreed—?"

Marjorie's chains quivered formidably. "You *can't* have forgotten about it. You put it in your diary, I know you did, because I stood over you while you wrote it down."

"Yes . . . but I don't always remember to look at my diary, you see." In fact Con had mislaid it. She seemed to spend most of her time, lately, searching for things she had mislaid and mislaying other things in the process. But she wasn't going to tell Marjorie that. No sense in asking for a further scolding.

"Do you mean you've done nothing at all to prepare for the show. *Really*, Constance, how can you be so irresponsible?"

Con began to worry. Not about the produce show, although she would never willingly inconvenience her fellow beekeepers, but about her memory. Mislaying things was a nuisance, but being unable to remember whether or not she had promised to do something was frightening. She felt that she was beginning to lose control of her own life.

"But I'm sure I asked you to find someone else to take charge of the honey this year, Marjorie. After all, I'm leaving. I told you that, I know I did. I may well have gone by the middle of September, and I thought we'd agreed that you would find a replacement for me?"

"Nonsense, we agreed no such thing. I told you at the time that it would be months before you move. You've been talking about it for long enough, but all you've done so far is to sell your bees. You haven't put your own property on the market yet, or been to view any others. Have you?"

"Er . . . no." Con took a deep breath to steady herself. "I've been waiting to discuss things with my nephew. I may go to look at properties with him. And if I find somewhere suitable, I could move from here almost immediately. I know it's a frightful nuisance for you, Marjorie, but you really must find someone else to take my place."

Her neighbour consented, grumbling. "But it's ridiculous to imagine that you'll be able to leave at short notice, even if you find a suitable property with vacant possession. You'll have to sell either this cottage or the one on the Horkey road first."

"No, I shan't." Con had always been reluctant to reveal much about herself to anyone, but she was tired of being browbeaten. "If you're wondering about finance, that's no problem. I have capital available."

"*Have* you?" Marjorie backed down, her tone a mixture of surprise and interest. "Lucky old thing," she went on, almost respectfully. Then she rallied. "Well, no wonder your nephew's prepared to come and help you house-hunt! I suppose he expects to benefit from your will?"

"You can suppose what you jolly well like," Con retorted, her thin face pink with heat and exasperation. "I'm very fond of Martin, and believe it or not he seems to be reasonably fond of me. Now if you're busy, Marjorie, don't let me keep you."

But her neighbour was listening to the sound of unmusical singing, a wobbly soprano coming closer as someone walked up the long garden path and round the side of the house towards the open back door.

"Help!" said Marjorie. "It's that *dreadful* Beryl woman. She really does drive me mad. If she asks me again whether I've found my Saviour, I shall be very rude to her."

What they could now both identify, shrilled out with joyous fervour and a persistent sing-along rhythm, was a gospel song that had been popularized by Cliff Richard. Beryl Websdell was an ardent Cliff Richard fan. She had once, on holiday years ago, seen and heard him live in concert at the Wellington Pier, Great Yarmouth, and had managed to get his autograph. His committedly Christian stance had helped to formulate her own belief, and she sang the chorus of his song—the only part of it she could remember—every day of her life.

This *is* my song,
My *Saviour*'s love to me-e:

How great *Thou* art,
How *great* Thou art!
This is my *song*, my *Saviour's* love to me-he,
How-great-Thou-art, how *great Thou art*!

This *is* my song—

Still singing it, Beryl appeared in the doorway, homely but
radiant. Her broad face and bare, fleshy arms were red and
damp from working in the heat, but her eyes were as full of
happiness as her voice.

Religious enthusiasm was rare in Fodderstone. Any other
woman who exhibited it—and expressed it so frequently, and
so off-key—would have been shunned. But Beryl was valued
as a very hard worker, and a lifeline for the old and disabled.
The cleaning she did on Saturdays at the Flintknappers Arms
was incidental to her local authority job as a home help. On
the left side of her sleeveless nylon overall were embroidered
the words *Home Help Service;* on the right she wore a large
badge proclaiming *Jesus My Joy.*

"Hallo, Constance dear," she cried cheerily. "I've just given
poor old Joey Wigg a good turn-out, and now I'm off to the
post office for his pension and groceries, so I popped in to see
if there's anything you need while I'm there. Good morning,
Marjorie," she added, beaming. "Lovely to see you."

Marjorie didn't acknowledge the greeting. She was the
kind of woman who made a point of addressing all the villagers by their first names while expecting to be called Mrs.
Braithwaite in return. She very much disliked being treated
as Beryl Websdell's sister in Christ, and she lingered only to
satisfy her curiosity.

"Have you heard from that daughter of yours yet?" she
demanded.

"Not yet," said Beryl, without a waver in her confidence or
a diminution of her smile. "Sandra will get in touch with us
when she's ready. But thank you for asking about her. God
bless you, Marjorie."

"Bah!" said Marjorie, stamping off to bully the pensioners
of the Ashthorpe Evergreen Club into eating bran for the
sake of their bowels.

She was slightly mollified, on her way down Constance's
garden path, by having the front gate held open for her with
proper deference by another of the villagers, the woodman,

who had just arrived in his old pick-up truck. "Good morning, Christopher," she said graciously; but it took him so long
to burst out with "Good morning, Mrs. Braithwaite," in
reply, that she couldn't wait to hear what else he was trying
to say to her.

Con was more patient with Christopher Thorold, and conse-
quently he found her easier to talk to. She listened to his
offer of winter firewood at special summer prices, and told
him that she wouldn't be needing any because she would
soon be leaving Fodderstone.

"I'm wholly sorry to hear that," he said sincerely. "Pa will
be sorry, an' all."

Christopher's father had regularly trimmed Con's garden
hedge for her in her early years in Fodderstone Green. She
enquired after his health.

"Fairly, thank you," answered Christopher, a reply that
Con, knowing her East Anglian comparatives, found satisfac-
tory. "Nicely" would have been preferable, "poorly" would
have been worse, and "sadly" would have meant at death's
door.

Beryl, who had been standing out of his sight, moved
forward and greeted him affectionately. She would be only
too glad, she reminded him, to come and give him and his
father a good turn-out whenever they needed her.

Taken aback by the unexpected encounter with her, Christopher began to blink. His boots trod up and down and he
burst out, " 'Tweren't me, Beryl! 'Tweren't me who threw
your gnome in a ditch."

"Bless you, boy," she said warmly, "I never thought it was."

"They say so at the Knappers. They've found him damaged, and they say I did it. But *'tweren't* me."

Beryl was visibly shaken. Her red cheeks lost some of their
colour and her voice wavered. " 'Course it wasn't you, Chris
dear," she said, trying to reassure him. "They were only
teasing . . . Just ignore them. God bless you—and your Pa."

But she gave the blessing mechanically. The disappearance of her daughter and the disappearance of her gnome
were inextricably linked in her mind. There was no logic, she
knew, in thinking that because Willum had been damaged,
Sandra had also been harmed; but for a few moments her
faith in her Saviour's loving care deserted her, and she felt as
concerned as any other mother for the safety of her missing
daughter.

9

She would give him one more chance to let her go. She would make one more attempt to persuade him to free her. It will save his pride, she told herself, thinking of the indignity he would suffer by having food thrown in his face; but in fact she was terrified by the prospect of having to put her plan into action. She knew that she was too shaky to aim straight, too weak at the knees to run far.

She began to plead with him as soon as he brought her midday sandwich. "You must let me go," she said. "I can't bear to be shut up in this heat. Can't you see that you're making me ill?"

He said that she would feel better if she ate her food.

"How can I eat, when you're keeping me prisoner? It's dreadful in here. You *must* let me go."

He said that he needed her. If he let her go he would lose her.

"But you can't keep me here indefinitely!"

He said that he had too much need of her to let her go.

"If you don't, I shall die," she sobbed.

He said that if only she would do as he asked, he would always take care of her.

He put the sandwich on the table. Then he went, securely fastening the door behind him.

10

Martin Tait arrived at his aunt's cottage on Fodderstone Green just in time for afternoon tea.

"I'm so glad you could come," said Con. "Gosh, you're looking awfully well."

He didn't feel well, after the way Alison had treated him. Healthy, certainly; but baffled, frustrated, angry. However, he had no intention of revealing any of that to his aunt. He kissed her with affection, noticing that she was wearing the scent that she had once admitted to having liked when she was young, the Worth *Je Reviens* that he had, as usual, given her for Christmas.

"I'm delighted to be here at last," he said. "And you're looking well, too."

It wasn't true. He was quite shocked by the change in her since his pre-Christmas visit. Con shared with him the characteristically sharp Tait profile, but her mouth was entirely her own. Dragged down at one corner by a muscular weakness, it had always given her what Martin remembered best about her, an engagingly lop-sided smile. But when her face was in repose her mouth gave her a melancholy appearance, and that was what predominated now. She looked as though she slept badly, and her hands were shaky. Instead of being the active, amusing woman he had always known, she seemed unfamiliar, depressed and elderly.

The ritual of afternoon tea seemed to revive her a little. They sat on the back lawn in the shade of an apple tree, drinking Darjeeling tea and eating cucumber sandwiches. Presently Con enquired after her sister-in-law, Martin's mother, a strong-minded widow who ran a secondhand bookshop in a village near Lavenham.

"Indefatigable, as always." Martin sighed. "She's into yoga now . . . I'm all for her keeping fit, but I do wish that at fifty she'd be a bit more dignified. Whenever I go to see her she's wearing a leotard and contorting herself on the sitting-room carpet."

He had in fact been acutely embarrassed at the prospect of taking Alison to meet his mother. The way the leotard clung to her lean body, tracing every fold of her pudenda, was he thought positively indecent. It would be so much easier and pleasanter to introduce Alison to Aunt Con—or, rather, it would have been. He fell silent, yearning angrily for the girl.

"Scones and honey?" offered Con. "Don't worry, *I* didn't make the scones. I bought them from the Horkey baker, so they're guaranteed edible."

"But the honey's most definitely yours," said Martin, helping himself. It was distinctively pale and scented, made by her bees from the nectar of the blossom of the lime trees that surrounded Fodderstone Green. "And I'm not sharing it with *you*," he added, swatting away a hovering wasp. He licked a smear of honey from his finger. "This is much too good to waste. How many pounds did you take this year, Aunt Con?"

"None at all. Didn't I mention it in a letter? I was sure I'd told you . . . I sold my hives in the spring."

He looked at her in surprise. "No, I'd no idea. You've always been so fond of your bees."

"Yes. But they're an awful lot of work, you know. And when I had to have Emma put down in March, I somehow lost the heart for it."

Emma, a golden Labrador, had been Con's companion throughout her retirement. Even to Martin, an infrequent visitor, the cottage seemed empty without the dog; as soon as he entered he had missed the click of her nails on the floorboards. And now, at tea-time, he recalled the way she used to come and lean against his legs, gazing up at him soulfully in the hope that he would give her a lick of honey.

"She was a beautiful creature," he said.

Con nodded. "That was a very kind and understanding note you sent me at the time. Jolly nice of you, Martin. I did appreciate it."

"Well, I remember how I felt when my poor old beagle had to be put down, not long after Dad died. I wanted to have another dog, but I couldn't because of being away at school. What about you, though—are you planning to buy a pup? A different breed, perhaps?"

"No." Con poured him another cup of tea, absent-mindedly adding both milk and sugar. Martin never took sugar (or ate honey, except to please his aunt) but he drank it without complaint.

"No," she continued, "I did think about getting a puppy, but I won't. The fact is, Martin, I've decided not to stay here another winter. I'm fond of the old cottage, but it's frightfully draughty and inconvenient. And the garden's much too big for me to cope with now. I've been happy here, but I feel I've had enough."

From the look of her, he thought, that was obvious. She usually liked hot weather but now she seemed distressed by the heat. Was she ill, he wondered? But it wasn't a question he could ever put to her. If she wanted him to know, she would tell him in her own way and her own time.

"I should jolly well think you have had enough of Fodderstone," he said heartily. Con's idiom was catching. "I've always enjoyed coming here to see you, but there's something

'—I don't know what—*odd* about the place. And it's so isolated. It'll be much better for you to move into a small town,
somewhere near the shops and a library and, er, dentists and
so on. Have you decided yet where you want to live?"

Con lifted the lid of the teapot and peered vaguely at its
contents. "Oh . . . Woodbridge, perhaps. Or Aldeburgh . . ."

"Good idea. There's plenty of property on the market, so
you should have no problem in finding somewhere suitable.
All the same, you'll need to start viewing right away if you
want to be out of here before the winter. Look, why don't we
go on a house-hunting expedition together, one day this
week?"

"Oh, no. Jolly nice of you, Martin, but you've come here to
fly your aeroplane. No, I can house-hunt by myself, after
your holiday."

"Well, the offer's there if you change your mind. And we
can at least look at the *East Anglian Daily Press* and see
what's advertised. What are you thinking of buying—a modern house? Or a bungalow? Or a flat?"

"Somewhere very small," said Con. "And that's a thing I
wanted to talk to you about while you're here. I've an awful
lot of furniture, you see. Some of it's modern, but there are
quite a few antiques and some of them are really good pieces.
I'll have to get rid of most of it, and I want you to have first
choice. Look it over during the week, and take whatever you
want. Make sure you have the best antiques, and enough of
the rest to furnish your house when you get married."

She spoke so urgently that Martin was completely taken
aback. It seemed such a strange offer. As his aunt knew, he
lived at present in a furnished flat; and now that Alison had
turned down his suggestion that they should live together—
had turned him down for good, as far as he could tell—he saw
no point in moving to a larger place. So what would he do
with a houseful of furniture? He had no intention of paying
for it to be kept in store. He rather liked some of his aunt's
antiques, but in general her taste in furniture was not his. By
the time he was ready to marry, Con might not be alive; and
in that event he'd be able to afford to go out and buy
whatever he wanted.

He thanked her with all his charm. "That's very generous
of you, Aunt Con. Don't think me ungrateful, will you—but
quite honestly I can't see myself needing to furnish a house.

Detective work and marriage don't mix, and I'm a career detective. A confirmed bachelor."

For the first time that afternoon, Con smiled her delightfully lopsided smile. "Phooey!" she retorted. "D'you want to bet on it?"

Martin had the grace to laugh. "Well, that's how I feel at the moment, anyway. I may change my mind, I suppose, but not until I'm established in senior rank. Really, it's very sweet of you, but I'm reluctant to accept your offer. Even if your new house isn't very big, you're still going to need to furnish it. You can't give everything away."

"But there's the furniture from my property in the Horkey road, too," said Con. "Don't you remember that pretty, derelict cottage I bought a few years ago? I've been letting it to summer holidaymakers since I restored it. It's empty at the moment, because I agreed that a local couple could rent it cheaply for a few weeks when they married, only the marriage never took place. The girl—my neighbour Beryl's daughter—disappeared."

Tait's sharp nose twitched with professional interest. "Disappeared?"

"Well, bolted. I can't say that I blame her—I don't think she would have been at all happy with Desmond Flood—but it's too bad of her not to have been in touch with her mother before now."

"Do the local police know about this?"

"Oh yes. Such a pleasant young woman detective came over from Breckham Market to make enquiries. But then Beryl discovered that Sandra had taken a lot of her clothes with her, so obviously her disappearance was deliberate. She's twenty-two, after all, and entitled to do as she likes. The only niggling worry is that she's usually a considerate girl. But then, she probably felt so frightfully embarrassed about messing up the wedding arrangements that she simply wanted to keep out of the way for a bit."

Martin relaxed. "Hardly surprising," he agreed. "Who was the woman detective, Aunt Con? A sergeant? Hilary Lloyd?"

"Oh Lord, I don't know! Beryl did introduce me—the detective wanted to look round the Horkey road cottage, so of course I went with them—but I can't remember. My head's like a sieve these days. I can never be sure—"

But Martin, alert again, was sniffing the air. "Could something be burning?"

Con frowned a denial. Then she jumped to her feet, slapping the crown of her greying head in vexed self-reprimand. "Oh what a coot I am! The casserole—I forgot the casserole—!"

She galloped off to the kitchen with a vigour that left her nephew reassured as to the state of her health, if not of his supper.

Hearing her captor approach the door, Sandra stopped her agitated walk about the room. This was it, then. This was the moment when he would bring her supper tray. She had to be ready, now, to pick up the bowl of fruit and custard, fling it accurately in his face and run for her life.

Poised for action, her skin prickling with sweat, her knees shaking, she stood and listened to the unfastening of the door; a strangely distant sound, diminished by the racing thump of her pulse. *Please, God*, she prayed, *give me strength*.

Her captor entered the room, tray in one hand, and closed the door behind him. "I have brought your supper," he said.

He placed the tray on the table. She moved slowly towards it, like a bather wading through deep water. Her vision was blurred. She blinked, trying to focus on the food. There was the usual plate of cold meat and lettuce . . . but for the first time in the whole of her captivity there was no bowl of stewed fruit.

She lifted her head with difficulty and stared at him. She tried to speak, but her mouth was so dry that it was difficult to get the words out. "Where . . . where are the plums and custard?" she whispered.

He opened a paper bag that lay on the tray and held it out to her, smiling. "I thought you would like a change," he said. "A treat."

The scent of fresh fruit, clean and fragrant in the stifling air of the room, rose to her nostrils. Inside the bag, their firm flesh yellow and crimson under the shining skin, were two large nectarines.

She closed her eyes against the disappointment. The tension drained out of her, running from beneath her eyelids. He sounded hurt, mystified: "I thought to please you," he said.

She shook her head and the tears rolled over her face, mingling with the sweat that stood on her upper lip and draining into the corners of her mouth. "I . . . I . . . I wanted custard . . ." she sobbed. "If you really want to please me, bring me some custard!"

His expression changed, and even in her distress she realized, for the first time, what pressure he must be under. Until now he had been patient with her. Even kind, according to his lights. But her rejection of his treat clearly angered him. She thought for a moment that he might even fling the fruit at her.

But he controlled himself. He stood for a moment, silent and frustrated. Then he put the nectarines on the table and left, fastening the door behind him.

11

"But gosh, it's been in the family for years, Martin. I can remember my grandfather telling me how he was given it by an old farmer in part-payment of a debt. It would be a frightful shame to let it go now."

"My dear Aunt Con," Tait put his hands on her shoulders—she was almost as tall as he was—and gave her a tiny shake, "I really can't give a good home to an oak chest as large as that, even if it is carved and dated 1709. Or to your early Victorian writing-desk, though I agree that the marquetry is very pretty. Or to a mahogany table that will extend to seat eight . . . I do appreciate your generosity, but I can't take any of your furniture. Thank you, but no."

Con sighed. "Dash it—I'd *counted* on your having the best pieces. They're worth a lot, you know, quite apart from their family interest."

"I'm sure they are. But you must keep the things with a sentimental value, and the rest can go to a good saleroom. Look, don't worry about having to make all the arrangements for your move, I'll do whatever I can to help. You know you can rely on me."

She gave him a small, sad version of her crooked smile. "Yes, and I'm grateful, though I'm hoping not to cause you too many problems . . ." Then she brightened: "Well, at least there are some nice small pieces that you can't possibly refuse. Come up to my room and see them. I'm afraid every-

thing's in a frightful muddle because I've been sorting through
drawers and cupboards—and I'm a terrible slut anyway, as
you've probably noticed."

"Nonsense," Martin lied, following her through a door in a
corner of the sitting-room and then up the narrow enclosed
stairway. He had noticed, of course. There was ample evidence that his aunt was no fonder of—or better at—housework
than cookery. He always took it for granted that her cottage
would be dusty and untidy, but on this visit it seemed positively dirty.

"My neighbour Beryl works as a home help," Con went on
over her shoulder as she climbed, taking the stairs more
slowly than he remembered from previous visits. "She has a
passion for cleanliness. I think she's been looking forward to
the time when age and infirmity would qualify me for her
services, and she could come and give me what she calls 'a
good turn-out.' She seemed quite disappointed when I told
her that I wouldn't be staying around for that to happen."

"I'm quite sure *that* wasn't the cause of her disappointment," protested Martin, laying on the gallantry with a trowel.
And why not? It was small enough to return for all that she
was giving him, poor old bat.

He edged after her into her bedroom. Here, preparations
for her move seemed to be well advanced. Much of the
available floor space was occupied by large cardboard cartons
that contained heaps of clean but tatty clothing, together with
torn diaries, letters and personal papers.

"I'm going to burn most of this lot," said Con. "I'll get you
to help me carry the boxes downstairs later in the week, and
then I'll have a jolly good bonfire."

"In this weather?" he asked. It was stiflingly hot, up in the
bedrooms under the eaves; the Gothic windows, with their
pretty leaded panes, were not designed to be opened more
than a few inches. He anticipated that, even naked with a
single sheet over him, he was unlikely to sleep well.

Con shrugged. "A bonfire won't be much fun in this heat,"
she agreed, "but I simply must get rid of this rubbish. Lord
knows why I've kept so many old underpinnings after their
shoulder straps have worn through . . . Anyway, the clothes
aren't fit for Oxfam so I'll have to put them out for the
dustman. The private papers must be burned, though. I'll
just have to make sure that the smoke doesn't offend my
neighbours."

"Is that bossy woman still at number 10?" asked Martin.

"Marjorie? Oh yes. She's kind, though, in her way . . ."

"She was a pain in the neck on my last visit. I remember her coming round here and telling you what you ought to do at Christmas. Come to think of it, I'm not surprised you're leaving Fodderstone, if only to get out of her way."

Con turned swiftly from her dressing-table, where she had been rummaging in a drawer. "Don't think that, Martin!" she exclaimed earnestly. "Don't ever think that it's because of Marjorie that I'm going. My reasons are my own, they're nothing whatever to do with anyone else."

Then she relaxed, embarrassed by her own vehemence. "Marjorie *means* well," she explained. "I'm quite sure that if I were ill she'd be round immediately to help in any way she could." Con gave her lop-sided grin. "I'd probably recover in record time, in sheer self-defence."

They laughed together, and Con lifted some jewellery boxes from a drawer. "*Now*, Martin—these you simply must have: your grandfather's watch and chain and cufflinks."

He took them with gratitude and surprise. The watch was a fine gold half-hunter, the cufflinks thin gold ovals.

"I had no idea that anything like this was still in the family," he said when he had thanked her. "I suppose I assumed that they would have gone to my father and been sold long ago."

"That was precisely why your grandfather gave them to me," said Con dryly. "Your father inherited *his* grandfather's gold hunter and—as you guessed—promptly sold it. Poor dear Robert—he had so much charm, and so few scruples . . . And no sense at all when it came to handling money. He couldn't know, of course, that he would be carried off by a heart attack in his forties, but that's no excuse for his failure to make any financial provision for his wife and son. I loved him dearly, and I still miss him, but I have to admit that he was a hopeless spendthrift."

Martin remembered what Alison had said to him only that morning on the subject of money. As a boy he had loved and admired his light-hearted father; as a sixteen-year-old, realizing that but for his grandparents' generosity his widowed mother would be in financial difficulties, he had been hotly critical of his father's conduct. Now he began to wonder, in the light of what Alison had said, whether his own attitude to

money was one of the few things he had inherited from
Robert Tait.

But at least he, unlike his father, would eventually have
ample capital. There would be no need for *him* to go to the
length of selling his grandfather's gold watch, thanks to Aunt
Con.

"Then there's some family silver," she went on. "I want
you to have the cigarette box and the candlesticks from the
sitting-room, and there's all this lot too—I never bother to
get it out because I'm too jolly idle to clean it."

She took a large box from a cupboard, opened it, un-
wrapped some protective chamois leather and revealed a
hoard of silver: christening mugs, photograph frames, napkin
rings, brandy and whisky decanter labels, a porringer, a
salver that had been presented to her lawyer father by his
partners on his retirement, and a handsome assortment of
Victorian knives and spoons and forks. Martin's eyes gleamed.
A dining-table was something that he could easily buy when
he married; any good mahogany table would do. But to be
able to set it with heavy silver bearing the initials of some
long-dead Tait would give him a distinct social edge.

He thanked his aunt. The last time he'd seen such a haul of
valuables, he told her, was in the possession of a professional
burglar.

"I'm awfully glad you're taking them all," said Con. "It
eases my mind a little . . . there's something I have to tell
you, you see. Let's go down and have a glass of sherry, shall
we? A pre-supper drink, even though I've burned the supper
so badly that we'll have to make do with bread and cheese."

She began to lead the way downstairs. Tait was about to
follow her when he noticed a sampler in a rosewood frame
hanging just inside the door of her bedroom. He stopped to
look at it.

"Jolly nice, isn't it?" said Con, returning to join him. "That
was made by your great-great—" she paused and slapped her
head despairingly "—oh, gosh, that's gone too. My memory's
gone completely . . ."

Martin was so interested in the sampler that he made no
reply. It was a beautiful piece of stitchwork, the colours faded
but still distinct, the design a delightfully formal and symmet-
rical assembly of trees and flowers and birds and dogs and
cats and hearts and cupids. At the top were the obligatory
letters and numerals; at the bottom, framed by blossoming

boughs, was the name of the needlewoman: *Maria Bethell, Aged 10 years, 1842.* And in the centre was a verse illustrating the emphasis placed on infant piety in an age when early death was all too common.

> Now in the heat of youthful blood
> Remember your Creator, God.
> Behold the months come hast'ning on
> When you shall say, My joys are gon.

Martin was silent for a moment. Then he said, with no thought of acquisition, "Oh, I do like that!"

His aunt, who had been searching through a deed box, produced an old notebook. "Here you are," she cried triumphantly, "the family tree. I worked it out years ago, and I want you to have this book and pass it on eventually to your children. Now, I'll show you where Maria Bethell comes in. She married—"

Con held the notebook at arm's length and screwed up her eyes. Marjorie Braithwaite was always telling her that she ought to wear her spectacles on a chain, and that was why she didn't. It was a nuisance, though, to be forever mislaying them; and not merely a nuisance but an increasingly frequent reminder of the way her mind was fraying at the edges. "Oh crikey, I can't read a thing without my specs. Where do you suppose I left them, Martin?"

"Oh, *Aunt.*" He sighed good-humouredly, and ran them to earth in the pantry.

"Thank you, dear," said Con vaguely when he returned them. "Such a help to have a detective in the family . . . Ah, that's better. Now look, here's Maria Bethell. She married your great-great-grandfather's brother George in 1853, but died a year later in childbirth. So the verse on her sampler was sadly prophetic, poor child. I say, would you like to take that, too, Martin? The sampler, I mean?"

He demurred; he said that he couldn't deprive his aunt of something she liked to keep hanging in her bedroom, something that would be perfectly easy to move to her new house. But he was careful not to refuse the offer.

The fact was that Alison would love the sampler. Martin had thought of her as soon as he saw it, and now he longed for an opportunity to show it to her. He wanted to see and share her pleasure in it—and he hoped too that it would make her realize that he wasn't the grasping, insensitive man she took him for. Surely, if she saw his appreciation of craft work and heard from him the moving story of Maria Bethell's short life, Alison couldn't help but soften towards him?

That is, if she ever spoke to him again.

"Of course," admitted Con, mistaking his unaccustomed quietness for reluctance, "I can quite see that the verse on the sampler isn't exactly appropriate for a modern bachelor. I don't want to embarrass you—"

"On the contrary." He gave her his best smile. He liked the sampler anyway, and if Alison was fool enough to throw away the prospect of being his eventual wife, to hell with her. There were other pretty girls; and pretty girls with better—more suitable—family backgrounds than Alison's. He'd been dreading the idea of having that dim, fussy, suburban little Mrs. Quantrill as his mother-in-law.

"In my job," he went on, "I have to spend a lot of time thinking about people who've come to untimely ends, so the verse is entirely appropriate. Really, Aunt Con, the sampler's quite the nicest thing you could offer me. Yes please, I'd love to take it. And you can be sure—"

"Constance!"

They both started as an authoritative voice called up from below. Marjorie Braithwaite had as usual marched into the house without ceremony. "Constance, where are you? Your casserole's burning!"

Aunt and nephew exchanged grimaces. "You're too late," called back Con, with some satisfaction. She went downstairs, turning her long feet cautiously sideways as she negotiated the narrow treads. "The casserole's burned to a frazzle already. Yes . . . yes, as you said . . . we'll be having a cold supper, which is what you suggested in the first place. Anyway, what brings you out now, Marjorie? Isn't this your usual suppertime?"

"Yes it is, but Howard's not back from fishing yet. Not that it matters—that's the advantage of having a cold meal, we can be flexible about our timing. But now look here, Constance, about the produce show: you really must—"

Tired of lingering on the scruffy stairway, Martin stepped down into the sitting-room. Glad of his intervention, Con introduced him to her neighbour.

"Ah yes, I remember you." Marjorie stood four-square and looked him over, the chains on either side of her cheeks swinging aggressively. "See here, young man, I know you're a detective, so answer me this: why was it that when my sister Helen, who lives near Colchester, was burgled, it was *over an hour* before the police arrived in answer to her 999 call? And although she gave the detective a detailed list of the missing items, not one single thing has been recovered! It's an absolute scandal—"

It was a well-known hazard of police work, being cornered off-duty and held responsible for the activities of every criminal and every police force in the country. As his former boss—Alison's father—Chief Inspector Quantrill had advised him, Tait smiled politely and said nothing. ("They don't want to listen to reasoned explanations," Quantrill had said. "They don't want to listen at all. Let 'em get it off their chests, and just be thankful that you don't work as an income-tax inspector. *Their* social life must be hell.")

"Excuse me, Marjorie," Con said firmly, going to his rescue, "but Martin is just off to the Flintknappers to collect some drink—I forgot to get in any lager for him. And while you're there, Martin, please ask Phil Goodwin the landlord if he's got that bottle of brandy I ordered."

"You don't drink brandy," objected her neighbour.

"It's for cooking with," said Con grandly. She accompanied Martin to the back door. "Actually," she whispered, "I asked Phil to get me a good cognac—but not a word to Marjorie, it's nothing to do with her."

Martin winked and went, glad to be out in the heat of the early evening sun instead of being cooped up and stifled indoors.

In the oven of her prison, Sandra Websdell shivered. The nervous sweat that had sprung as she stood poised in front of her captor, ready to blind him and run, now felt deathly cold on her skin. She huddled in a corner listening, sick and afraid.

Would he come back with the dish of fruit and custard she had asked for? Would he come back that evening at all?

If he didn't, then she would have to wait a whole twenty-four hours before she had another opportunity to escape. By that time, would she still be capable of taking the opportunity? Would she be capable of taking it now, even if he came back?

A sudden sound in the gloom startled her. But it was only a rustle, a scrabble of tiny feet and a squeaking as her room-mates found her supper. She wept again, in weakness and despair.

And then, when she was no longer listening for it, a noise came from outside. With a pounding heart and a plug of fear in her throat she forced herself upright and waited for the door to be opened.

12

When Phil Goodwin hadn't returned home to the Flint-knappers Arms by six o'clock, his wife's attitude of cross acceptance began to corrode into anger. As if it wasn't bad enough of him to leave all the bar work to her at lunch-time—not to mention the subsequent clearing and washing-up, in this heat! And now it was time to open again for the evening . . . Damn Phil and his little bits on the side! Damn the woman, whoever she was . . .

The fact that Charley Horrocks failed to make his usual entrance soon after six o'clock did nothing to cheer Lois. If anything, it deprived her of a really good reason for giving her husband a piece of her mind. If she'd had to put up with Charley twice in one day, or if she'd been run off her feet by an early-evening coachload of unexpected customers, how she would have been justified in letting fly at Phil when he returned!

But at six-thirty the Flintknappers Arms was still empty. Lois went to the open doorway. The street was empty too. The whole of Fodderstone village, now that the day workers had returned home, had an air of exhaustion, as though it had been baked into silence by the unclouded sun.

She flounced back into the bar, her neat medium-high heels clicking on the floor. It was such a complete waste of time, hanging about waiting for customers. The children had brought home two rumbustious friends, and she had had to leave them to forage for their own tea; heaven knew what they were all up to. But if she journeyed to the kitchen to sort them out, someone would immediately materialize in the bar and shout for service. Damn the customers, damn the Flintknappers Arms . . .

By six-forty when her first customer—a young, fair, sharp-featured stranger—appeared, Lois could have screamed at him. "Yes?" she snapped, her hamster cheeks crimson above the lilac pie-frill of her blouse.

"Is the landlord anywhere about?" asked the man.

Lois would have enjoyed announcing exactly what she thought of her husband's absence, but loyalty and discretion made her guard her tongue. "I'm afraid my husband isn't in," she said, putting a belated welcome into her voice, though her neatly rounded buttocks were quivering with the effort of restraint. "He had to go into Breckham Market to see his accountant this afternoon, and he must have been held up. I'm expecting him back any moment."

Martin Tait told her that he had come about his aunt's brandy. Lois recalled Mrs. Schultz as an occasional buyer of a bottle of sherry, but she knew nothing about the brandy. Tait, who was in no hurry, bought a half-pint of lager to drink while he waited for the landlord to return, and carried his glass out into the sun.

There were no benches outside the Flintknappers Arms, which fronted directly on to the quiet village street. He leaned with consciously negligent grace against the doorpost and watched a young woman who was dismounting from a fine black horse. She hitched it to a convenient garden fence and then walked across the street towards him, making straight for the pub.

Tait moved away from the door with what appeared to be nothing more than casual courtesy, though the blood had begun to shift through his veins at an unprecedented gallop. He couldn't remember when he had last seen a combination quite as stunning as this: natural ash-blonde hair, dark-blue eyes, slim body inside nothing but a thin shirt and cream-coloured stretch jodhpurs; and over all an air of expensively bred self-assurance.

She stepped through the door without appearing to notice his existence, let alone returning his smile. Tait was momentarily crestfallen, realizing that he'd just been on the receiving end of an upper-class put-down. But to hell with that: she was probably no more than upper-middle, and he was middle class himself—only middle-middle, perhaps, but *old* middle-

middle, with family silver to prove it. His public school, Framlingham College, might not be in the Eton and Winchester league, but it had a good solid reputation in East Anglia. And with a university degree behind him and a Chief Constable's appointment somewhere up ahead, he had no intention of being put down socially by anyone.

He followed her into the bar, where she was buying cigarettes.

"You're not, by any chance, Charlotte Spencer-Davenport?" he asked, inventing a name that sounded like a pedigree.

"No," said the horsewoman, picking up the packet of cigarettes. The negative, expressed in two drawling syllables, could have been a further put-down, but Tait had calculated that his public-school voice would save him from that fate. She turned to him and looked him over, from his properly cut hair to his shoes that passed for Guccis, and evidently decided that he was sufficiently civilized to merit a longer reply. "No—I don't think I know Charlotte Spencer-Davenport, actually."

At close quarters she was a little less stunning than he had thought: in her early thirties rather than her twenties, with a wedding ring, hooded lids that made her eyes seem permanently supercilious, and a sharp-angled jaw. Her otherwise healthy skin was marred by a cold sore at one corner of her mouth. But she couldn't help having suffered from a summer cold, and none of those minor defects could detract from her style.

"Ah, sorry to bother you, then," he said pleasantly. "One of Charlotte's friends told me that she might be staying in Fodderstone, and asked me to look out for her." Inventing cover stories was on occasion an essential part of a detective's job; Martin Tait did it fluently, and with enjoyment. It was a practice that infuriated Alison, who called it lying. That had been one cause of their first parting, two years ago.

Alison . . . He recalled the girl with a sudden, painful vividness: so lovely, so warm, so young, so sweetly serious. But so uncompromisingly *honest* about everything, so stubborn, so censorious! She'd disapproved of him and said that she never wanted to see him again. Well, she needn't. He drove her out of his mind and concentrated on making a good impression on the woman in the second-skin jodhpurs.

"I'm here for a few days' duty visit to an elderly aunt," he went on. He avoided mentioning Aunt Con's undistinguished foreign surname, which would cut no social ice at all. "I don't expect you know her—she lives very quietly on Fodderstone Green, and isn't able to introduce me to anyone but equally elderly neighbours. My name's Tait, Martin Tait. May I buy you a drink?"

The ash-blonde woman looked him over again. He looked back at her, frankly but without being pushing; if she should snub him, he wanted to be able to retreat without undue loss of face.

But although she was hardly enthusiastic, she didn't put him down. "I don't see why not," she said coolly.

"Gin and tonic, with ice and lemon?"

She gave him a nod of probationary approval. "But we'll drink outside," she said with piercing clarity, moving to the door. "It's foully stuffy in here."

Imprisoned behind the bar counter, Lois Goodwin twitched with fury. First Phil's defection, and now the ultimate insult from that Mrs. Annabel Yardley. Oh the arrogance of the woman, treating people beneath her own class as if they weren't there! And all the time, while her husband was abroad, she was using her borrowed house to entertain men at weekends. She brought her noisy friends to the Flint-knappers for drinks on Saturday mornings—sometimes a mixed party, sometimes just one man. And not always the same man either.

But in spite of her air of superiority, Mrs. Yardley wasn't too particular—if you could believe the drunken boasts of young Andrew Stagg, the farrier from Horkey—about keeping to her own class, as long as the man was sufficiently good-looking. And if she could get away without paying for any of her pleasures, she would.

"Mrs. Yardley!" shrilled Lois. "You didn't give me the money for your cigarettes!"

"Really?" The voice that floated back from the doorway conveyed disbelief rather than apology, together with a suggestion that the woman behind the bar was being tiresomely petty. "Oh—see to it for me while you're there, will you—ah—Martin?"

Tait observed the affronted look on the landlady's round flushed face, and smiled an apology as he made what he hoped would prove to be a good investment. Then he hurried outside, carrying a large gin and tonic and his own refilled glass.

Lois Goodwin watched him go. *Another man running after her like a puppy dog,* she thought. *I wonder how far* he'll *get?*

The fair-haired stranger's accent would help him, of course. But he wasn't particularly good-looking, and Lois didn't imagine that a posh voice alone would take him very much further with Annabel Yardley than Phil had ever got; or any of their customers—with the possible exception of Andrew Stagg—though they all kept trying.

The vexatious thing about so many men was that they didn't know when to give up. Phil hadn't a ghost of a chance with Mrs. Yardley, but he was too vain to see it. Despite the number of times she'd snubbed him, he always preened himself and tried to chat her up when she came into the pub.

Male arrogance, concluded Lois crossly as she wiped the bar counter, was every bit as infuriating as social arrogance. Once men had set their sights on something—or someone— there seemed no way of convincing them that it was out of their reach.

Her captor re-entered Sandra's prison carrying a small bowl in blue and white willow-patterned earthenware. She pressed her hands flat on the table, trying to keep her trembling body upright. The combination of heat and nervous strain had exhausted her.

"I—I didn't think you'd come back," she whispered.

He told her that he had brought what she wanted. He reminded her that he had promised to look after her.

He stood there holding out the bowl, and smiled at her. Sandra pushed herself away from the table and moved towards him without being conscious of movement, banging her shin against the chair but feeling no pain.

She was still trembling, but she no longer worried about the physical difficulty of making good her escape. She was beyond rational thought. Her brain had switched off, leaving only instinct. The whole of her attention was concentrated on the weapon he was offering her, the blue and white bowl and its nauseatingly yellow contents.

She reached out her right hand. Smiling still, he gave her the bowl. As she took it, feeling its weight and the snug fit of the base in the palm of her hand, her nerves calmed and she sensed for a moment an extraordinary detachment. There was just such a bowl at home, and when she was a child her mother had taught her a verse about it. Even in the gloom of her prison, Sandra could pick out the details of the pattern with perfect clarity: the swallows, the Chinese temple, the bridge with three men—or was it four?

She raised her eyes to look dispassionately at her captor's face, judging angle and distance. Her pulse quickened, her mouth fell open as she breathed more deeply. Realizing what she intended, his expression started to change, but the change acted as a split-second trigger to her adrenalin supply. Before he could move she flung the bowl, heard his spluttering shout and glimpsed the viscous mess that covered his face. Then she tugged open the door and stumbled out, gasping, into the hottest August day for half a century. And ran, or tried to run; and screamed for help, or tried to.

"You're a detective? You mean you're what the Americans call a private eye? How very amusing."

"No," said Tait, nettled but taking care not to show it. Casual self-assurance, that was the only attitude that would impress a woman like Annabel Yardley. "I'm a police officer—a detective inspector in the regional crime squad."

The hooded dark-blue eyes widened with genuine interest. "But how riveting! You mean you investigate murders, and rapes and so on?"

"Frequently. We're called in by the county police forces to handle their difficult cases." It was not entirely true; the squad's primary job was to gather information about professional criminals engaged in organized crimes that extended beyond individual county boundaries, and most of the cases concerned burglary or breaking and entering. But crimes against the person were always more fascinating to the civilian mind, and Tait was out to fascinate.

He had already discovered that, whatever Annabel Yardley's relationship with her husband, she felt perfectly free to encourage other men. The only problem as far as Tait was concerned was that she appeared to be outrageously choosy. She had quizzed him about his background, and had then made it clear that the combination of Framlingham College and the University of Sussex was amusing rather than socially acceptable. She had also made it clear that she found him no more than mildly attractive.

But Tait had too much masculine pride to abandon hope. Annabel Yardley presented a challenge that he couldn't resist. She was, he guessed, easily bored; meeting a detective was obviously a new experience for her, and he intended to exploit the interest he had aroused. He would have to work fast, though, because he could spare her only this one week of his leave.

"Another drink?" he suggested. "While I tell you about an intriguing murder I investigated last year?"

She handed him her empty glass. "Thank you, but I really have to dash. You must tell me some other time."

She unhitched her horse from the garden fence she had temporarily commandeered, ignoring the housebound elderly resident who was glaring at her from behind a windowbox of geraniums. Her animal had passed the time by chewing absently at a rambling white Alberic Barbier rose. It had however deposited a pile of steaming knobs of high-grade organic fertilizer immediately outside the garden gate, by way of compensation.

Tait watched Annabel Yardley swing herself into the saddle. "I like your gelding," he said, hoping to sound knowledgeable.

She looked at him. "Do you ride?"

"Not since I was a boy." He had no intention of making a fool of himself in front of her. A horse was an unreliable beast, and uncomfortably tall: a long way up and—if it threw you—a hell of a long way down.

"I haven't time for riding now," he went on. "I spend every spare moment flying. I have a private pilot's licence, and a two-seater Cessna. I keep it hangared on Horkey airfield, and I'm hoping to notch up a few flying hours while I'm here."

"*Really?*" It was a very different "really" from the one she had used on the landlord's wife. She looked at Martin Tait with renewed interest.

"Would you like to come for a flight?"

"I don't see why not. . . ." She gathered up the reins and smiled at him in a way that concealed the cold sore at the corner of her mouth. "Yes, that might be amusing. Call me on the telephone and we'll arrange something." She pressed her calves against the horse and it began to walk, flicking Tait with its tail as it went.

"Tomorrow morning?" he called after her.

"I don't know *when*. Ring me."

"But what's your number?" he cried, running to catch up.

She turned in the saddle and looked him over. The early evening sun was in his eyes and he squinted up at her, suddenly conscious that there was sweat on his upper lip and that flies were buzzing round his head.

"I thought you were a *detective*," she mocked him. Then she leaned forward in the saddle and the horse broke into a canter, bearing her off with a clatter down the empty village street.

She had made him feel like a stable lad. All the more reason, then, for him to prove that he wasn't.

Sandra Websdell had been penned so long in the gloom that the sun struck her like a physical blow. Its heat hurt her head, its light dazzled her eyes. She tried to run, but she could manage only a drunken stagger. She tried to scream for help, but all that emerged was rasping breath.

He was coming after her. She could hear the thump of his feet on the sun-hardened earth. She tried to spurt through the burning kaleidoscope that surrounded her, but she tripped and fell. And once she was down she stayed down, her remaining strength seeming to ebb away from her into the dusty grass.

Ants immediately swarmed over her skin, and the effort of brushing them away was beyond her. But at least her vision cleared. Lying with her cheek against the ground, her nostrils filled with the peppery smell of dry earth, she opened her eyes and observed with complete detachment the differing green-ness of each blade of grass, and the tiny, separate, coloured grains of which the dust was composed. She could see more ants, scurrying through their grass forest; a red ladybird with six black spots, swaying on a grass stem; a small brown butterfly, taking to the air . . .

She raised her head a little, following the flight of the butterfly, and saw a wider world. Against the blue of the sky was an apple tree with apples on, and just beyond the tree was a fence. Beyond the fence, something was moving. No, not just something, someone. Someone passing by, on foot, on a horse, on a bicycle—

She tried to push herself into a sitting position and call for help, but a dark shadow fell across her, blocking the sun. Her captor, his face and shirt smeared with the mess she had thrown, was gazing down at her.

"No use trying to run away," he told her. "I need you too much to let you go."

She found a voice to plead with him. "Please—oh *please*."

He bent as if to lift her in his arms. He stank of stress and sweat, and his hands were slimy from wiping the mess out of his eyes.

She began to scream. He slapped his open hand across her mouth. She looked up at him, and what she saw in his face reduced her voice to a whimper.

First she said, *"No no no."*

Then she said nothing.

13

"Sorry I've been so long, I—oh, sorry."

Martin Tait had talked his way into the sitting-room before he realized that his aunt was listening seriously to music. Con stood at the open window gazing towards the lime trees that surrounded the Green, their upper branches golden in the last of the light from the evening sun. She was listening to a small battery-operated cassette player, concentrating so intently on soaring strings, harp and voices that if she heard her nephew she took no notice.

He sat down and waited quietly for the piece to finish. It was not his kind of music at all—too smooth, too choral, too full-bodied. Martin liked music to be modern and inventive, jazz for preference. The music that his aunt was listening to was solemn, even liturgical; yes, he could hear words in ecclesiastical Latin, "Pie Jesu" and "sempiternam requiem". Not what he wanted to listen to on a summer evening just when his social life was moving into top gear.

He wouldn't have thought the music would have any appeal for Aunt Con, either. When, in her younger days, he'd heard her singing as she went about the house, it had usually been something jolly from Gilbert and Sullivan. As for religion, she was—like all the Taits—plain Church of England and an infrequent attender.

And yet, obliged as a matter of courtesy to keep quiet and listen, Martin found himself acknowledging that the music of her choice had its own beauty. The high pure voice of the boy soloist was strangely moving in its expression of innocent faith. It made him feel sad: dissatisfied with his rootless life, aware for the first time of the fact that he had already lived for more than a quarter of a century, and that he was not immortal.

He thought of his newly acquired sampler, another expression of infant piety. And then he thought of the girl he had wanted the sampler for, because he knew she would love it. She would love this music, too.

But his sentimental affair with Alison was over. *"Now in the heat of youthful blood,"* the sampler said. Right: now in the heat of youthful blood he was going to make the most of whatever opportunities came his way, and he couldn't ask for a more attractive opportunity than Annabel Yardley.

So where did Aunt Con keep her telephone directory?

The music faded and died. His aunt didn't move; didn't even know he was there. He slipped out quietly, and came in again talking.

"Sorry I've been so long. The landlord of the Flintknappers was out and his wife knew nothing about your brandy, but she eventually found me a bottle. I hope it's the one you wanted."

Con expelled her breath in a long sigh, then turned away from the window. "Thank you, I'm sure it will do," she said in a sad, strained voice. She switched off the player. "I've been listening to music."

"So I heard. What was it?"

"The Fauré *Requiem*."

"Of course," said Martin, who hated to admit complete ignorance of anything.

"It's one of the most sublime pieces of music I know," she went on dreamily. "So reassuringly confident of the prospect of eternal rest . . ."

The prospect of eternal rest held no attraction for Martin at all, but it seemed unkind to break his aunt's mood by changing the subject. "May I?" He took the cassette out of the recorder and looked at the label. "Ah, the choir of St. John's College, Cambridge—yes, it's a beautiful performance."

"Isn't it?" Con gave her thin shoulders a shake and resumed the artificially bright voice she had used for most of the day. "I belonged to an amateur choir when I lived in Ipswich, and we did the Fauré just before I left—awfully well, too, though I sez it. But a female soprano had to sing the treble solo, and a boy's voice is so much more moving. That's why I love this recording. If you'd like to play it—or any of my other tapes or records, of course—do help yourself."

He thanked her, and settled for the immediate use of the telephone directory. Con switched on a table lamp, poured two glasses of sherry and took hers into the kitchen. There she found that Martin had brought back from the pub not only the cognac and lager she had sent him for, but a bottle of her favourite Amontillado sherry as well.

Enjoying the sensation of generosity, he refused payment for any of the drinks: "A thank-you-for-having-me present," he insisted.

"That's jolly nice of you, Martin. You shouldn't've, but thank you." Con began to break eggs into a bowl; despite—no, because of—Marjorie's strictures, she intended to cook something for her nephew. The dratted boy was leaning against the kitchen dresser watching her, as he invariably did when she was trying to concentrate on cookery, but even so she thought she might be able to produce some edible scrambled egg.

"Actually," she continued, "there is something I'd be awfully glad if you'd do for me while you're here."

"Anything at all, Aunt Con." Martin inserted a finger between two pages of the directory he was holding, and prepared to combine gallantry with patience. He always felt obliged to keep his aunt company when she was working in the kitchen because he knew that she liked having him there to chat to.

Con put two slices of bread under the grill. "Well, it's my car—"

"*Not* still the same white Ford Escort?" Martin was always amused by his aunt's reluctance to spend her money. All the more for him, eventually; but he felt that he could well afford to be generous with it. "Go on, be a devil and get yourself a new model!"

"What ever for? She's usually a very reliable car, and that's all I need. But I've just had her serviced, and I'm not entirely happy with the result. When I slow right down, or go into neutral, the engine tends to stop."

"Sounds as though the timing needs adjusting. It'll have to go back to the garage."

"That's what I thought. I've booked her in for 8:30 tomorrow morning. But dear old Mr. Rudge who used to be their mechanic has retired, and I'm not very good at explaining things to the new man—he's very young and impatient. So I'd be awfully grateful if you'd take the car in for me, and before you bring it back make absolutely sure that the engine won't cut out when it's in neutral. Do you mind?"

"Not a bit. Glad to help. Hey, watch it, the toast's burning—"

"Oh *gosh*," said Con. She made it sound like a major disaster. Martin laughed, until he saw how her hands were shaking as she turned the bread over. If it wasn't absurd to imagine that anyone would ever make a production number out of two slices of burnt toast, he could have sworn that she was very close to tears.

Revived by a second glass of sherry, Con scraped the toast, buttered it and piled it with rubbery scrambled egg. They ate at the kitchen table, using limp linen napkins, clumsily hemmed, that had once been part of a tablecloth; another of Con's endearingly absurd economies.

"Right," said Martin, eager to get his aunt organized so that he could pursue his own affairs. "I'll carry your boxes of rubbish down to the garden after supper, ready for your bonfire. And tomorrow morning I'll get your car seen to. What else can I do for you while I'm here?"

"Well, I *would* like you to come with me to look at the furniture in the cottage on the Horkey road. I know you said you don't want any of it, but I shan't be easy in my mind until you've seen it. Perhaps we could go there as soon as you bring back the car from the garage? But after that, you must go and fly your aeroplane and enjoy yourself. Did you find the telephone number you wanted, by the way?"

"No, I didn't. I met a girl at the Flintknappers—I expect you know her, Annabel Yardley. She asked me to ring her, but forgot to give me her number, and it doesn't seem to be in the book. Do you think she's ex-directory?"

"Annabel Yardley?" Con looked wryly amused. "I've never met her, but I know who she is. She won't be in the book because she's living here only temporarily—she's a friend of the Seymours. They're away in New Zealand, and she's

come down from London to look after their horses. You'll find
her number under their name—the address is Beech House.
Actually she has family connections with Fodderstone, because she was born a Horrocks. Her father is a brother of the
present Earl of Brandon and her great-grandfather, the third
Earl, was the last of the family to live at Fodderstone Hall.
But I imagine she's deliberately keeping quiet about her
connections because there's an uncouth Horrocks, Charley,
still living in the village."

"You seem to know a lot about her," said Martin, trying to
conceal his elation at the prospect of becoming intimately
acquainted with the niece of an earl. He wasn't entirely
surprised by his aunt's knowledge because she had always
taken a lively and respectful interest in those members of the
aristocracy who lived in Suffolk. She knew none of them
personally but she had—still had, apparently, despite her
forgetfulness about more pertinent matters—an extensive
knowledge of who was related to whom, how and when their
peerages had been obtained (mostly in the nineteenth century, after they'd made fortunes from brewing beer or manu-
facturing carpets) and their reported social activities. Her
table linen might be tatty, but she enjoyed spending money
on glossy magazines like *Country Life* and *Harpers & Queen*.

"Oh well, I know the Seymours slightly. I usually help
with Elizabeth Seymour's fund-raising events for the RNLI,"
said Con. Having been brought up near the coast, she had
always taken an interest in the lifeboat service. "Annabel
Yardley's married," she went on, offering her nephew a word
of caution. "Her husband's abroad with the army."

"I'm glad she *is* married," said Martin. "I couldn't possibly
afford to keep a woman like her entertained on a regular
basis. But it could be amusing to see something of her during
my leave."

Con put down her knife and fork. Her long narrow face was
earnest, her eyes slightly unfocused. "You haven't a regular
girlfriend, then?" she asked.

"No," he said without hesitation.

"And no foreseeable plans to marry? I'm not just being
inquisitive, I do have a good reason for asking."

He laughed and crunched burnt toast with his strong teeth,
enjoying the knowledge that he had no ties, no encum-
brances, and in the long term no financial problems. "*Definitely*
no plans of that kind!"

"And yours is a good career, isn't it?" Con persisted. "I mean, as a senior police officer you'll be well paid? And eventually you'll get a comfortable pension?"

He'd never given much thought to it, knowing that he had his aunt's money to come. He shrugged cheerfully, "Oh—we never think we're well paid, considering the responsibilities society puts upon us. But at Chief Constable level the money's not bad—and if I become Chief Commissioner of the Metropolitan Police I can always make a small fortune when I retire by selling my memoirs."

"Oh good . . ." said Con seriously. She had abandoned the greater part of her supper and was now concentrating her attention on some spilled grains of salt, pushing them about the table with her bony forefinger.

"You see, Martin . . . the thing is this: if you had a steady girlfriend and were planning to marry, I might feel that I was being unfair to you by altering my financial arrangements. As I'm sure your mother has told you, I made a will in your favour when your father died. You were still a boy, and I wanted to make sure that your education would be safeguarded if I fell under a bus.

"But the situation's different now, isn't it?" She raised her eyes and peered at him anxiously, urging him to agree with the logic of what she was saying. "You're independent. You're well established in your career, and you've a brilliant future. And now you've set my mind at rest by assuring me that you have no commitments, I'd better tell you what I've planned." She took a breath, and plunged. "I'm not going to leave you my godmother's money after all."

Martin's jaw stilled in mid-chew. He stared at her, rigid with disbelief.

"I'm not cutting you out of my will, don't think that," Con assured him with a nervous laugh. "But, well, £350,000 is an awful lot of money to leave to any one person, isn't it? It doesn't seem right, when it could be put to good use in helping people in distress, and saving lives. So now I know that you really aren't in any need of the money, I feel a sort of moral obligation to give it to charity instead."

14

Con had given a great deal of thought, over the years, to the problem of what to do with her embarrassing inheritance.

Her godmother, Alice Simpson, had been one of Con's mother's oldest friends and the wife of the owner of a large fishing-fleet that had sailed out of Lowestoft in the heyday of the herring. On her husband's death, Alice had taken shrewd advice and sold up the fleet while the herring was still king. Childless, and with no near relatives, she had made a sizeable bequest to the Royal National Lifeboat Institution for the purchase of a boat in her late husband's name, then willed the remainder of her fortune to her god-daughter Con Schultz, *née* Constance Alice Tait.

When Con had inherited the money in middle age, she was astonished and alarmed to find that it amounted to over £200,000. She had known that her godmother intended to leave her something, and she had thought in terms of buying herself a car, and perhaps travelling a little. But £200,000 was more than she knew what to do with.

At the time Con was living in the family home in Woodbridge, where she had returned after her brief marriage to help her mother care for her ailing father. She was able to meet all her living expenses from her salary as a deputy librarian, and though she bought a small car for journeying to work in Ipswich, and took holidays-of-a-lifetime with an old schoolfriend in Venice, Florence and Athens, she used very little of her godmother's money. Her greatest extravagance had been to retain the services of a good accountant and a stockbroker. With sound investment advice, and the conscientious re-investment of most of the interest over a period of twenty years, her godmother's money did nothing but grow.

When her father died, Con had faced the prospect of looking after her ageing mother. She knew that she was far more fortunate than most middle-aged women in her situation, in that she had no financial need to go on working, but she enjoyed her job and valued the company of her colleagues. And so she sold up the house in Woodbridge and moved her mother with her to a small house in Ipswich not far from the library, so that she could hurry home every lunch-time to attend to the old lady.

It was at this stage in her life that her much younger brother Robert, Martin's father, had succumbed to a heart attack and left his wife and schoolboy son almost penniless. Con was already paying her nephew's school fees and expenses: Robert had relied on his father to pay for the boy to follow the family tradition and go to Framlingham College, and Con had taken over that responsibility—without her nephew's knowledge—after the old man died. And on her brother's death she immediately arranged, with her mother's agreement, that his widow should receive the whole of the proceeds from the sale of the Woodbridge house.

Robert's death in early middle age had put Con in mind of her own mortality. Accordingly, she had made her will in her nephew's favour and she told her sister-in-law what she had done; but she had never until now made any mention of the amount of money involved.

Throughout her financial transactions, Con had instructed her accountant to keep a clear distinction between the money she regarded as her own (her salary, and after she retired her pension); the family money (a small bequest from her father, and anything she handled on her mother's behalf or inherited after the old lady's death); and her godmother's money. This was the point that she tried to make to her nephew as he sat opposite her at the kitchen table, white-faced, still clutching a fork to which clung some cold scrambled egg.

"You see, I'm not talking about my own money, Martin. Or about family money. The £350,000 grew out of money that George Simpson, my godmother's husband, made from his fishing-fleet. It has no connection at all with the Taits, and I don't think we have any moral right to go on keeping it in our family. It ought to be used to help those in peril on the sea, and so I'm going to give it to the RNLI. When you think of the tremendous work the lifeboats do without any government grants, and the bravery of the volunteers who risk their lives—*give* their lives—to save others . . . well, you can see why I've made this decision, can't you?"

Martin unclenched his jaw and attempted to speak. The muscles of his throat were so tight that he felt close to suffocation. He thought perhaps—hoped fervently that—he was dreaming.

"Family money?" he heard himself croak. "You mentioned family money?"

"Why, yes." Con was growing increasingly nervous. She hadn't looked forward to having this conversation with her nephew, but she had been completely convinced by her own logic. It had never occurred to her that Martin would be so shocked by the news.

"All that's left of the family money," she gabbled brightly, "and my money, of course, will come to you after I'm dead. My accountant did a valuation for me last month. It's not an awful lot, I'm afraid. But it will buy you a good car, and perhaps an exotic holiday. I've always thought that it would be interesting to go to China . . ."

A *car?* A *holiday?* When she'd just mentioned £350,000 . . . Martin dropped his fork and gripped the edge of the table. "How much?" he demanded hoarsely.

"Er—" Con's encouraging smile faded. The amount that she would be leaving her nephew, though surely acceptable to a bachelor, was nothing in comparison with her godmother's fortune. She knew now that she should never have mentioned the £350,000. She had done so because Martin was an intelligent and responsible man—a police officer, no less—and she had felt that he would be sure to agree with her that such a large sum must be put to a worthy use. But although she was still convinced that logic and morality were on her side, she could see that the amount she was offering him must seem insultingly small.

"Um—well, about £10,000—"

Her nephew stared at her, the shocked whiteness of his skin changing to an indignant red. *"Ten thousand?"* he repeated. "You're not serious, Aunt Con. You can't be! You can't possibly—"

He paused in mid-sentence, his face beginning to clear but his voice still wary. "Oh, but of course—you're talking just about *cash*, aren't you? There's this house, too. And the one on the Horkey road—" He did a quick mental estimate; yes, with luck he might still come out with something approaching £100,000. Nothing like that tantalizing £350,000, but almost what he'd originally expected. Not good, but not too bad either.

But his aunt was shaking her head. "I'm afraid not. I didn't spend much of my godmother's money, but I did buy these two houses with it. Their value is included in the £350,000. And you see, I need every penny of that to buy a lifeboat."

"You're going to *buy* a lifeboat?"

"Oh, yes." The thought of what she planned to do restored Con's confidence and enthusiasm. "That's what I've set my heart on. I've checked with the RNLI, and they've told me approximately what it will cost to build and equip a boat. Not one of the biggest, they cost half a million; but the kind that was lost with all its crew off the Cornish coast a few Christmases ago. If I buy a new boat, the RNLI will let me name it in someone's memory, and that's what I intend to do. The money came from my godmother, so I shall name the boat the *Alice Simpson*. It'll be a jolly good memorial to her, won't it?"

Martin pushed himself away from the table and began to stride about the kitchen, his mind in a turmoil. Then he turned on his aunt, his eyes gleaming with anger, his voice rising. "But what happened to the family money, for God's sake? My grandfather was a man of property—there was that big house in Woodbridge, and a scattering of smaller houses and shops in the centre of the town. Grandfather must have left a small fortune. And that was Tait money, it should have come to me!"

Con rose uneasily to her feet and backed against the sink, alarmed by the change in her nephew. This was an aspect of his character that she had never seen. "Don't shout, Martin, please. Yes, your grandfather did once own a lot of property, but he sold it some years before he died. He left what at the time seemed to be a substantial amount of money—but you must remember that property values were a great deal lower then than they are now. And when your father died, your mother had to be provided for. Her house and the bookshop were bought with your grandfather's money, and I expect you'll eventually inherit them. And then there was your grandmother—"

"Granny? What did *she* want with money? She lived with you for years, and she was virtually housebound. Good God, she was ninety when she died! What did she want money *for?*"

Con faced him, her back straight, her eyes and voice bleak. "It was the nursing home," she said. "Don't forget that your grandmother spent her last five years in a private nursing home. That was what took all the money."

"But why the *family* money?" Martin exploded. "You had all that capital of your own: why did you use up money that should have been kept in the family? I'm the only grandchild, the only living Tait, and one day I shall marry and have children to carry on the name. I had an *entitlement* to grandfather's money."

"But your grandmother had a prior entitlement," snapped Con, angry in her turn. "My father left me with the responsibility of looking after my mother in her old age, and with the means to do so. That was how he intended his money spent. It never occurred to me to use Alice Simpson's money for that purpose. It wouldn't have been right. The pity was, of course—from everyone's point of view, including her own—that your grandmother should have lived so long in the nursing home."

"And that's another thing," stormed Martin. "Why did Granny have to go into a nursing home at all? I know she was frail, but she wasn't actually ill. A bit muddle-headed, perhaps, but I remember her as a nice little old body, no trouble to anyone. You looked after her for long enough while you were working—surely you could have gone on doing so after you retired? Good grief, Aunt Con, she was your *mother*. How *could* you shove her away in an expensive nursing home? Christ, how can you talk about it not being 'right' to use the money your godmother left you? Was it *right* to put your own mother away? Was it *right* to use up all the family money in order to get rid of her, just because the poor old dear was a bit of an encumbrance?"

Con flinched as though he had struck her. "Martin," she pleaded, "you don't understand—"

"No I bloody well don't! I've always thought you were kind and generous towards the family, but I'm beginning to see things differently now." He strode to the open door. "Well, you must do as you please with all your money. But if your conscience tells you to give a third of a million to charity and only a measly ten thousand to your own flesh and blood, don't expect *me* to help you in your old age. You can die alone for all I care."

He swung out of the cottage and along the darkening path towards the front gate, too furious to see or hear an eavesdropper scuttle away behind the cover of a rose hedge to the garden of the cottage next door.

*   *   *

Martin Tait's first thought was to go to the Flintknappers
Arms and get drunk. But he was a cerebral man: too clever to
pickle his wits in alcohol, he sat alone in a corner of the noisy
bar room, brooding over one small gin and tonic.

His thrusting stride through the woods between Fodderstone
Green and the Flintknappers had worked some of the blind
fury out of his system. Now he was cold, resentful, calculating.

And what he calculated was that there was still time to
retrieve his rightful fortune. He didn't know whether his aunt
intended to give her money to the RNLI while she was still
alive, or leave it to them in a new will; but from what she had
said, it seemed as though the money was still in her possession. It ought to be possible, then, for him to devise some
way of extracting it from her. It must be possible. His whole
future, the way of life that he had planned for himself, was at
stake.

He made a decision, and went to the bar. The man behind
it, loud-voiced, catfish-moustached, shifty-eyed behind tinted
spectacles, was presumably Phil Goodwin the landlord.

"I suppose you wouldn't happen to have a bottle of champagne I could buy to take away?" Tait asked.

His bucolic fellow-customers stared and sniggered. A pot-
bellied darts player missed the double, lost his match and
swore roundly. Tait ignored them.

Phil Goodwin, mentally and physically exhausted after a
difficult day out, and angered by his wife's nagging over his
lateness, shouted in astonishment. Unlikely as it seemed, he
did have some champagne. The crafty brewery rep, taking
advantage of Phil's inexperience to increase his own sales
commission, had persuaded him that he would need to stock
some for the Christmas trade in his first year at the Flintknappers; but of course no one had bought it. Ordinary local
people didn't drink champagne, and the rich could always get
it cheaper by the case elsewhere. Half a dozen gold-foiled
bottles, representing a wasted investment of pounds of Phil's
inadequate capital, were gathering cobwebs in his cellar.

"Seriously?" he demanded. "For cash?" The fair-haired,
posh-voiced stranger sounded genuine, but Phil had learned
enough about pub-keeping and about customers' bloody stupid jokes to be wary of outlandish requests.

"Seriously," confirmed Tait, pulling his wallet from his hip pocket. "In fact make it two. And is there a telephone I can use?"

Five minutes later Martin Tait left the Flintknappers, a slight smile on his face, two bottles of champagne under his arm, a complete plan of action on ice in his mind.

15

Con felt utterly wretched. She had been so sure that what she intended to do with her godmother's money was both fair and reasonable, but now she was in a complete muddle, not knowing right from wrong. *Was* she treating Martin shabbily? She had always, from her schooldays, been notorious for her clumsiness. Had she, in her effort to do good, made a monumental hash of everything?

As for what her nephew had said about her treatment of her mother: he was too young, too inexperienced to understand. What he had shouted at her was cruelly unfair. And yet . . .

He didn't understand and he wasn't being fair, but she knew in her heart that he was right. He had voiced the reason for the guilt that had been her constant companion for ten years. Acknowledging it, overwhelmed by regret and the sense of failure, Con found that only the Fauré "Pie Jesu" —that ravishingly tender combination of organ and woodwind, strings and harp and treble innocence—could give her any comfort. She had played the *Requiem* almost continuously ever since Martin had walked out.

And now he was back. Con flinched as she heard him approach, dreading another row. She hadn't known that he had so much anger in him.

But astonishingly—thankfully—the anger had all gone. Martin was himself again, courteous, charming, abjectly apologetic. He'd even brought a bottle of champagne!

He stood with his hands behind his back, as he used to do when he was in trouble as a boy, and made a speech that he had obviously rehearsed. "Inexcusable behaviour . . . unjust, abominably rude, thoroughly ungrateful. You've been a splendid aunt to me, always. And Grandpa and Granny were

wonderfully kind and generous to my mother and me. Can't
expect you to forgive me . . . deeply ashamed . . . And now
I'm going to pack and clear off."

He made for the stairs, but Con couldn't let him go. He
had so much of his father about him, and just as she had
always found it impossible not to forgive her brother Robert,
so she couldn't not forgive his son. After all, her nephew's
failings were nothing in comparison with her own.

"Martin!" she called. "Don't leave—stay and finish your
holiday, *please*."

He hesitated, then turned. "If you really mean that . . .?"

"Oh, I do," she said, her face brightening. "Oh golly, yes,
I do."

"Then of course I'll stay," he said, smiling a boyish smile.

During the next twelve hours Martin Tait took every opportunity to devote himself to his aunt. He carried the boxes of
burnable rubbish from her bedroom to the garden, washed
up the supper things, chatted to her amusingly and made her
a late-night cup of Ovaltine.

The following morning he was up and about soon after six,
unrefreshed after an airless, wakeful night. The day promised
to be as hot as ever. He watered the garden thoroughly,
mowed the grass and took his aunt an early morning cup of
tea. Then, as he had promised, he attended to her car.

The tranquil appearance of Fodderstone Green had been
preserved by keeping the twentieth-century residents' cars
and garages out of sight at the far end of their long, leafy
gardens. Martin backed the white Escort out of his aunt's
discreet timber garage and on to the dirt lane that gave access
to the road through the Green. He drove to the village
garage, and explained to the mechanic how Mrs. Schultz
wanted the engine to be adjusted. When the work had been
completed to his satisfaction he filled the tank with petrol,
paying for it out of his own pocket rather than putting it on
his aunt's account. And after he returned the car to her he
drove her, again as he had promised, to the property she
owned in the Horkey road.

The cottage, standing entirely alone beside the quiet country lane, with harvested fields on either side and a belt of
woodland at the back, had no name. Surprisingly, it had a
number instead. Built at the same time as the cottages on

Fodderstone Green, number 15 had once been part of the
first Earl of Brandon's estate.

As it was not a showpiece, the cottage had been plainly
built, with no porch, pantiles instead of thatch, and a service-
able mixture of brick and rough flint for the walls. Even so,
the front door and windows had been constructed in the
Regency Gothic style, and it was this architectural quirk—
together with the absurdity of the number on the door when
there was not another building in sight—that had made Con
Schultz fall in love with the cottage and decide to rescue it
from dilapidation.

She had spent plenty of money on it, that was obvious. Tait
glanced sourly at the renovated roof, the renewed woodwork,
the recent paint. An extension at the rear, presumably contain-
ing a new kitchen and a bathroom, had been architect-designed
to be in sympathy with the rest of the cottage.

The garden, though, was showing signs of neglect. The
grass was shaggy. Roses, geraniums, lobelia, clematis, were
all wilting from lack of water. And on the cottage door, the
original brass numerals that had been worn thin by a century
and a half of polishing were now dulled.

"Oh crumbs," sighed Con. "What a shame . . . My own
fault, of course. When I used to let the place to summer
visitors, I took the trouble to look after things. But it was a
frightful bind, rushing over between lets to clean the house
and keep the garden tidy. I was jolly relieved when Sandra
Websdell and her fiancé decided that they wanted to start
their married life here, and I haven't done a thing since I
gave them their key. And then when Sandra disappeared, I
was so concerned about her that I didn't even notice the
garden when I came over here with Beryl and the detective.
Oh, those poor thirsty plants . . ."

"Don't worry, Aunt Con," said Martin. "I'll water them.
And then I'll cut the grass—"

He took the key from her hand, unlocked the door and
held it open for her. She went in, giving the numerals an
apologetic rub with her handkerchief in passing. A stone-
paved lobby, with a staircase bending up from it, opened on
to what had originally been the only ground-floor room of the
cottage. It was furnished comfortably enough, but the narrow
pointed Gothic windows with their leaded panes gave the
room a dim, ecclesiastical air—not unpleasant on a hot day,
but in more typical English weather it would almost certainly

seem gloomy. A passable place, Tait thought, for a short secluded honeymoon, but a dump to live in.

His aunt turned to him, her thin face flushing with anticipated embarrassment. They had neither of them made any allusion, since Martin's apology, to their quarrel; but there was something Con felt the need to say.

"About the furniture, Martin. Here and in my own house. You see, I'd *counted* on your taking as much of it as you wanted. After all, a houseful of good furniture isn't to be sneezed at. It'd save you a great deal of money when you do eventually get married. Won't you please think again? Look, this small oak table is really rather a nice piece—"

"No thank you, Aunt Con."

"Or what about kitchen equipment?" She galloped ahead of him into the extension and pointed out a nearly new electric cooker and a fridge-freezer. "Won't you take these?"

"Thank you, but no." He moved to her side and put an arm across her bony shoulders so that she could no longer see his face. "I do appreciate your offer, but I made my decision yesterday and nothing has happened to make me change my mind." He spoke gently, almost sadly, in furtherance of the plan he had made last night, but his eyes were angry. It was not, he knew, her intention to insult him; but he felt insulted.

Con twisted away and faced him again, desperate to explain her meaning. "But I wouldn't expect you to keep the furniture, if you really don't want it. What I thought, you see, was that you could make quite a lot of money by selling it."

Then she saw her nephew's expression. Realizing how far her well-intentioned clumsiness was hurting his pride, she tried to retrieve the situation by babbling on: "Selling the *antiques*, I mean. I wasn't suggesting that you should go round trying to flog a second-hand cooker . . . Oh gosh!" She stood for a moment in the middle of the room, angular, awkward, pink with mortification. Then, muttering something about taking a look at the bedroom, she made a dash for the stairs.

Tait kicked the chintz-covered sofa, and swore under his breath. The prospect of playing the devoted, forgiving nephew for the remainder of his holiday was almost more than he could endure; and yet to leave now, when he was in an obvious huff, might well ruin his plans.

And then he heard her calling from upstairs, in a high,

strange voice. "Martin—come quickly! This is incredible! I can hardly believe—"

He took the twisting stairs at a run, and met his aunt on the tiny landing. There was a look of amazement, of mystery, on her face. She put a finger to her lips and whispered breathily, jerking her head towards the open door of the only bedroom.

"It's Sandra! Sandra Websdell, my neighbour's daughter, the girl who bolted just before her wedding. She's come back! She's here now, tucked up in bed and fast asleep!"

Tait gave his aunt a shrewd glance. Con Schultz was no fool. He could see that she was in shock, and that she was saying only what she desperately wanted to believe.

He strode past her into the low-ceilinged bedroom. There, as his aunt had described, apparently snug under the bed-clothes, was a girl in her early twenties. Her eyes were closed, her face was shadowed by the sheets, her pretty brown hair was spread out over the pillow.

Inspector Tait was an experienced detective. One close look, touching nothing, and then he ushered his aunt out of the house and set in motion a police investigation. He knew at once, by sight, by sense, by smell, that the girl was dead.

16

The unenviable duty of informing the missing girl's parents that she had been found dead in suspicious circumstances fell to Detective Sergeant Lloyd. Normally it would have been done by a uniformed policeman or policewoman; a uniform gives grave news its necessary authenticity. But Hilary Lloyd went to tell the Websdells because they already knew her. She was the detective who had interviewed them when they first reported that their daughter was missing.

Both Websdells were out at work that hot morning, Wednesday 9 August. Geoff was deep in the forest, one of a gang helping to fell a block of mature Scots pines. He was summoned by Forestry Commission radio, and was returned to his home by Land Rover. Beryl was in Fodderstone village, where Hilary Lloyd found her in a council-owned bungalow, washing an old widower's linen.

When the couple were together in their own home, number 8 Fodderstone Green, Hilary broke the news. She stayed with them for half an hour; not attempting to question them, because she already knew as much as they could tell her, but letting them talk, sharing a pot of tea, reassuring them that their daughter would have died quickly. Until the post-mortem had been completed she had no means of knowing whether this was true, but she knew that it was what they wanted to hear.

Beryl Websdell had a sister who lived in Horkey, but she was away on holiday with her family at Lowestoft. Hilary Lloyd arranged for the sister to be notified. When a police car arrived to take Geoff Websdell to identify his daughter's body, Hilary asked Beryl if there was a friend or neighbour who could keep her company until her husband returned. Beryl opted immediately for her neighbour at number 9. Hilary had some doubt about involving Mrs. Schultz, who was still shocked after discovering the body. But she fetched her, and then left the two women together.

Con was glad to be able to do something useful. Her nephew, pleased as a two-tailed police dog, had returned himself to unofficial duty. In his absence Con felt very much alone, distressed by what she had seen, grieved for the girl and her family, overwhelmed by sadness.

But Beryl had asked for her support, and Con gladly gave whatever she could. She was too awkward and shy to touch the bereaved woman; but Beryl, cuddly as she looked, was equally shy, equally inhibited, and she neither expected nor wanted an embrace. Instead they sat together, talked a little, wiped their eyes, dabbed their noses, drank more tea.

Beryl was too numbed to be able to cry properly. Her grief was too deep for her to begin to express it. She talked brightly, off the top of her head, about what she would give her husband to eat now that he was unexpectedly at home, and what she would do that afternoon. She was concerned, she explained, about poor old Tom Vout's long-johns; she'd have to go back and finish washing them, or he wouldn't have a clean pair to his name.

Con promised to deal with the problem. Not to go and do

the laundering, because that would embarrass the old man as much as it would embarrass her, but to telephone the home-help organizer and arrange for Beryl to be temporarily replaced. Her mind at rest on that score, Beryl set about cooking a large meal that neither she nor her husband would eat; although later in the day Geoff would sneak into the larder and help himself guiltily to some cold food, ashamed to be seen eating when his only child had been found dead, when he'd had to identify her body on the mortuary slab, but wholly hungry just the same.

Con went home as soon as Geoff returned. She called back later in the afternoon and found him busy in his garden, sowing spring cabbage and onions. Life had to go on, and the seasons must be served. And in the kitchen, on hands and knees, her red face and arms running with sweat, Beryl was washing her already immaculate floor. Why not? thought Con, and tiptoed angularly away.

But she spent the afternoon in her own garden, dead-heading roses, so that she would be within call if Beryl needed her. There was a good deal of coming and going at the Websdells' house during the afternoon: the police, twice; the Horkey parson who was in charge of five parishes including Fodderstone and couldn't hope to know all his flock, but who did his best to keep an eye on them; and a number of local people who, too shocked and embarrassed to attempt to voice their feelings, pushed envelopes through the letter-box and hurried off. The village shop must have had an unprecedented run on its stock of condolence cards.

And that, Con thought, was almost certainly the way Beryl and Geoff would want it: seeing as few people as possible, but receiving Fodderstone's silent sympathy. Just as well that Marjorie Braithwaite was out for the day and knew nothing of what had happened, or she would be in number 8 taking over the Websdells' lives!

The only villager who went to call was Christopher Thorold. Con saw him park his truck at the gate and tramp heavily up her neighbours' garden path, his shock of greying hair partly tamed, his broad face newly shaven. He was tieless, but wearing a stiff dark suit. Obviously he intended to offer sympathy in person, and for a moment Con was surprised; but then she remembered having heard Beryl say that Christopher's late mother was her cousin.

When Beryl answered his knock on her back door, she

seemed to Con to be fairly well composed. More so than Christopher himself. Con could hear the nervous shuffling of his boots on Beryl's doorstep.

"P-pa sent me," Con heard him burst out, "to say we're sorry about your Sandra. Wholly sorry."

"You're a good boy, Christopher," said Beryl, her voice a little higher than usual but otherwise steady. "Thank you for coming. And thank your Pa for me, too."

Christopher shifted his boots again. "An' he told me to say, if there's anything we can do . . ." His voice trailed off uncertainly. Beryl assured him that there was nothing, and he sounded greatly relieved. "That's all right, then. I'll bring your load of firewood tomorrow, Beryl, an' it'll be free. Pa says I'm to take nothing for it, to say how sorry we are."

He backed out of his bereaved relative's presence and tramped off, having delivered his own form of condolence card. Con, touched by so much clumsy good-heartedness, and relieved that Beryl was coping so well, went indoors and consoled herself by playing once again the Fauré *Requiem*.

Towards dusk, though, she felt that she ought to slip back and see whether Beryl needed her in any way. Geoff was still in his garden, talking over the fence to his forester neighbour at number 7 who had expressed himself as well as he could by offering the Websdells a bowl of late raspberries.

Con found Beryl sitting in the kitchen. Her elbows on the table, her head on her hands, she was crying at last. Deep sobs came wrenching up from her stomach; great tears oozed through her fingers and ran down her forearms, until each rough-skinned elbow rested in salt water.

Con hesitated in the doorway. A private person, she had always been accustomed to bear her sorrows alone. She was unwilling to intrude on Beryl's grief, uncertain what to do for the best.

But at least there was some practical help she could give. Observing that Beryl's handkerchief was sodden Con hurried home, returned with an open box of man-sized tissues, and offered them wordlessly.

Silenced at last by sheer exhaustion, Beryl sat up and accepted a handful of tissues. She blew her nose, mopped her swollen face, and pushed her damp hair off her forehead. She even tried to smile. "God bless you, Con dear," she said.

Con didn't reply. Over-sensitive to others' emotion—she always wept at televised funerals—she was too choked to

speak. Instead, nervously, awkwardly, she placed what she
hoped would feel like a comforting hand on Beryl's shoulder.

The "God bless you" had reminded her of Beryl's religious
faith. The bereaved woman hadn't mentioned it to her today;
hadn't until now spoken of God, wasn't wearing her *Jesus My Joy*
badge, certainly hadn't sung her song. And yet, if her faith
really had any meaning, today was the day when it should be
of most help to her. If, nominal Christian that she was, Con
herself could derive so much comfort from the *Requiem*, then
Beryl would surely be comforted by her own choice of religious music.

Con gave her friend's plump shoulder an experimental pat.
She cleared her throat—it was still tight with lurking tears—
and said, "You haven't sung your song today."

Beryl shook her head.

"I've missed it," said Con. "I've missed hearing you sing it.
Why not give it a try?"

"I couldn't," said Beryl. "I still believe, don't think I don't.
I've prayed and prayed, and I know that whatever's happened, Jesus still loves me. But I wouldn't be able to find the
voice to sing."

"I'll help," said Con. "Let's sing it together."

The younger woman shook her head again but Con, her
arm pressed more confidently round the bowed shoulders,
began to hum. Beryl hiccuped, sniffed, and then, drawn
irresistibly by the tune, attempted a few words:

"This is my—"

Her voice wavered and broke. "I can't," she said. "I can't."

"Yes, you can," said Con. "Come on, Beryl dear—'This *is*
my song—' "

They made an uncertain start. Beryl had a poor singing
voice at the best of times. But with Con's true contralto
supporting her, bearing her up, she gradually lifted her head
and began to sing:

"This is *my song*
My Saviour's *love to me-e,*
How great Thou *art,*
How great *Thou art.*"

And that was how Sergeant Lloyd found them when, making

a late evening call, she passed the open kitchen window. It was a strange, almost a ludicrous sight: two women, one middle-aged, one elderly, one fat, one very thin, sitting side by side at the table, staring straight ahead and clinging to each other unselfconsciously as they swayed to their own vocal rhythm:

> *"This* is *my* song, *my Saviour's love to me,*
> *How great* Thou *art, how* great *Thou art!"*

Hilary Lloyd listened to their soaring voices for a few moments, saw their rapt faces, and went discreetly away.

17

When, in the bedroom of the cottage numbered 15 on the Horkey road, the covering sheets and blankets were carefully lifted from the body of Sandra Websdell, she was found to be fully clothed.

She was a tall girl, slim but well built. Her feet and legs were bare, but otherwise she was dressed appropriately for hot weather in light briefs and brassière, and a sundress. She lay curled on her right side, with the skirt of her sundress arranged tidily and modestly over her legs. Her shoes—a pair of espadrilles—were standing neatly together on the floor beside the bed.

There were traces of dusty earth on the left side of her face, but they were smoothed over her cheek as though an attempt had been made to wipe them away. More extensive traces of earth, and also of grasses and grass seeds, were present in her hair, on her arms and legs and on her dress.

The only visible injury on her face was a slight swelling on the lower lip. There was also one small bruise on the front of the throat, at the level of the larynx, consistent with her having been gripped by the neck.

The pathologist's estimate was that the girl had died between six and eight o'clock the previous evening, Tuesday 8 August. In his opinion she was already dead when she was placed in the bed.

At the post-mortem examination, conducted on the afternoon of Wednesday 9 August, no evidence was found of recent sexual intercourse or any form of sexual assault. The only marks on the body took the form of a narrow line of faded bruises across the girl's back at waist level. Her fingernails had been damaged in use, and scrapings from them yielded shreds of rope fibre.

At the time of her death the girl had been suffering from an acute respiratory infection.

Despite the evidence of bruising on her throat, she had not died by manual strangulation. The pathologist's finding was that the cause of death was reflex cardiac arrest—the sudden stoppage of the heart following pressure on the nerves and arteries of the neck.

The pressure had been minor; insufficient to asphyxiate the girl, and probably applied without the intention to kill. Sandra Websdell had died not by violence, but from shock. She had literally been frightened to death.

18

Detective Chief Inspector Douglas Quantrill, head of Breckham Market CID, looked with disfavour at Detective Inspector Tait. He respected the younger man's professional abilities, but that didn't mean he had to like him. Or that he had to welcome Tait's reappearance at the Horkey road cottage early on Wednesday afternoon.

"You've no business to be in on this investigation, Martin," he said. "It's nothing whatever to do with the regional crime squad."

"Ah, but I'm not here in my regional crime squad capacity," said Tait blandly. "I found the body this morning, so I'm helping you with your enquiries. And because I'm staying in the village, I can provide you with the local information you're going to need."

Quantrill snorted. "According to her statement, and to your own, it was Mrs. Constance Schultz who found the body. And as she's an established resident, I've no doubt she knows a good deal more about the village than you do."

"Arguably. But this is her—my aunt's—cottage, and as her representative I'm entitled to remain here. If there's anything further you want to know from her, I'm the best person to do the asking."

The Chief Inspector scowled. As if the blasted boy didn't have enough going for him, with his superior voice and his university degree and his guarantee of accelerated promotion! All Tait had to do was to keep his nose clean, and in a few months' time he'd also be a chief inspector. Another couple of years—perhaps less—and he, Quantrill, would be outranked. So much for the value of experience. So much for his own twenty-five years' hard slog as a detective . . .

And then there was his daughter Alison. That was another grievance he had against Martin Tait. There was something going on between the two of them, and Quantrill didn't like it. He suspected Tait of trifling with his daughter's affections. Only yesterday she'd called at home on her way back to Yarchester, seething with fury over something Martin had said or done when he took her flying. Damn his conceit . . . and damn his impudence for barging in on this enquiry expecting to run rings round the investigating officer! Quantrill tried to think of a reply that would cut Tait down to size, and was mortified that he couldn't.

The scene of crime team was still at work, concentrating their attention on the lobby, the stairs and the bedroom where the body had been found. They were handicapped by the fact that the cottage had been used by holidaymakers, and had not been cleaned between lets by a conscientious housewife. None of the doors had been dusted for months. There were so many latent fingerprints in the cottage that they had become superimposed and blurred.

Chief Inspector Quantrill summoned the investigating detectives to assemble in the gloomy sitting-room with the Gothic windows. "We've already got a start with this one," he told them. "Miss Lloyd knows the background, and she—"

He looked up as Detective Inspector Tait entered the room, wiping fingerprinting ink off his fingers. "Sorry to interrupt, sir," Tait said. "Someone left a good dab on the front door, but I'm afraid it turns out to be mine. I held the door open for my aunt when we arrived this morning." He smiled and sat down. Detective Constable Wigby stared at him aggressively.

Ian Wigby, a blond, beefy man in his mid-thirties, had been an opponent of Tait ever since the younger man had first arrived at Breckham Market as a detective sergeant, straight from police college and supremely confident of his own ability. "Sir!" protested Wigby, turning to the Chief Inspector, "since when has the regional crime squad been allowed to interfere at the start of an investigation?"

Tait looked at him with disdain. "Oh, grow up, Wigby," he said.

"Mr. Tait is on leave at the moment, so he has no regional crime squad status," said Quantrill firmly. "He's here because of his local connections. He may be able to help us with information, but he won't be taking part in the investigation."

"Of course not," said Tait, trying to sound as though it had never entered his head to do so.

"Har-bloody-har," muttered Wigby. Tait looked down his nose at him. Quantrill glared at the pair of them, and asked Hilary Lloyd to begin her briefing; thinking as he did so, and not for the first time, how glad he was to have her as his CID sergeant.

Not because she was a young woman and he found her attractive. Far from it. Douglas Quantrill didn't care for thin women, no matter with what straight-backed grace they held themselves, nor how good their bone structure was. And she wasn't all that young, anyway. He happened to know that she was nearly thirty-one.

No, Quantrill wasn't in the least attracted by her. He approved of her, that was all. She was extremely efficient at her job—inclined to be argumentative, but experienced, resourceful, thoroughly competent. An asset to his team. He had already read the report she'd made when Sandra Websdell first went missing, but now he listened intently—Hilary had an attractive voice, he had to admit that—as she went over the facts.

For the past four years Sandra Jane Websdell had worked in Saintsbury at a florist's shop, latterly as manageress. She had shared a flat in the town with a girl friend. Last April, on a weekend visit to her parents, she had met Desmond Flood. He had recently come to live in temporary accommodation in Fodderstone village. After their first meeting she had seen him frequently. They became engaged in June, and planned to marry at Saintsbury register office on Saturday 21 July.

Sandra had arranged with her parents' neighbour, Mrs. Constance Schultz, to rent the cottage in the Horkey road from that date. Mrs. Schultz lent Mrs. Websdell a key to the cottage a week in advance, so that Sandra would have time to prepare it before the wedding.

On Saturday 14 July, Sandra had begun two weeks' leave from her job. She moved out of her flat, and went back until the wedding to her parents' home. Rather than unpack all her belongings there, she took two suitcases full of clothing straight to the cottage. She spent most of the next three days with her fiancé, either out and about or at the barn he rented as a studio.

On Wednesday morning 18 July, Sandra told her mother that she had things to do on her own at the cottage, and that she didn't know when she would be back. Mrs. Websdell assumed that her daughter was talking about doing the cleaning. Sandra left Fodderstone Green just before 9 a.m. in her car, a green Ford Fiesta 950, registration number FNG 245R. She never returned.

"She was twenty-two, so she had a right to disappear if she wanted to," went on Sergeant Lloyd. "The Websdells were naturally concerned because it happened just three days before her wedding, and she'd given them no indication that she might not go through with it. But they stopped worrying as soon as they realized that the suitcases she'd left here had gone. They assumed she'd simply ducked out of getting married, and they weren't sorry about that. They didn't actually tell me so, but it was obvious that they weren't at all enthusiastic about their prospective son-in-law. Desmond Flood used to be the assistant art director of a London advertising agency. He now describes himself as a self-employed artist. He's lethargic, divorced, and fifty-one."

"A most unsuitable husband for a twenty-two-year-old," pronounced Quantrill, reminded of his own daughter. He glanced with momentary approval at Martin Tait; come to think of it, there was no doubt that Alison could do worse. "But Flood himself told you, when you interviewed him after Sandra disappeared, that their relationship was happy?"

"Very happy, so he said. And I wouldn't for a moment discount the possibility," added Hilary, taking the opportunity to give Douglas Quantrill's old-fashioned prejudices a passing knock. "But I didn't believe him. I thought he was incapable of being happy himself, or of making anyone else happy.

"So I went to Saintsbury and talked to Sandra's former flatmate. She said that Sandra had wanted to marry Desmond because she thought he was very handsome and lonely and needed someone to look after him. But as the date of the wedding approached, Sandra admitted to her friend that she was afraid she was making a terrible mistake. When I pressed Desmond Flood, though, he insisted that she'd said nothing to him about changing her mind."

"He would say that, wouldn't he, if he'd got something to hide?" DC Wigby, bored and fidgety, wanted some action. "It looks to me a perfectly straightforward case. The man's first marriage had broken up, he'd lost his job, and he couldn't face the thought of losing Sandra Websdell. When she told him she wasn't going to marry him, he abducted her, and she died in the course of a bit of rough and tumble. Why don't we just bring the man in?"

"We will, when we find him," said Quantrill. "According to the elderly couple he rents his studio from, Flood left early yesterday afternoon saying that he was going to Saintsbury and that he might stay away overnight. We've since found out that he travelled on the 2:30 bus from Horkey, and got off at Saintsbury bus station. What he's been doing since then, we don't know. I've alerted the Saintsbury division, and as soon as this briefing's over, Ian, you'd better get down there and try to trace him."

"Will do," said Wigby with relish, studying the photograph and description that Sergeant Lloyd passed to him. Making enquiries on his own initiative in Saintsbury, where Greene King brewed a very drinkable Abbot Ale, was just the kind of job he liked. He certainly hadn't fancied tramping from house to house in the village in this heat, still less searching the fly-ridden forest.

"The bus journey to Saintsbury must be very inconvenient for anyone from Fodderstone, if Horkey's the nearest stop," commented James Bedford. He was a fresh-faced, eager detective constable who often had difficulty in convincing members of the public that he was old enough to be a real policeman. "Do you think, sir, that Flood went by bus in order to set up an alibi for himself, and then sneaked back some other way?"

"Perhaps so," agreed Quantrill. "But don't read too much into Flood's use of public transport—apparently he sold his car soon after he came to live in Fodderstone. And don't take DC Wigby's guesswork as gospel, either. Yes, Flood's the natural suspect; but there are other possibilities. Sandra Websdell was an attractive girl, and no doubt she had other admirers. Someone might have abducted her just before her wedding—not knowing that she was thinking of calling it off—because he didn't want her to marry Desmond Flood."

"It wasn't her previous boyfriend," said Hilary Lloyd. "I've already eliminated him. They split up at the beginning of the year, and he's now working in Saudi Arabia. According to her girlfriend, Sandra hadn't mentioned any other men in particular. She certainly hadn't mentioned anyone who lives in Fodderstone. But perhaps there was someone who'd had a long-term yearning for her—for example, someone who couldn't approach her openly because he was married. Or possibly someone who was even less suitable for her than Desmond Flood, and hadn't approached her before because he wasn't prepared to risk being rejected."

Wigby looked up from the cigarette he was lighting. "A local weirdo?" he asked.

"Not necessarily one you'd notice," said Hilary. "But he must have held her captive because he wanted something from her that he couldn't—or wouldn't—take by force. And he'd have to have a weird streak to imagine that he could ever win her over, if the only way he could keep her was by tying her up with a rope round her waist."

The Chief Inspector outlined his tactics.

He wanted house-to-house enquiries made in Fodderstone and Fodderstone Green, principally to establish whether anyone had seen Sandra after she left home on the morning she disappeared, but also for the purpose of finding out who were her likely admirers. In addition, he wanted all empty buildings, sheds and barns in the village to be thoroughly searched.

"We're looking for several things. First, traces of occupation. Secondly, the rope that was used to tie her. Then the two missing suitcases—Sergeant Lloyd will give you their description. We know what clothes the girl was wearing when she disappeared, and they're not the ones she was wearing when she was found, so she must have had access to the suitcases during her captivity.

"We also want to find the key to this cottage. The door was locked when the owner came here this morning, so the girl's captor must have locked it behind him after he brought back her body. It's possible that he then threw away the key. The garden's already been searched, and I want the search extended to the fields round the garden, and also the roadside verges.

"And then we need to find the girl's car. I've put out a watch for it on the roads, but I think it's more likely to be hidden somewhere."

"Probably deep in the forest," said Wigby, blowing cigarette smoke down his nose. "God knows how big an area that covers . . ."

Martin Tait tapped him on the shoulder and handed him an ashtray. "Kindly stop flicking ash on to my aunt's carpet," he said. "And for your information, the forest area's about eighty square miles."

"Bloody know-all—" muttered Wigby under his breath. He scowled, and disposed ostentatiously of his already spilled ash by rubbing it into the carpet with the sole of his shoe.

"The forest's a big problem," Quantrill agreed. "There are a surprising number of isolated old properties scattered about in it—keepers' and warreners' cottages and barns, some occupied and some disused. If necessary we'll extend our search to them, and it'll take time. But the forensic lab should be able to help when they've analysed the earth and grasses found on the girl's clothing. She must have died somewhere out in the open, probably not far from where she was held captive, and forensic will be able to tell us whether or not it was in the forest."

"One thing's puzzling me about that," said James Bedford. "If Sandra died in the open air, in the forest or wherever, why did her captor go to the bother of bringing her back here and putting her to bed?"

"Because he's weird," said Wigby impatiently.

"Weird he may be," said Hilary Lloyd. "But I think he did what he did because he loved her."

The briefing finished with the allocation of duties. Naturally enough, Martin Tait was excluded.

"Anything I can do to help, sir?" he enquired politely.

"No—you're on leave, remember?" said Quantrill. "Go and get on with it." Then he added, with some suspicion, "You've been unusually quiet."

"As you wanted me to be. I was listening, though. And thinking."

"I don't doubt it."

Tait smiled. As usual, he looked pleased with himself. No one would guess that within the past twenty-four hours he had heard that he'd been cut out of a large fortune; but anyone who knew him well would also know that Martin Tait was not a man to accept defeat if he could possibly plan his way out of it.

"Give my love to Alison when you see her," he said. "And now—if you really can't think of anything else you want me to do—I'll go and fly my aeroplane."

Wigby, who had overheard the conversation, glared at the younger man's departing back. "*His aeroplane* . . . who does he think he is?" the detective constable seethed aloud. "Just who does he bloody think he *is?*"

It was something that Quantrill often—especially where his daughter's, and his own, future relationship with Martin Tait was concerned—wondered himself.

19

There was only one possible topic of conversation in Fodderstone on Wednesday 9 August. The Websdells were well liked and respected in the village, and the news that Sandra had been found dead had shocked the whole community.

No one was in any doubt about the identity of her killer. And because Desmond Flood was an outsider, no one had any hesitation in condemning him within earshot of a reporter from the local paper, a trainee journalist who looked like a cherub with acne. He had been sent to Fodderstone in a hurry, late on Wednesday morning, not so much to cover the story as to hold it until a senior reporter arrived. But the young journalist was tired of reporting village fêtes and sports events. Determined to prove that he could handle a murder story unaided, he followed the most vocal of the villagers to the Flintknappers Arms and offered to buy drinks all round.

Phil Goodwin was behind the bar. Lois had told him that she was too upset on Beryl's behalf to stand there listening to gossip. She had intended to insist that Phil must for once stay at home, but to her surprise he hadn't even suggested going out.

Taking advantage of the fact that her husband was unusually subdued and co-operative—and too thankful for it to wonder why—Lois had also declared that she had no intention of preparing a cooked meal. It was too hot, and she felt too sad, to bother. Her only regular customer for lunch, since Desmond Flood had stopped coming after Sandra's disappearance, was Howard Braithwaite; and he, Lois told her husband, could for once eat salad whether he liked it or not.

Phil Goodwin gave a surly reply to the reporter's greeting, refused a drink for himself, and tried with frowns and scowls to prevent the regulars from taking up the invitation. But knowing a good offer when they heard it, Charley Horrocks and Stan Bolderow and Reg Osler all asked for pints.

"O' course Flood's the man the police want," declared the balding and belligerent Stan. "Who else could it be? You can never trust a feller who comes from London and says he's an artist—stands to reason he's peculiar. And Desmond Flood's the most miserable sod I ever met. God knows why Sandra ever got engaged to him. She must ha' realized in the end that she'd made a mistake, but by then he wouldn't let her go. That must ha' been how it happened."

"It was him, definitely," concurred Stan's sidewhiskered sidekick, Reg. Phil Goodwin, secretive behind his tinted spectacles, nodded in reluctant agreement; so did Howard Braithwaite, who had just come in. And from his usual bar stool Charley Horrocks made upper-crust sounds of approval, the baying "Wah wah wah" noise that appals sensitive listeners when they hear it being made by Members of Parliament during broadcast debates from the House of Commons.

Then they all fell silent. Charley buried his purple nose in his pint. But Stan and Reg, though they were smoke-blackened and thirsty as usual, drank more circumspectly.

"What about Sandra Websdell herself?" asked the cherubic reporter, pen poised. "What can you tell me about her?"

"Nothing!" intervened Phil Goodwin fiercely. "She'd lived

away from the village for years. There's nothing any of us can tell you."

Stan and Reg exchanged glances. "That's right," agreed Stan, though he sounded surprised.

"True enough," confirmed Reg. They drank cautiously.

"Yes, quite." Howard Braithwaite moved up to the bar and put on a pair of gold-rimmed half-moon spectacles so that he could read the menu chalked on the blackboard. He was a spare, grey man: grey hair, grey skin, grey suit, completely urban despite the fishing tackle propped against the wall beside what he considered to be his private corner table. Everyone at the Flintknappers knew that fishing was his excuse for getting out of his wife's way, and having heard from their own wives about the organizing habits of Marjorie Braithwaite they couldn't blame him.

"But what about when Sandra Websdell was younger?" persisted the reporter. "Surely some of you—?"

"*Salad,*" barked Howard Braithwaite, staring with disbelief at the blackboard. "Ham salad! Is there no hot dish?"

"No there isn't," snapped the landlord, who even at the best of times found it difficult to take kindly to the proposition that the customer is always right. He used the forefinger and thumb of one hand to make a simultaneous tour of both sides of his catfish moustache. "Lois didn't feel like cooking today."

"*Didn't feel* like it?" Braithwaite exploded. "Your wife knows perfectly well that I detest salads. I'm a regular customer here, and I expect a hot meal. If she's prepared nothing else, then tell her that I'd like bacon and egg. Crisp bacon, two eggs, fried bread and fried tomatoes."

The two men glared at each other across the bar counter. Phil Goodwin's eyes slid in the reporter's direction. "Oh well—I'll ask Lois to do you a fry-up," he agreed sulkily.

"What about you, sir?" the reporter appealed to Charley Horrocks. "Do you remember Sandra Websdell?"

Horrocks raised his nose from his mug and reached for his copy of the *Sun*. "Good-lookin' gel," he mused with some regret. "Well developed . . . Titillatin', you might say. Pity about what happened to her, but there's no doubt she arsked for it."

The reporter's eyes popped. "What makes you say that?"

"He said it," broke in Stan Bolderow, bristling ominously,

"because he's a dirty old fool." He advanced slowly on Horrocks, his bald head glistening with sweat, his muscular body stretching the holes in his string vest to their limit. Charley Horrocks was twice Stan's size, and perched up on a bar stool; but Stan was younger and very fit. He took a sudden rush at the third Earl's grandson, butting Charley's beer-barrel of a body so hard that the man was knocked backwards, his purple face incredulous, his khaki arms and legs flailing as he fell.

"And as for you, boy—" said Stan, breathing hard as he turned; but the spotted cherub was already half-way to the door, having decided not to pursue this particular story until he had the support of an experienced reporter.

"Did you have to do that, Stan?" said Phil Goodwin angrily as he went round the counter to help heave Charley Horrocks on to his stool again. "The last thing we want is to draw attention to ourselves."

"The last thing we want is to have this stupid bugger shooting his mouth off to the press," Stan retorted. "He might say anything. Besides, I'm not going to stand by an' listen to his dirty talk about the girl. I was fond of her. If you want to know, I'm wholly upset that she died."

"You're not the only one," said Reg Osler.

"We're none of us exactly happy about it," snapped Howard Braithwaite. "It was extremely inconvenient for us, to say the least. There'll be reporters and policemen all over the village now, and I for one am going to keep my head down. As far as I'm concerned, the rest of the project's cancelled."

"Oh no, it's not!" Phil Goodwin shouted. "We've gone to a hell of a lot of trouble to set it up, and there's too much at stake to cancel it now."

"Then don't attempt to include me. I've finished with it—and with all of you. We've never been equally involved, and I have no intention of being dragged down with you if you're caught."

"Haven't you, Mr. Braithwaite?" Reg gave a jeering laugh. "Well, you'd better have another think about that, because you *are* involved. Doesn't matter which of us did what, or when or where. You played your part, and you're not going to wriggle out of it."

"I'd like to see him try," threatened Stan.

"He can't get out of it," asserted Phil Goodwin. "He's in as deep as we are, and he knows it. That's why we've got to stick together. When the police come round asking questions, we must all be ready with the same story. Right?"

He suggested a communal alibi for the previous evening. Braithwaite and Bolderow and Osler argued hotly, but could think of no better alternative.

"Right, Charley?" Goodwin demanded.

The third Earl's grandson lifted his nose from his mug and bayed his agreement.

20

When Desmond Flood left Fodderstone the previous day, he had told his landlady that he expected to return on the 5:15 bus from Saintsbury on Wednesday afternoon.

He could, of course, have been lying. That was one reason why Chief Inspector Quantrill had sent DC Wigby to Saintsbury in an attempt to trace the man. But on the off-chance that Flood would do as he'd said—either because he was innocent of Sandra Websdell's abduction and death, or because he was cunning enough to try to avert suspicion from himself by returning—Quantrill decided to go to Horkey and wait for the bus to arrive.

Horkey was a bigger, busier village than Fodderstone, with several shops, a post office, a school, and the invaluable bus service. The bus stop was outside a small brick and flint house in whose weedy garden a couple of tables and benches were parked in the shade of an elder bush. The garden was staked with hand-painted signs offering everything the owners could think of to tempt passers-by to stop and buy: *Country Crafts, Bric-a-Brac, Herbs, Victoriana, Hamsters, Salads, Teas*.

"And not a bad cup of tea, either," Quantrill admitted with grudging surprise. On his own, he would not have gone near the place; but Hilary Lloyd had made straight for it, and he had followed out of courtesy and thirst. "I never trust anywhere that advertises 'country crafts'," he went on. Suffolk born and bred, he recognized the hallmark of incomers and regarded them with the traditional countryman's mixture of suspicion and derision. "You can bet it's run by townies, playing at what they think is country life."

"That doesn't mean they can't make a perfectly good cup of tea."

"Hmm. I expected it would turn out to be herbal."

Hilary had worked with him long enough to realize that she would never shift his prejudices, though she kept on trying. "I might have known you'd think that," she said.

She smiled at him as she said it, and he took no offence. Although she was lively and womanly, she usually made a point of keeping her distance. She laughed easily, but she didn't often give a wholehearted smile. And that was a pity.

Quantrill knew that she'd been attacked, years ago when she was a uniformed policewoman in Yarchester, by a villain wielding a broken bottle. Although she wore her dark hair in a sideswept fringe, she couldn't completely hide the faint residual scar on her forehead. It jagged down towards her nose, just missing her eyes, and puckered her right eyebrow in a way that gave her what seemed from a distance to be a permanent frown. Really, he thought, she looked quite plain much of the time; but her smile, when it came, was a beauty.

Suddenly conscious that he had been looking at her for too long, he stood up and moved away. "Now there's a *real* country craft," he said, pointing across the road to an old brick-built, pantile-roofed shed. It stood at a right angle to the road, facing an open yard that seemed to be part coal-dump, part ironmongery junk-heap. On the gable end of the shed, in painted letters so faded as to be barely legible, was the name STAGG, and underneath it the words VETERINARY SHOEING FORGE. And below, in bold paint on a modern display board: *Andrew Stagg, Farrier*.

"A proper old-established country business," Quantrill approved. "Good to see it continuing. No one would have thought, thirty years ago, that there'd be any future for farriers—but then, no one realized how popular riding would become."

A dismounted girl rider stood in the yard of the forge holding her horse's head. At the blunt end of the animal, examining its off hind hoof, was a broad-shouldered young man in jeans and a leather apron, with a widespread distribution of dark curly hair on his head and bare chest.

"Andrew Stagg himself, presumably," said Hilary, rising to

join Quantrill. The young man now stood with his hands on his narrow hips, chatting and laughing with the girl as she remounted, and Hilary was looking at him in a way that Quantrill found disturbing and improper; that kind of frank appraisal of a member of the opposite sex was a man's prerogative.

"I should think Andrew Stagg's services are very much in demand," she went on, oblivious of—or disregarding—her companion's disapproval, "as far as all the female riders in this part of the county are concerned. He's a very well-built young man."

Douglas Quantrill turned away, straightening his shoulders and sucking in his stomach muscles until they ached. "This dratted bus is late. We're wasting time," he said irritably.

A loud buzzing somewhere up above drew their attention to a piston-engined aircraft flying downwind at 800 feet. Quantrill squinted up at it and identified the yellow and white high-wing monoplane as one of the Cessnas that flew from Horkey's old wartime airfield. He could just read—his eyesight would still be perfect if it weren't for the fact that there was more small print about now than there used to be—the letters on the aeroplane's wings: G-IRSR.

"That's Martin Tait," he complained. "Showing his skills to some girlfriend, no doubt . . ."

"My impression, at the end of the briefing, was that he intended to do an aerial search for Sandra Websdell's car," said Hilary.

Quantrill snorted. "If I know Martin, he'll be doing both. Showing off to a girl and trying to solve this case for us at the same time. Mind you," he added fairly, "it'd be a great help if he could find Sandra's car, and I certainly wouldn't raise any objection because he'd done it unofficially. But he needn't think he can put in an expense sheet for a tankful of aircraft fuel!"

"A light aeroplane isn't really the right machine for the job, though, is it?" said Hilary. "Couldn't we borrow an army helicopter? After all, this *is* a murder enquiry."

Quantrill shook his head. "Not a chance. The force has to pay for the use of army machines, and you know how tight our budget is. The ACC would turn the request down flat. And I really couldn't argue with him—it'd be different if we were looking for a vicious murderer, a psychopath who might kill again. From what you've said about Flood—"

"That he's lethargic? Yes, he moves as though he's trying to wade through treacle. The Websdells say he's been like that ever since they've known him, and so does his landlady. In fact, you know, it makes me doubtful that he's the man we want. Whoever abducted Sandra and held her for three weeks against her will would have needed a lot more energy than Desmond Flood seems to possess."

"Is he ill?" Quantrill demanded. "Mentally, I mean?"

Hilary Lloyd had qualified as a State Registered Nurse before joining the police force. The Chief Inspector knew it and was inclined, to her annoyance, to regard her as a medical authority.

"I'm not a doctor," she pointed out, "still less a psychiatrist. I simply don't know. It's textbook wisdom that people who are apathetic, or clinically depressed, are unlikely to use any form of violence against anyone else; but I'm not qualified to say whether or not that applies to Desmond Flood. I'm just guessing."

"But according to the pathologist," persisted Quantrill, "whoever killed Sandra used a minimum of violence. And from the way he arranged her body on the bed, he was obviously filled with remorse over what he'd done. Couldn't that have been Flood, however lethargic he may seem?"

"Yes, it's possible. That's the point I'm making—your guess is just as good as mine." Hilary paused, thinking, her brow vertically ridged by the combination of frown and scar. "If Desmond Flood really is acutely depressed—and regardless of whether he was responsible for Sandra's death—we do need to find him for his own sake. Because the person a depressive is most likely to kill is himself."

"That's what I was afraid of," said Quantrill. "It's one reason why I asked the Saintsbury division to try to find him, with or without Ian Wigby's help."

The Saintsbury police had failed to find Flood. So too had DC Wigby, though he was still enjoying the job of looking. But their failure gave the Chief Inspector no problem. Guilty or not, depressive or not, Desmond Flood was alive and a passenger on the 5:15 bus from Saintsbury to Horkey.

Flood was the last to alight, and the slowest. A man of medium height and slim build, he walked with dragging steps and bowed shoulders. His looks were potentially striking:

strong features, a fine head of prematurely grey hair, dark eyebrows above dark eyes; but his head was down, his eyes dull, his demeanour defeated. He wasn't just wading through treacle, he seemed to be up to his neck in it.

Flood took the news of his fiancée's death without any change in his expression. Sitting in the back of the Chief Inspector's car, next to Sergeant Lloyd, he stared dully out of the open window at the tree they were parked under, and said nothing. His only reaction, after a few minutes, was a deep sigh.

"You haven't asked us how or when Sandra died," said Quantrill, turning sideways in the driving seat to look at the man. "Don't you want to know?"

"I suppose you're going to tell me she was murdered," said Flood, his voice so dreary that it made him sound indifferent. "It's what I expected, when she didn't get in touch with her parents."

"But why did you think that? Why should she have been murdered?"

"Because it's what seems to happen to girls who go missing."

"Very often, yes. But usually they're killed almost immediately. Sandra wasn't though. She was kept against her will for three whole weeks before she died. What do you make of that, Mr. Flood?"

He said nothing at first. Then he asked distantly, "Was she . . . ill-treated?"

"_Ill-treated?_" Quantrill made an effort to control his anger. "Good God, man, don't you count being held against her will as ill-treatment? Perhaps you'd like me to go over the details. For part of the time she was tethered with a rope, like an animal, and she bruised her back by tugging the rope forward in her attempts to unfasten it. She tore every one of her fingernails in her efforts to undo the knot. She—"

"We know she wasn't sexually assaulted, Mr. Flood," Hilary said quietly. "Her captor didn't behave with brutality. But ill-treatment isn't necessarily physical, is it? Sandra must have gone through three weeks of mental torment. Mustn't she?"

Flood gave another of his deep sighs. Still staring out of the car at nothing he said dully, "Poor kid. She didn't deserve that . . ."

"What did she deserve, then?" asked Quantrill quickly, leaning over to grip the man's shoulder in an attempt to seize his attention. "If she didn't deserve the anguish she must have gone through before she died, what *did* she deserve? Did you have some other punishment in mind for her because she'd rejected you?"

"Rejected me?" Flood sounded puzzled. Then he gave a curious neighing sound, a kind of mirthless laugh. "Oh, you're wrong if you think I minded because she decided not to marry me. I liked Sandra—she was a nice girl. Very sweet, very kind. I suppose I was quite fond of her. Marriage to her would certainly have been a lot more comfortable than going on living on my own.

"But I didn't want to remarry at all. For one thing, I couldn't afford it. My ex-wife took our house as part of the divorce settlement, and I haven't any money apart from what I can scrape up by selling my paintings. And for another thing, I don't want to acquire any new responsibilities. That was the whole point of getting a divorce and chucking my job. I'd had enough of pressures, of families and mortgages and clients and deadlines—I came here to be free."

"Then why did you ask Sandra to marry you?" said Hilary.

"I didn't. It was her idea, not mine."

Hilary frowned at him. "Why didn't you tell me all this when I spoke to you three weeks ago, Mr. Flood? You said then that you and Sandra were happy about the marriage, and that there were no problems between you."

Flood shrugged. "What I told you was the truth, in a way. There *were* no problems by then. We'd sorted things out, on the evening before she disappeared, and we parted happily, as friends."

"So why didn't you tell me that you'd agreed to part?"

"Because I didn't think you'd believe me. If I'd told you the truth, you'd have imagined what you're imagining now, that we'd quarrelled and I'd abducted her. And I didn't want to be bothered by questions. I just want to be left alone."

Police officers have an inbuilt disinclination to believe people who have previously lied to them.

And what, they asked Desmond Flood suspiciously, was he doing yesterday afternoon and evening?

Flood said that he had gone to London. He traveled from Saintsbury by coach and went to see his ex-wife, who lived in Camden; but she was not at home. Quite possibly she was away on holiday. He still had a key—after all, he'd worked hard enough to buy the house—so he let himself in and spent the night there. This morning he went to the Tate Gallery for a couple of hours—no, there hadn't been an admission ticket—and then returned by coach to Saintsbury.

"Why did you have this sudden urge to visit your ex-wife?" asked Quantrill.

"It wasn't sudden. I'd been contemplating going back ever since Sandra called off our marriage."

Hilary's feminism surfaced sharply. "What makes you think your ex-wife would want you back?"

Flood knotted his dark eyebrows in an attempt to understand what evidently seemed to him a superfluous question. "I was the one who left," he said. "I was the one who wanted my freedom."

"Then why on earth are you thinking of giving it up?" demanded Quantrill, genuinely wanting to know. He was a little younger than Desmond Flood, not yet fifty, and freedom was something he had dreamed of at intervals throughout his humdrum married life.

Flood looked at Quantrill for the first time. "You should give it a try yourself," he advised sardonically. "When you get your freedom, it isn't what you thought it was going to be. I used to despise my job and resent the fact that I never had time to paint—but now I've got all the time in the world, I've lost the urge. I used to row with my wife and hate the waste of spirit involved. But when you've got someone to be angry with, you do at least know that you're alive."

The Chief Inspector drove Flood to his studio, a small flint barn in the main street of Fodderstone village. Flood had rented it for the summer from a retired farmer. It suited him well enough—it was cheap, and the skylight gave a good north light for painting. Yes, he got his own meals, after a fashion. He used to eat lunch at the Flintknappers Arms, but he gave up going there after Sandra disappeared. He couldn't put up with Lois Goodwin's relentless sympathy.

Quantrill took a cursory look inside the barn. It was basically a single high room, with whitewashed walls and a wooden half-loft reached by a ladder. On an easel in the middle of the room was a half-finished, half-hearted canvas; the portrait of a woman, though not of Sandra Websdell. Other unfinished canvases, chiefly Breckland landscapes, were propped against the walls. The palette looked dusty, the paint on it dry and cracked.

Presumably Flood slept in the loft, but Quantrill had no intention of climbing the ladder. Ladder-climbing was an ungainly activity for a man of his size, and Hilary Lloyd was watching.

"I don't imagine you've held Sandra here in secret for the past three weeks, Mr. Flood," he said. "It's too close to other houses for that."

"I haven't held her anywhere," said Flood. "I told you, I didn't want her."

"So you say. But you admit to being fond of her—and so was the man who was responsible for her death. We have evidence of that. If it wasn't you, then you must have had a local rival."

"Half a dozen, for all I know . . ."

"But who? Did she mention any names?"

"If she did, I didn't listen. I didn't take a *personal* interest in the girl. We discussed painting most of the time—she had a good eye for line and colour. That was why she did well in the florist's shop. You'd better try talking to the woman in charge of the business, she knew Sandra better than I did."

"I was told that the owner of the shop is away in New Zealand," said Hilary.

"There's another woman, then. She's in Fodderstone for the summer."

"Would that be Mrs. Annabel Yardley?"

But Desmond Flood was deep in treacle again. "I don't know . . ."

21

Beech House, the home of Mrs. Elizabeth Seymour who owned the Saintsbury florist's shop, was an early nineteenth-century gentleman's residence of grey brick, with a hipped slate roof and a pedimented porch on two Tuscan columns. It stood on its own about half a mile out of Fodderstone on the Saintsbury road. On one side of the house, a beech hedge concealed the garden from the quiet road; on the other side was a paddock in which two horses were grazing. A large beech tree grew beside the open entrance gates, and parked on the gravel drive in front of the house was a red Alfa Romeo Alfasud.

Hearing voices coming from outside the house, Quantrill pushed open an ornamental iron gate in the beech hedge and followed Hilary into the garden. There, sitting on the terrace enjoying a drink in the early evening sunshine, were Martin Tait and a slim ash-blonde woman who was wearing a cotton sundress of such stunning simplicity that it couldn't have cost much less, Hilary estimated, than a hundred pounds.

As soon as he saw them, Martin Tait leaped to his feet. He looked pleased with himself, and at the same time slightly guilty and slightly defiant, as though he had been caught in a compromising situation with a more attractive woman than his fiancée by his prospective father-in-law.

He introduced his colleagues to Annabel Yardley, who greeted them with a distant, amused civility. "The Detective Inspector has quite a talent for making Pimm's," she added, indicating a glass jug that contained an innocent-looking combination of pale liquid, fresh fruit salad and decorative greenery. "I'll have another, Martin—and perhaps you'd like to offer some to your visitors."

Tait refilled her glass, and then raised the jug and an eyebrow at Sergeant Lloyd.

Hilary shook her head. She enjoyed the taste of Pimm's, but hadn't drunk it for years; not since that May Ball at Clare College, Cambridge, when she was a final-year student nurse at Addenbrooke's hospital and Stephen was still alive. Just for a moment the smell of the Pimm's brought back that long lovely night on the river—the distant music, the softly spotlit stonework of the ancient walls and bridges, the ripple and plash of the water as their punt drifted along the Backs under the willow trees—and Stephen beside her, so brilliant and brave that they could both pretend for a few hours not to know that he was dying.

No, she never wanted to drink Pimm's again . . . And as for Douglas Quantrill, her unpretentious, stick-in-the-mud, salt-of-the-earth boss, she had already seen the look of horror on his face as he stared at Martin Tait's frivolous concoction and identified the slices of orange, lemon, apple and cucumber, and the topping of sprigs of mint. His thoughts were as clear as if he'd voiced them: *You'll never catch me drinking that!*

"Thank you for the offer," Hilary said pleasantly to Annabel Yardley, "but I'm afraid we haven't time to appreciate a Pimm's." The Chief Inspector beckoned Tait aside, and Hilary sat down on the vacant garden chair. "We're investigating Sandra Websdell's death—as I'm sure Martin has told you—and we wondered whether you could give us some information about her."

Mrs. Yardley opened her hooded eyelids wide, changing her amused expression to one of serious concern. Even though her family had left Fodderstone years ago, as a niece of the fifth Earl of Brandon she felt a certain responsibility towards the villagers, whether they were aware of it or not.

"Yes, I do know about Sandra's death, of course. I'm really sorry—quite shattered, actually. I did try to do my bit this afternoon, while I was flying with Martin, to spot her car in the forest. But no luck, I'm afraid. How else can I help you?"

"You knew her because she ran Mrs. Seymour's shop, I believe?"

"Yes. She was competent, and Elizabeth thought highly of her. I got to know the girl because she did all the buying of the flowers that Elizabeth arranges for friends' weddings and dances. I'm a flower-arranger too, for my sins, so Elizabeth roped me in to stay here and take over while she and her husband went orf to New Zealand. Life was absolutely hectic in June, and I don't know how I'd have coped without Sandra's help."

"What did you make of the girl, Mrs. Yardley?" asked Hilary. "Was she having some kind of secret affair, do you think, at the same time as she was engaged to Desmond Flood?"

Annabel Yardley gave a well-bred snort of laughter. "God, no! What *ever* gave you that idea? She was a conventional, romantic girl—I doubt if she even went to bed with her fiancé, though *he* probably wasn't up to it anyway. He was quite wrong for her, of course. I think the poor child saw him at first as some kind of brooding romantic hero who would be transformed by her love. I told her that he was a lost cause."

She sat back and took a cigarette from a packet that was lying on the garden table beside her glass. Martin Tait materialized in a moment, picking up her lighter and flicking it for her. Hilary watched them both, amused in her turn; glad to be self-assured enough to know that her own inexpensive clothes—a striped cotton shirt and a denim skirt worn with a good leather belt—were in no way inferior to Mrs. Yardley's because they were absolutely right for her job. A police-woman would look conspicuous if she went out detecting in rural Suffolk in a designer sundress.

But Sergeant Lloyd found Annabel Yardley interestingly decorative: stylish, elegant, with an unmistakable aura of expensive sexuality. No wonder Martin Tait, although he had returned to his conversation with the Chief Inspector, couldn't keep his eyes off her. Pity about that cold sore on the corner of her mouth, though . . .

"As far as you know then, Mrs. Yardley, Sandra Websdell had no other attachments. But do you think she might have had a secret admirer?"

"Very probably." Annabel Yardley began to sound a little bored, tired of being questioned. "Sandra was a big girl, you know. She had a simply enormous bosom, 38 if it was an inch. It seemed to embarrass her terribly—but the men loved it, of course."

"Which men?"

Jolted out of her boredom, Mrs. Yardley blinked with surprise. "My goodness, you're quick off the mark, aren't you? Actually I meant the regulars at the Flintknappers Arms. They're the only men I've seen her with. I happened to visit the pub one weekend early in the summer, and Sandra was there with Desmond Flood. She obviously felt shy and out of place, and because she was a Fodderstone girl she was being teased by the regulars. They were positively mauling her with their hot little eyes."

Hilary took her notebook from her shoulder bag, but Mrs. Yardley waved it away. "I have *no* idea of their names," she said firmly. "The landlord was one, though—I do dislike him, he's so conceited and familiar. Really, the Flintknappers is such a crude pub that I wouldn't go there at all if it weren't the only one in Fodderstone. I'd say that the regulars are thoroughly untrustworthy—almost without exception."

"And who is the exception?"

"Charley Horrocks. He's an eccentric cousin of Daddy's, actually. I prefer him not to know who I am because he'd be a serious social embarrassment. But I can vouch for the fact that he's absolutely harmless."

*   *   *

The conversation between Chief Inspector Quantrill and Martin Tait had not at first gone well. Tait, unsure of how much Alison's father knew about their relationship, was on the defensive.

"Mrs. Yardley rides," he said. "She knows the bridleways on this side of the forest. So it seemed a good idea to take her up to do some observing while I flew over the area."

"Oh yes? I thought it was your *aunt's* local knowledge you were going to make use of."

"*Ground* knowledge. Aunt Con doesn't like flying."

As he said it, Tait realized that he had no idea whether or not it was true; he'd never even thought of offering his aunt a trip in his aeroplane. He certainly didn't want her with him this week, not when Annabel Yardley was available. On the other hand, it was important to keep Aunt Con sweet. He'd better suggest it. With luck—considering how ill she looked—she would refuse.

"I've spotted some possible hide-outs within a mile of the village," he went on quickly. "There's nothing left of Fodderstone Hall—Mrs. Yardley's old family home. The park where it stood is arable land now, though there are crop marks that show the site of the house. But in the surrounding woodland I noticed two derelict buildings that must have belonged to the Hall at one time. One's a partially roofless house, and the other is an old boathouse beside an ornamental lake. The area's called Stoneyhill wood. I'll pinpoint it for you on your map. As for Sandra Websdell's car, it could have been driven along any one of the forest rides and hidden among the trees. It would take a helicopter to make a proper search, but I'll do what I can."

"I'm glad of your help," acknowledged Quantrill. "One thing, though, Martin—any aerial observing that you do has to be entirely unofficial and voluntary. It must cost you a small fortune to keep that aeroplane flying, but I can't possibly wangle any expenses for you."

Tait gave a confident shrug. "What makes you think I can't afford it?" he said.

Quantrill and Hilary said good-bye to Mrs. Yardley, and Tait excused himself from her for a few minutes. He went with them to their car, and marked their large-scale map. When he left them to return through the iron gate that led into the garden, Hilary hurried after him.

"Martin—"

They had once, for a short time, been sergeants together at Yarchester; colleagues rather than friends. Hilary found his air of professional superiority irritating, and his conviction that he was God's gift to any attractive woman under the age of thirty-five tiresome. But at the moment she felt some concern for him, and even more for his girlfriend, Alison Quantrill.

"You're not going to like this," she went on, keeping her voice low. "But having once been a nurse I can't get out of the habit of noticing health hazards."

Tait looked puzzled. "What do you mean? What's happened?"

"Nothing's happened yet, I hope. That's why I'd better say this now, before you get involved. You're spending this evening here, I imagine?"

"Annabel's invited me to stay for supper, yes."

"She's a very attractive woman. And she obviously enjoys the company of interesting men. You could be in with a chance."

"I think so."

"And the fact that she has a cold sore near her mouth doesn't worry you? I know you must have noticed it."

"I have noticed it—and it doesn't worry me in the least."

"That's what I was afraid of. Listen, Martin—cold sores are caused by a virus that's closely related to a much more dangerous one. Most of them are quite innocent, of course. If Mrs. Yardley were faithful to her absent husband, there'd be no problem. But she isn't, is she? From what I've heard—and you must have heard it, too—she's known to lead an active and varied sex life. And because of that, it's just possible that her particular cold sore is a symptom of herpes."

Tait gaped. *"Herpes?"* He glanced over his shoulder to make sure that they were standing far enough from the garden hedge for their voices not to carry over it. "For God's sake," he hissed indignantly, "she's the niece of an earl!"

"Blue blood doesn't seem to provide immunity," said Hilary dryly. "The fact is, you don't know where she's been. If by any chance she has got it, and you come into physical contact with her, the Earl's niece's cold sore could become your genital herpes. And surely you don't want to risk catching *that*?"

Tait became agitated. He strode up and down the gravel drive, a few steps one way, a few steps another, trying to recall what he'd heard about the uncontrollable, incurable by-product of sexual freedom. Then he stood still, and stared at Hilary with suspicion.

"Catching genital herpes from someone with a cold sore . . . ? You're trying to fool me, aren't you?"

"No. It's a medical fact that the virus is highly contagious. It can be spread by kissing, even by finger contact. That's why I had to mention it to you. Don't you see, Martin? It's not just yourself you're putting at risk, it's Alison too."

"It's nothing to do with Alison," Tait snapped. "That's finished."

"It's not just Alison I'm talking about. If you should contract genital herpes, you'll be a danger to any woman you ever fall in love with. For their sakes, if not your own, you really ought to steer clear of the Earl's niece."

Tait scowled. His eyes were cold with anger. "Damn you, Sergeant Lloyd," he said. "Who the hell do you think you are, to interfere in my private life? I'll choose my own friends, thank you."

He turned and strode to the gate that led into the garden where Annabel Yardley was waiting for him.

"I thought you were going to stay for supper."

"Sorry, Annabel. Duty calls—I've just remembered my poor old aunt. She's the Websdell family's neighbour, you see. She was with me this morning when I found Sandra's body, and it was a nasty shock for her. Much as I'd love to stay with you, I really feel obliged to spend the rest of the evening with Aunt Con."

Mrs. Yardley looked a little piqued that her arrangements had been altered, but not disappointed. "As you please," she said. "The flight was amusing, though. You did suggest that we might go up again tomorrow—?"

"Ah, that was before Chief Inspector Quantrill came barging in," said Tait. "He wants my help with this murder enquiry, so I'm afraid it looks as though I'm going to be completely tied up for the next few days."

"Really?" The fifth Earl's niece's voice had dropped to

freezing point. She picked up a copy of *Harpers & Queen* and flicked dismissively through it. "Then what are you waiting for? Why don't you eff orf?"

Tait went, congratulating himself on his narrow escape.

22

When Martin Tait returned after sunset to number 9 Fodderstone Green, he found that although the back door was unlocked his aunt was not at home. She must, he guessed, be with one or another of her neighbours.

He noticed that she had been busy during the day. Propped beside the dustbin, not far from the back door, were three or four bulging plastic sacks, their necks fastened with elastic bands, that presumably contained the things she had decided to throw away. And he could smell smoke coming from an almost extinct bonfire at the end of the garden.

He walked down to the site of the bonfire. The private letters and papers that he had carried out of the house that morning had already been reduced to a smouldering heap. But paper in bulk burns slowly and incompletely, and some of the thicker items—account books, diaries, photographs—were charred rather than burnt. Tait made himself useful by fetching a garden fork from the shed and turning the papers over, lifting them so as to get enough air underneath to rekindle the flames.

"What on earth are you doing?" demanded an authoritative female voice. He looked up from his task and saw his aunt's neighbour Mrs. Braithwaite bearing down on him. She was wearing her summer lecturing ensemble, a floral dress and jacket in an unbecomingly shiny material, together with a pair of stout shoes. "What are you *doing?*" she repeated, the retaining chain on her spectacles swinging on either side of her cheeks with the vigour of her questioning.

Martin Tait felt that he'd had enough to put up with, during the past twenty-four hours, without being bothered by a stupid old bag like Mrs. B. "As you see," he said coldly, "I am having a bonfire."

"In this weather? What are you burning?" Marjorie Braithwaite peered at the revived fire. Then, with an exclamation of horror, she darted forward and snatched a half-burned hard-covered notebook that he had just lifted on the tines of his fork. "But it's my diary—this year's desk diary—the one I gave Constance at Christmas! What do you mean by burning this? Where *is* your aunt? Does she know what you're doing?"

Martin stirred the fire, hoping that the smoke would drive the wretched woman away. "No, I don't know where my aunt is," he said through his teeth. "And no, she doesn't know that I'm doing this."

"Then how dare you? How *dare* you? Words fail me," spluttered Marjorie, though this was audibly untrue. Tait let her go on protesting for some moments while he fed papers to the flames. When he could endure her company no longer, he turned to her with a cool smile.

"Look, Mrs. Braithwaite," he said, recalling the effectiveness of Annabel Yardley's remark to him an hour earlier, "why don't you eff orf?"

He had almost completed the burning when his aunt returned from the Websdells' house. She looked very sad and tired, raw-nerved after doing what she could to comfort Beryl.

Con didn't at first see her nephew. The garden seemed to be swirling with black swifts and she stood for a few moments watching them wheeling and screaming as they trawled for insects in the gathering dusk. Her nephew called to her. She started, peered, then trudged down the long garden towards him.

"Hope I've done the right thing, Aunt Con," he said cheerfully. He explained that Mrs. Braithwaite had taken exception to the burning of her gift. "I assumed that you wouldn't have put it on the bonfire in the first place if you'd wanted to keep it, but I thought I'd better salvage it in case you'd made a mistake. It really is this year's diary, and there are some entries in it."

He offered her the charred remains of the *Healthy Living* yearbook. Con shrugged it away. "Yes, I did begin using it as an engagement diary, but I haven't bothered with it for weeks. It might as well be burned with the other rubbish. I'm sorry that Marjorie knows I've got rid of it, though—poor dear, she must be frightfully offended. What did she say?"

Martin told his aunt what Mrs. Braithwaite had said to

him. Then, after a moment's hesitation, he told his aunt exactly what he had said to Mrs. Braithwaite.

"Oh Martin—how could you? Poor Marjorie . . ." But Con's look of shocked surprise slowly gave way to a lop-sided, naughty grin. "I bet it did her a world of good," she said. "I ought to have told her that myself, long ago."

She went into her kitchen to forage for supper. Martin finished burning the diary, scraped through the ashes of the bonfire to make sure that nothing legible remained, and then followed his aunt.

"How are the Websdells taking their daughter's death?" he asked.

Con told him. "What's particularly upsetting them at the moment," she added, "is the fact that they can't make any plans for burying Sandra. The coroner's officer told them that it might be some time before her body can be released. Is that right, Martin?"

"Yes—it's entirely at the discretion of the coroner, and he has first to satisfy himself as to how, when and why the girl died. No one can say how long that will take, so I'm afraid her parents will have to be patient."

"That's what they were told. But it does seem to make her death even harder for them to bear. The funeral service will be such a comfort, to Beryl in particular."

Con finished assembling bread, cheddar cheese, lettuce and tomatoes, and a jar of Beryl's home-made chutney. She was too preoccupied with the Websdells' bereavement to think of apologizing to her nephew for the scratch meal. Martin went to the bathroom to wash away the bonfire smuts, and then joined his aunt at the kitchen table. She was still talking about funerals.

"Our own church at Fodderstone isn't used any longer," she said. "Such a pity—it was small and comforting, just right for a funeral service. When we want church services now we have to go to Horkey, and their church is a big, gloomy place. The windows are filled with some late-Victorian stained glass, all greenery-yallery, and I find it terribly depressing. Still, a great many of the Websdells' relatives and friends will want to go to Sandra's funeral service, so they'll need a large church to fit them all in."

Her nephew, who was hungry, made polite sounds of agreement and got on with his supper. Con, who was not hungry, fiddled about with a lettuce leaf.

"When I die, Martin," she said abruptly, "I don't want to be buried. I want to be cremated."

Inspector Tait had recently been required to be present at an exhumation. Recalling it—the hair, the mould, the smell of putrescence—he put down his bread and cheese. "Me too," he said, assuming that they were having a general conversation.

Con's narrow face flushed as she tried to make her nephew realize the purpose of her statement. "I'm telling you this because you're my nearest relative, and no doubt you'll find yourself having to arrange my funeral. I'm sorry to burden you with that, but it can't be helped. So I thought it best, while you're here, to say exactly what I want. Would it help if you took some notes?"

Con's wishes were for simplicity and the minimum of inconvenience to her family and friends. She would have liked, she told her nephew, a short service in Fodderstone church and the hymn "Dear Lord and Father of mankind, forgive our foolish ways"; but she specifically did not want a service at Horkey, not just because of the ugly stained glass but because she was convinced that only three or four people would attend. It would, she said, be embarrassing to think of a handful of people trying to sing a hymn in that great barn of a church.

And so she opted for a service in the crematorium chapel, with no attempt at a hymn at all, and no address. She wanted music, though. "I think they usually play taped music anyway, in crematorium chapels, and what I'd really like is the second half of the Fauré Requiem. Do you think that would be possible?"

"I don't see why not," said Martin. "Yes, certainly, I'll organize it."

"Thank you. And I particularly want the prayers to be taken from the Book of Common Prayer. I may not be much of a churchgoer but I was baptized and confirmed in the Church of England, and the words of the old prayerbook are important to me. I don't suppose I always understand their meaning, but I know them by heart and they're a great comfort. After all, life and death are mysteries. A modern-language service offers no real explanation, and no comfort either."

She fell silent, her thoughts far away. Martin waited, pen poised, for her to return.

"Perhaps you'd better put notices in the East Anglian

Daily Times and the *Daily Telegraph*," she resumed briskly.
"Just a plain statement of my demise, and the arrangements
for the funeral. No need to say 'Aunt of—' or anything like
that. And be sure to put 'no flowers'. Otherwise someone
might feel obliged to send a wreath, and I always think that's
a terrible waste. I'd much rather they gave the money to
charity instead."

Martin stopped writing. He looked up at his aunt. "To the
Royal National Lifeboat Institution?" he asked in a carefully
neutral voice.

"Gosh, no," said Con promptly. "If anyone does want to
make a donation in my memory, I'd rather it went to cancer
research. The RNLI will be getting more than enough from
me as it is." She paused, realizing what she had said and to
whom. "I mean—oh, crikey . . ."

Martin let her talk herself into an embarrassed silence.
Then he said, in the same level voice, "You must do whatever is fair and right, Aunt Con."

"That's just what I want to do . . . only it's so difficult to
know what *is* fair and right," she lamented.

He smiled at her affectionately and reached across the
table to press her hand. "I'll make you some coffee," he said.

While they drank their coffee, Con returned to the subject of
Sandra Websdell's death. "I'm so thankful you're here, Martin. If you hadn't been, I wouldn't have gone to the Horkey
road cottage this morning—I probably wouldn't have gone
there for days, and then it would have been on my own . . ."
She shivered at the thought. "You've been such a help. I
really am grateful."

"Always glad to help, you know that. Tell me, Aunt, what
do you make of the girl's death? Who do you think was
responsible?"

In common with the other inhabitants of Fodderstone, Con
assumed that it was Desmond Flood. Martin explained that it
could have been someone else. "That's why I asked for your
opinion. After all, you've lived here for ten years. You must
know most of the local people, and you're a good judge of
character. If it wasn't Desmond Flood who abducted Sandra,
who do you think it might have been?"

"If it *wasn't* Desmond? Golly—" Con bit her lip as she

tried to assimilate that possibility. "I really can't imagine who else would have done such a thing."

"Someone who's a bit of an odd man out in the community?" suggested Tait.

"Ah well." Con gave her lop-sided grin. "Fodderstone's an odd place—you said that yourself. Most of us are a bit eccentric, one way or another. It's perfectly ordinary people who are the exception round here."

Her nephew murmured something diplomatic. "The man we're looking for," he went on, "was probably very fond of Sandra. She might not have known that he loved her, but we think he did, in a rather peculiar way."

"Oh, that's different," said Con immediately. "If you're talking about affection, it could have been—"

She stopped abruptly. "More coffee?" she asked.

"Could have been whom?"

His aunt said nothing more. Her colour high, her mouth tightly closed, she rose from the table and began to wash the supper dishes.

Tait stood up and gave her a lecture. It was, he said sternly, her duty as a citizen to tell the police all she knew.

"That's just the point," retorted Con. "I *know* nothing. I have absolutely no idea who was responsible for the poor child's death. Anything I say would be speculation, and I'm jolly well not going to offer you that."

"For God's sake, Aunt Con—you can't shield a murderer!".

"Don't be silly, dear. Of course I'm not shielding a murderer—I don't believe for a moment that any of the village men would have harmed a hair of Sandra's head."

"But—"

"I'm saying nothing more, Martin. What you must remember is that Fodderstone is my home. I'm a part of this community. We may be a bit isolated, a bit odd—but the people here have given me as much friendship as I've ever known, and I wouldn't dream of tattling about what I suspect to be their private yearnings. Gosh, I've quite enough on my conscience without that . . . No, I'm not going to try to make things easy for you. You must do whatever you have to do without any help from me."

Ordinarily, Tait would not have accepted such a refusal. Ordinarily, he would have pressured her until she told him what he wanted to know. But Constance Schultz wasn't an ordinary witness. She was his aunt, and the possessor of a

fortune, and he wanted her money far more than he wanted
her opinion on the Sandra Websdell case.

"Of course," he agreed, soothing away her annoyance. He
picked up the tea-towel and began to dry the dishes for her.
"Don't worry, Aunt Con, I will."

23

The morning of Thursday 10 August was oppressively humid.
The sun failed to appear at all, the sky was uniform light
grey, the air tasted ready-breathed. Visibility was too poor for
Martin Tait to go flying.

A mobile incident room manned by a uniformed police
sergeant and a constable was now parked near the centre of
the village. The prematurely balding constable, in a shirt that
was already damp with sweat, was collating the statements
that had been obtained by house-to-house enquiry. The combined population of Fodderstone and Fodderstone Green was
so small that the enquiries had already been completed. Not
one of the residents had provided information of any immediate significance, but without exception—and without being
asked—they had expressed the opinion that Desmond Flood
was the man responsible for Sandra Websdell's death.

"It's what I expected," said Chief Inspector Quantrill. He
and Hilary Lloyd were in the caravan, reading through statements. Martin Tait was with them, having thought it essential
to go and tell them that he wouldn't be able to continue his
aerial search that day.

The caravan was a good deal pleasanter to work in than
Quantrill remembered from previous summers, because the
resourceful Sergeant Lloyd had brought with her an electric
fan. Quantrill assumed that she had done this out of a proper
womanly consideration for the comfort of her colleagues. In
fact she had brought the fan in self-defence, knowing that in
warm weather there always hung about the hard-working,
balding PC Carpenter a miasma of sweaty socks.

"In an isolated community like this," the Chief Inspector
went on, "the local people often close ranks. They're pointing
at Flood not necessarily because they think he was responsi-

ble for the girl's death—they may know that he wasn't—but because he's an outsider."

"And therefore expendable?" said Hilary.

"Exactly. They want us to arrest him and then go away and leave them alone. So if Flood's alibi holds, we'll have to be very devious and patient to get the truth out of any of them."

The Chief Inspector had at first thought of following Flood's alleged trail himself; but as he very much disliked London—an overcrowded, foreign place at the best of times, and no doubt stifling in this weather—he had sent DC Wigby straight there from Saintsbury.

Wigby had reported by telephone from London the previous evening. As instructed, he had gone to Camden and found the address of Flood's ex-wife. There was no one at home, as the man had said; but on the other hand, none of the neighbours had noticed a man of Flood's description entering the house on Tuesday evening or leaving it on Wednesday morning.

The Detective Constable had asked for time to make further enquiries, but Quantrill had spiked his plans for a night on the town by recalling him. A better line, the Chief Inspector decided, would be to try to establish whether Flood had been seen on the journeys he alleged he had taken. Wigby had already questioned the coach drivers, without success. Some of the passengers, though, might have noticed Flood; and some of them might be regular travellers. Without waiting for Wigby to return from London, Quantrill had asked Saintsbury CID to undertake the routine of checking Desmond Flood's alibi.

For his part, the Chief Inspector had been looking forward to following the line of enquiry that Mrs. Yardley had suggested to Sergeant Lloyd. In particular, he had wanted to interview the man she had tried to eliminate, Charley Horrocks. An outsider herself, Annabel Yardley had no reason to protect any of the villagers; but she was related to Horrocks. It was impossible to know, at this stage, whether she was trying to protect him because he was family, or to draw the attention of the police to him because he was a potential nuisance. Either way, the Chief Inspector had been interested in him. But according to Horrocks's statement, he had spent the whole of Tuesday evening from approximately 6:05 p.m. in the Flintknappers Arms. He had named other customers who were there at the same time, and Quantrill's interest had receded.

There had been no luck so far in any of the searches: for the key to the cottage, for Sandra Websdell's car, or for the place where she had been held captive. All empty buildings in the village had now been searched, and Quantrill had directed the searchers to spread out.

The forensic science laboratory had reported that the smudges of dirt on the dead girl's face had been caused by a mingling of sweat with the sandy soil typical of the forest area. The seeds and grasses on her clothing did not, however, include pine needles, and a small quantity of sawdust that had been found in the folds of her dress was hardwood, not softwood. A fragment of twig found in her hair, though yet to be positively identified, was definitely not from a conifer.

"It's a waste of time to search the Forestry Commission plantations for the place where she was hidden, then," advised Martin Tait, unasked. "Better to go straight to the place I spotted from the air, Stoneyhill wood."

The Chief Inspector ignored the advice. Stoneyhill wood was more than a mile from Fodderstone, and he intended to do things his own way, systematically.

"I see that Mrs. Websdell's garden gnome has reappeared," said Hilary. She was reading a report from DC Bedford, whose enquiry patch the previous day had included the Flintknappers Arms. "It was found on Tuesday, damaged, in a ditch along the Horkey road."

"Was it," said Quantrill. He took no interest in gnomes. Molly had been keen on having one when they first moved into their semi-detached house in Breckham Market, but he had refused to give it garden space. In his opinion, gnomes were a stupid waste of money. They were also, in residential areas, an open invitation to practical jokers, and he was damned if he would ever make himself a laughing-stock at divisional HQ by having to report that a gnome of his own had gone missing.

But Sergeant Lloyd persisted. "I'm beginning to wonder whether the Websdells' gnome is significant," she said. "I didn't think so, when it disappeared—but at the time we all believed that Sandra had gone off of her own accord. Now, though, it seems odd. Apparently the gnome had stood in the Websdells' garden for the whole of their married life. No one had larked about with it in twenty-three years—understandably, in a quiet place like Fodderstone Green. So surely it can't be a coincidence that it went missing just after Sandra did, and then turned up again, damaged, on the morning of the day she died?"

Quantrill put down the report he was reading, and scratched his jaw. "Hmm. There was the usual silly ransom note, wasn't there? I'd better have a look at it."

Hilary went to the file. Martin Tait couldn't resist offering some further advice. "I wouldn't pin any hope on anything to do with a garden gnome," he said. "Stealing gnomes is the kind of thing Hooray Henries do, and I think Mrs. Yardley has been entertaining some of them at weekends."

"Hooray who?" said Quantrill.

"Henries. Well-bred twits who've never grown up," explained Tait with contempt. He'd gone off the upper classes. "You know, the ones who get drunk and behave like hooligans, and then try to charm their way out of court by pleading youthful high spirits."

"Oh, *them*," said Quantrill.

"It's certainly a literate note. Isn't it?" said Hilary, offering it in its plastic evidence bag to the Chief Inspector. "Greek e's and all."

"I wouldn't know about that." Quantrill was growing increasingly irritated. He was a senior police officer who'd come up the hard way. His own village-school education had finished when he was fourteen, and he didn't care to be reminded of the fact that a new generation of better-educated, more sophisticated detectives was about to overtake him. "What I *do* know is that people who fool about with gnomes in Breckham Market are usually the Young Farmers' Club type—they enjoy a prank, but they're responsible enough not to damage other people's property, or to throw it away. They usually just swap gnomes round. But if they left a ransom note I'd expect them to return the gnome later, whether the sweets were put out for them or not. So this doesn't look like a standard practical joke."

"That's how the Hooray Henries would see it, though," said Tait. "They're mindlessly arrogant when it comes to other people's property. That's why I suggested Mrs. Yardley's friends. They probably took the gnome for a laugh, drove it about until they got tired of it, and then pitched it out of the car window."

"Yes . . ." agreed Hilary. "But there's something you don't

know, Martin. The ransom note didn't appear until two days after the gnome went missing. The gnome disappeared during the night of Friday 20th July, and the note was found stuck conspicuously on a rose bush by the Websdells' garden gate on the morning of Sunday 22nd. How do you account for that?"

"He's not required to account for it." Chief Inspector Quantrill slapped crossly at some midges that were scudding over his face on their maddeningly tickly microfeet. "You'd better send the gnome and the note to the lab, Hilary. As for you, Martin—all right, you've offered a suggestion that needs following up. You're on visiting terms with Mrs. Yardley, so you might as well make yourself useful by asking her whether any of her guests ever mentioned the gnome."

Tait hesitated. Alison's father knew nothing about the subject of his conversation with Hilary Lloyd the previous evening, then. Good for Hilary; he'd always thought well of her, and he felt a momentary embarrassment for having sworn at her, a twinge of guilt because he hadn't since apologized. Fortunately she was behaving today as though nothing had happened.

The fact that she hadn't blabbed to the old man did create a problem, though. It was going to be impossible, Tait realized, for him to get out of going to see Annabel Yardley again. The DCI had been very decent in offering him this chance to stay with the investigation, and he could see no way of turning down the invitation to question Annabel without telling Alison's father more than he wanted him to know.

"Of course," said Tait confidently. "I'll be glad to help."

Quantrill simmered down. "Mrs. Yardley's already suggested that we might take a look at the regulars of the Flintknappers Arms," he said. "Do you use the pub at all, Martin?"

"I was there on Tuesday evening. Twice. It was where I met Annabel Yardley, as it happens. I know the men she means, by sight anyway. They were all in the bar when I went there the second time—they're a noisy, unsavoury-looking bunch." Tait paused, thinking. "Now that's interesting. Tuesday evening . . . That was when Sandra Websdell died. The pathologist says that her death would have occurred somewhere between six and eight o'clock. I was at the Flintknappers on my first visit from—oh, about six-forty to seven-thirty. And in all that time there wasn't a soul in the pub apart from myself and Mrs. Yardley and the landlady behind the bar. Not a regular in sight."

"There wasn't?" Quantrill brightened visibly. "We could be on to something, then. Did you hear that, Chips?" he asked the perspiring collator. "How many alibis does that demolish?"

PC Carpenter extracted a list from one of his files. "Four, sir. According to their statements, four men spent the whole of Tuesday evening in the Flintknappers Arms: Howard Braithwaite, Charles Horrocks, Stanley Bolderow and Reginald Osler."

"Five men," said Quantrill. "The landlord as well."

"Oh, right—Philip Goodwin. He said that he opened the pub at the usual time, six o'clock. The other four said that they all arrived between six and six-fifteen. Each one of them said that the others were there, and that they all stayed in the bar until closing time."

"*Five* men, sir?" protested Hilary. "Surely you're not suggesting that they were all involved in Sandra's death?"

"Possibly not," said Quantrill. "But they wouldn't have lied to us if they weren't up to something at the time she died, and I intend to find out what it was."

"No, Martin. Sorry, but that's definite. You've been extremely helpful, and I'm obliged to you, but I'm not going to have this case taken over unofficially by the regional crime squad. Yes, I'll be glad if you'll still have a word about the gnome with Mrs. Yardley—you're certainly the best man for that job. But apart from that, all the investigating will be done by members of Breckham CID. To which you no longer belong. Damn it, man, you're on leave—go away and fly your aeroplane."

Tait pointed out that visibility was too hazy for flying.

"Then go and entertain your aged aunt. Take her out to lunch—no, *not* at the Flintknappers Arms. Treat her to a day out, right away from Fodderstone. Alison told me how fond of the old lady you are, but I've seen precious little evidence of it."

"I've already offered to take my aunt out, but she doesn't want to go," said Tait. "She doesn't feel like coming for a flight, either—she's not at all well, I'm afraid. And Alison's quite right, I *am* fond of Aunt Con. I may not mention her very often, but I think about her a great deal."

"Excuse me, Mr. Quantrill," interrupted the heavily moustached sergeant in charge of the caravan. He had just received a radio message from the crew of the police Land Rover that had been searching for Sandra Websdell's car. "The girl's Fiesta's been found in the forest, about a couple of miles north-east of Fodderstone Green. It looks as though the car's been there for some time—probably ever since she was abducted."

The sergeant went to the map displayed on the wall and pointed out the approximate location, in a Forestry Commission plantation that lay to the north of, and parallel with, the Horkey road. Whoever had abducted the girl could have driven her car into the forest along an unmetalled track that led across the fields from the road, not far from the cottage for which she had set out on the morning she disappeared.

The fact that the car had been abandoned so comparatively close to the village suggested that Sandra might have been held captive somewhere in the same area. The map showed that there was another track leading to—and from—the plantation where the car had been hidden. This track ran west from the plantation, going by a roundabout route to Fodderstone Green. And the roundabout route went past Stoneyhill wood, which Tait had already advised the Chief Inspector to search.

"Looks as though I might as well take the rest of the week as leave," grumbled Quantrill to Sergeant Lloyd, "and hand this whole case over to the Flying Detective . . ."

"Ready when you are, sir," said Inspector Tait.

24

Thursday lunch at the Flintknappers Arms was cold meat and salad again.

Lois Goodwin was too worried about her husband to bother with cooking, or with the customers. Yesterday she had heard Phil deliberately lying to the police about where he had been

on the evening of Sandra Websdell's death. Surely he hadn't—?
Surely he couldn't have—?

No. Definitely not. For all his faults, not Phil.

But why had he lied? Where had he really been on Tuesday? She hadn't seen him from 11 a.m., when he'd rushed off saying that he had an appointment in Breckham Market, until just before eight in the evening when he'd rushed back, noisy with excuses. She hadn't believed his complicated story about being kept waiting between business appointments because she'd heard similar stories from him before; she knew that shifty-eyed look behind those tinted spectacles. She minded about his attempted deception, but she'd comforted herself with the thought that the affair he must be having wouldn't last. They never did.

But that was before she knew that Sandra had been found dead. Before she'd heard her husband telling a completely different story about Tuesday evening to the police. She had longed to challenge him about it last night, but she realized that if he knew anything about Sandra's death—not that he would have, could have, been personally involved, but if he *knew* anything—he wouldn't tell her. She wasn't even sure that she wanted to know.

Phil had certainly been edgy when a customer had looked into the pub just as they were closing after lunch yesterday to tell them that the police were working their way through the village making enquiries.

"Nothing to worry about, love!" her husband had exclaimed as soon as they were alone, although his habit of fingering his catfish moustache into shape when he was agitated was a complete giveaway. "No need for you to be pestered by the fuzz, though. You go and put your feet up, and leave the talking to me."

So she'd left him to it; but she'd listened from behind the lobby door. And of course Phil was good at talking. The fuzz had turned out to be a ridiculously young-looking detective, no match for a former Fitted-Kitchen-Salesman-of-the-Year, and he'd happily written down the lies Phil told him. Her husband had often said that all policemen were as thick as two short planks, and Lois hoped that he was right.

But the boy detective had sharp eyes. He'd spotted the gnome that Lois had cleaned up and left ready to be returned to Beryl Websdell, and he'd asked when and where it was found, and by whom. Her husband hadn't known. Lois, forgetting that Phil didn't know that she'd been listening, had immediately gone to his assistance. While the detective was writing down her answers, Phil had given her a peculiar look—at once annoyed, guilty and anxious for her support. But he ought to realize by now, after fourteen years of marriage, that however much she disapproved of his lies, however alarmed she was by them, she would never let him down.

Lois hoped, of course, that the police would not come back. When they did, just on closing time at two-thirty on Thursday afternoon, her stomach tightened with anxiety. Phil had been serving behind the bar again that lunch-time, but when the detectives arrived he happened to be down in the cellar disconnecting an empty beer cask and connecting a full one. Lois was glad he was out of earshot. She intended to confirm the statement he had made, but she thought she might find it easier to lie for him if he wasn't there to hear her.

This time it was not the boy detective who came, but the dark-haired woman sergeant with the scar on her forehead who had made enquiries when Sandra first went missing. With the sergeant was a middle-aged chief inspector, a big man with a slow Suffolk voice and a patient manner, but unnervingly watchful green eyes.

The sergeant gave Lois a pleasant enough greeting, and explained that they were puzzled about some facts that didn't seem to match. "For instance, our information is that you yourself, Mrs. Goodwin, were alone behind the bar from at least six-thirty to seven-thirty on Tuesday evening. And during the whole of that time you had only two casual customers. Is that right?"

Oh God. So they knew that Phil had lied.

Lois swallowed nervously. The air in the bar room was unbearably stuffy now that the front door was closed. Her forehead and upper lip felt damp, but she thought it unwise to be seen to mop her face. "Yes!" she said, trying to sound brightly co-operative. "Yes, that's right."

"And where was your husband at the time?"

Lois gripped the edge of the counter to hold herself steady. "He was here," she said. "At home, in our private quarters."

The chief inspector stared at her. "Our information," he said, "is that you told a customer that your husband was out."

Oh *God*. So it was the fair-haired young man who'd given them the information. He'd come to the Flintknappers for brandy for his aunt, Mrs. Schultz. And now she came to think of it, Lois could remember having heard Beryl Websdell mention that Mrs. Schultz's nephew was a detective . . .

"Yes—yes, I did say that," Lois babbled, stretching her lips in what she hoped would look like a smile. "I thought my husband was out because he'd had to go to Breckham Market to see his accountant, and I had no idea that he'd already returned. But in fact he'd slipped indoors without my knowledge. In the late afternoon. About five o'clock, I believe. And when I happened to go upstairs about half-past seven I found him fast asleep on the bed."

It sounded feeble, but it was the best she could do. The detectives said nothing, but looked at her as though they didn't believe a word of it.

"Apparently he'd had a drink in Breckham Market," she plunged on. "Rather more than one, I expect. And then with all this hot weather . . ."

"I don't mind admitting that I didn't feel too good! So I sneaked in, as my wife's just told you, and tried to sleep it off without her knowledge. Some hope!" Phil, who must have heard what she was saying, took the cellar steps at a run and came to join Lois behind the counter. Out of sight of the detectives, his arm slipped round her waist. She would have been glad of that simple act of support, but he chose to supplement it by squeezing her bottom; she pushed his arm away, hating herself for lying and hating her husband for handling her so conspiratorially.

"Quite honestly," Phil added to the detectives, moving verbally into top-salesman gear, "I'd better tell you that I'd fibbed to my wife about having to see my accountant—" He proceeded to explain that he found Fodderstone a dreary hole, the customers primitive, and that he sometimes felt the need to spend a few hours in civilization. "Just walking on pavements, looking in shops, having a drink here and there. And now I've confessed to that, I'm in the dog-house as far as Lois is concerned. Aren't I, love?"

He gave his wife another squeeze. Lois moved out of his reach and busied herself by putting clean glasses on the shelf, turning her back on the detectives to avoid their sceptical eyes.

"Nothing wrong with taking a few hours off," said the chief

inspector, "though Mrs. Goodwin may well feel aggrieved that you lied to her. But why did you lie to the detective constable who took your statement yesterday? What was your reason for telling him that you were here behind the bar, if you were really upstairs in your pit?"

"I'd have thought that was obvious," exclaimed Phil with a smile. "I may not like this place, but it's my only source of income and I don't want to lose my licence. Your young detective was writing down everything I said. I wasn't going to have him putting it on record that I was too drunk to serve my customers at opening time! Have a heart, sir and madam . . ."

Phil was laughing now, inviting the straight-faced detectives to laugh with him, trying to jolly them along. Lois glanced at them, and knew that her husband was doing the wrong thing. She sidled up to Phil and tried to nudge him surreptitiously into silence.

"Your licence to sell alcohol is of no interest to us, Mr. Goodwin," said the chief inspector sternly. "And the death of a young woman is no laughing matter."

"Of *course* not!" Sobering immediately, Phil expressed sorrow over Sandra Websdell's death and assured the detectives that he knew nothing whatever about it. But the trouble was, thought Lois as she listened to his fluency, that once people had taken a dislike to Phil they disbelieved everything he said. She could see that the detectives assumed that he was lying again.

For herself, though, she felt a lightening of her heart. As he spoke of his sorrow, Phil had taken off his tinted spectacles in an unconscious gesture that she recognized as a sign of sincerity. She was right about him, then, thank God. And for a moment she was so relieved that she forgot that his absence on Tuesday evening was still unexplained.

But the chief inspector pursued her husband with questions. Why had he alleged that four of his customers were in the bar with him on Tuesday from opening time onwards?

Phil put on his spectacles again. "Because they're regulars. I naturally assumed they'd have been here."

"But they weren't. Do you know where they were?"

"Do *I* know? Of course not! I went out to get away from them."

"Ah yes: you don't like them, and you have nothing in common—you've already told us that. But each one of them stated, when he was interviewed, that he came here just after six o'clock and that you were serving behind the bar. They all tried to provide you with an alibi, Mr. Goodwin, just as you tried to provide alibis for them. So it seems to me that you do have something in common after all. What is it? Where were the five of you on Tuesday evening?"

For once in his life Phil was wordless. Lois could sense that he had sagged, body and spirit. Heaven knew what kind of a mess her husband had got himself into . . . but she knew that there were limits to his follies. She gripped his hand and appealed to the sergeant; a woman detective—particularly one who wore a diamond eternity ring on her wedding finger and therefore had an emotional attachment of her own—would surely understand.

"You *must* believe my husband when he says he knows nothing about Sandra! He would never have harmed the girl—he isn't that kind of man. Please believe me. *Please*."

The sergeant shook her dark head reproachfully. "How can you expect us to believe you, Mrs. Goodwin, when you haven't been honest with us? Your story about your husband being asleep upstairs wasn't true, was it? You lied to us to protect him. But if he knows nothing about Sandra's death he doesn't need any protection. Does he?"

Anguished, Lois bit her lower lip. She tried to think what to say next, but the only words that came into her head were, *Oh God, what are we going to do?*

Beside her, Phil kept licking the second finger of his right hand and nervously pressing down each alignment of his moustache, as though it was a false one that might drop off at any moment. He still said nothing; but he returned his wife's grip.

The chief inspector gave each of them a hard green look. "We'll leave you to think it over," he said. "Next time we come, we shall want the truth from both of you."

As the detectives reached the door, the sergeant glanced over her shoulder and gave Lois a smile of sympathy and understanding. It was so completely unexpected that Lois felt unnerved. For a moment she longed to call the sergeant back, sit down with her over a cup of tea and tell her everything she knew—except of course that she knew nothing . . .

Phil, having locked and bolted the door behind their visitors, was coming back to her with a look of gratitude and triumph on his face. He praised her and thanked her. "If we both stick to our story," he insisted, "everything will be all right. And everything *will* be all right—things are going to be better for us in the future, I promise. Trust me!"

Lois wished that she could. But at least he had taken off his tinted spectacles again, and that token of sincerity was a small comfort.

25

Before going to interview the Goodwins at the Flintknappers Arms, Chief Inspector Quantrill had directed all the police officers at his disposal to make a thorough search of Stoneyhill wood.

The searchers—some uniformed, some in civilian clothes, all shirt-sleeved and sweating in the humid air—worked their way through the wood looking for huts or shelters where Sandra Websdell might have been held captive. They made slow progress. Stoneyhill wood had been neglected for years and was rank with undergrowth and booby-trapped by fallen boughs too rotten to bear a man's weight. The police officers were clawed at by brambles and stung by nettles, and each one was accompanied by a living, buzzing, biting halo of flies.

Eventually they converged on an open area in the centre of which were the ruins of a small house, probably once a keeper's cottage. The house was plainly built of grey brick, and the reason for its ruined state was immediately obvious: the walls were partly blackened, partly scorched pink by some long-ago fire. Most of the roof had been destroyed, and elder trees growing inside the ruins had forced their way towards the light until they sprouted out at the top.

What must once have been the garden, all round the house, was now elbow-high with vicious vegetation. The police had armed themselves with sticks, and after their struggle through the trees it would have been a comparatively straightforward job for them to hack their way through the nettles and giant thistles to reach the house. But instead of moving forward they lingered at the edge of the open area, panting and sweating and smarting and swearing, and surveyed the greenery with disgust.

There was no need for them to go any further. No one could have made use of the ruined house without beating a path through the vegetation, and they could all see that it was pathless. Frustrated, they sat down at the edge of the clearing—the non-smokers edging near the smokers in the hope that newly lighted cigarettes would drive away the flies—and awarded themselves a ten-minute break to lick their wounds and grumble.

The loudest grumbler was Detective Constable Ian Wigby. Having to his annoyance been recalled from London, he was further disgruntled to hear that in his absence the job of checking Desmond Flood's alibi had been passed over to the Saintsbury division. To add injury to the insult, he had been sent out with the search team as soon as he reported back, and had ripped his trousers on a bramble in Stoneyhill wood. And all for nothing.

No, not for nothing. That was what really made Wigby feel riled. He'd been required to search the wood for the benefit of Detective-bloody-Inspector Tait who, it seemed, had flown over in his aeroplane—his *own* bloody aeroplane—and had thought from on high that this looked a likely place. So Wigby had damaged his clothes, been scratched, stung, and eaten alive by flies, just to satisfy Mr. Martin Tait . . . The beefy detective constable smoked and scowled and tried to think of a suitable way of getting even.

DC Bedford was the only policeman who didn't sit down and complain. He insisted on thrusting through the thistles and goose-grass so that he could search the derelict house, and his colleagues let him get on with it. When he returned and made the expected report that there was no sign that the ruins had been in recent use, he was given a slow handclap.

Undeterred, James Bedford reminded his lounging colleagues that there was still the old boathouse to be searched. They seemed to have no heart for it and so he set off on his own, to the accompaniment of ironic cries of "Well done, Jim-lad," and "We're right behind you, boy." Bedford blushed, but kept going.

The detective constable found that the northern edge of the wood was skirted by a little-used dirt lane. He remembered that according to the map the lane led eastwards to the Forestry Commission plantation where Sandra Websdell's car

had been found; to the west it led the mile and a bit to
Fodderstone Green.

On the other side of the lane was what had once been an
ornamental lake, now surrounded by a strip of rough grass.
Beyond the lake, where Fodderstone Hall had once stood in
parkland, were harvested fields.

Like Stoneyhill wood, the lake was neglected: choked with
matted reeds at the edges, weedy in the middle. Beside
it drooped a few round-shouldered old willow trees. At the
western end, where the lane passed close to the water, was
the boathouse that Bedford had come to investigate.

He observed it from the shelter of the trees. At first sight
the wooden building looked unused and unusable. Holes
gaped in the plank walls, the roof of the boat dock had fallen
in, the staging that led out across mud and reeds to the open
water was broken. Nothing had been painted in years.

But a Rover 2600 was parked in the shadow of the willow
clump. The back door of the boathouse looked comparatively
new, and had a large hasp and a padlock. And mounted on the
gable end of the building was a radio aerial.

DC Bedford's message reached Chief Inspector Quantrill over
his car radio as he and Sergeant Lloyd were driving away
from the Flintknappers Arms. Quantrill had intended to interview Charley Horrocks next, but now he drove out of
Fodderstone, through Fodderstone Green, and along the
bumpy lane that led to the old boathouse. What drew him
was the information that the owner of the Rover 2600 was
another of the pub regulars who had lied about his whereabouts on the evening of Sandra Websdell's death: Howard
Braithwaite.

As Quantrill and Hilary approached the boathouse they could
hear the sound of a radio. There was a great deal of background noise coming over the air, and an excited voice giving
what they realized, as they stood at the door, was a racing
commentary. Quantrill waited until the race finished, then
knocked loudly. No one answered or came to the door, and
so he opened it and walked in.

The room they entered, a man-sized dog kennel construction inside the shell of the dilapidated boathouse, was neat

and businesslike. To the detectives coming from out-of-doors the room seemed gloomy, though the roof at the far end, above the window, was patterned by shifts of reflected light. The open window looked north, over the lake, and through it drifted the sweetly rotten smell of warm mud and decaying reed, and the sound of water slopping about in the boat dock.

Howard Braithwaite, grey and cross-looking, sat at a desk with his back to the window. The radio was now off, and he was in the act of making a call on the cordless telephone he held in his hand. The nature of his occupation was obvious: his pile of racing reference-books, his battery-operated radio and calculator, his spread copy of the *Sporting Life*, all made it clear that he was a dedicated off-course punter.

He glared at the intruders over his half-moon spectacles. "Who the hell are you? What do you want?"

Quantrill told him. Braithwaite looked even more furious. He slapped his telephone on to the desk, pushed aside the *Sporting Life*, and denied, in short sharp barks, that he knew Sandra Websdell. Yes, her parents lived two doors away from him, or so he understood from his wife; he took no notice of his neighbours, hardly knew what any of them looked like.

As for where he had been on Tuesday evening, he had already given a statement about that. Quantrill pointed out that his statement was at variance with other information. Braithwaite immediately defended himself by launching a verbal attack.

"Your constable was officious and insolent. I intend to make a formal complaint about him. I wasn't able to be accurate about the timing of my movements, and I declined to make guesses. He tried to insist. If he added any specific times to the information I gave him, that's his responsibility. Not mine."

The Chief Inspector asked the man to repeat his account of his movements on Tuesday afternoon and evening. Braithwaite said crossly that he had spent the afternoon there, in the boathouse, working. Yes, of course alone. That was why he'd rented the place and had it made habitable, so that he could have somewhere to work without interruption. After the results of the last race—the 4:40 from Newmarket—were broadcast, he had, as usual, done some fishing. It helped him to relax. Yes, for pike; no, he'd caught nothing; no, he had no idea how long he went on fishing. He'd packed up his rod

some time in the early evening, and gone straight to the
Flintknappers Arms.

"I wouldn't have thought the Flintknappers was the right
pub for a man of your background," commented the Chief
Inspector.

"It isn't. But I find it convenient. I go there every lunch
time to collect my copy of the *Sporting Life.*"

"Why not have the paper delivered to your home?" asked
Hilary.

Braithwaite glared at her. He seemed not to like women;
certainly not those who asked him questions. "Domestic reasons," he barked.

Quantrill required no further explanation. There were domestic reasons for some of his own practices . . . working later
than he sometimes needed to, for one. "Even so," he said, "I
find it difficult to believe that you can enjoy spending whole
evenings in the Flintknappers Arms. *Every* evening?"

"No. Occasionally."

"And why that particular evening?"

"Why not? It was hot, I was thirsty."

"And presumably you enjoy the company of the other
regulars. But I really wouldn't have thought you had much in
common with them."

"Racing. We talk about racing."

The Chief Inspector picked up the books on Braithwaite's
desk, one by one: *Horses in Training* by Raceform, Timeform
Computer Timefigures, Ladbroke's *Racing Year,* Timeform
Horses to Follow, The Sporting Life Racehorse Ratings, Timeform *Black Book,* Raceform *Up-to-Date Form Book* . . . The
man would need to be an extremely serious punter to recoup
what he spent on books every year, let alone make a profit.

"But you don't actually go racing, Mr. Braithwaite? Or
watch on television?"

"I make no claim to like horses. Or horsey people. I bet
because I enjoy backing my own judgement."

"And pitting your wits against the bookmakers—you have a
credit account with one or more of them, I expect?"

"What the devil has that got to do with the police?"

"It has nothing to do with our reason for being here,"
Quantrill agreed. "What we've come for is to ask your permission to search this building. We're looking for the place
where Sandra Websdell was held captive."

Braithwaite jumped to his feet, barking furiously. "Good

God, you needn't imagine she was here! I had no connection
with her. None at all."

"Then you won't object if our men make a thorough search?"

"I do object! I object most strongly!"

Sergeant Lloyd picked the man's outspread copy of the
Sporting Life off the desk and folded it up. The two detectives looked pointedly at the telephone that Braithwaite had
tried to conceal as soon as he knew who they were.

"Very useful things, cordless telephones," said Quantrill.
"You couldn't place bets from an isolated office like this
without one, could you?"

Braithwaite growled unintelligibly.

"The only problem with them," Quantrill went on, "is that
the models approved for use with British Telecom equipment
have a very modest range—not much over 700 feet from the
base telephone, I believe. But this boathouse is over a mile
from your home on Fodderstone Green. An approved cordless telephone would be no use to you, so you bought a far
more powerful set—even though you knew that its use was
illegal."

"I know nothing of the kind. The set was on open sale in a
reputable shop in Saintsbury."

"It's not illegal to supply the sets," explained Hilary. "But
no reputable shop would have sold you this one without
warning you that it's illegal to use it."

"That's utterly stupid. It's the most stupidly illogical thing
I've heard in my life!"

"It's the law," said Quantrill impassively. "By using this
set, you're committing an offence by transmitting on a
waveband reserved for other users. I shall have to charge you
to appear before the magistrates, and your equipment will
automatically be confiscated."

Braithwaite's aggressive bark changed to a worried yap.
His spectacles had slid to the end of his nose and he peered
over them anxiously. "A court appearance? Oh no . . . My
God, I'll never hear the last of this from my wife . . ." His
facial muscles creaked as he forced the corners of his mouth
apart in an unaccustomed smile. "Look, er—Chief Inspector—
supposing I allow you—*invite* you—to search this place. Will
that help?"

"No, sir. But thank you for the invitation."

*   *   *

The old boathouse was searched minutely; but nothing was found to indicate that Sandra Websdell had been held captive there.

26

"That's not a bad set-up, for any retired man," said Quantrill as he drove away from the boathouse. He spoke thoughtfully, almost enviously. "Somewhere snug and private, where he can follow an indoor hobby without interruption or interference, and do a bit of fishing whenever he feels like it."

"Nice for the retired man's wife, too," pointed out Hilary. "I don't suppose she wants him hanging about the house all day."

Quantrill hadn't thought of it like that. For a moment he felt miffed; he'd expected his sergeant to be on his side.

"Anyway," he said, "it clears up one thing that's puzzled me ever since I read the report of the initial interview with Braithwaite. He didn't sound the type to spend the whole of his time fishing. A man who'd been used to managing his own industrial firm would need a hobby that challenged him and kept him mentally alert. Serious gambling would certainly do that for him. I still can't believe that he enjoys the company of the other regulars at the Flintknappers Arms, though. He's obviously not a gregarious man. I suppose they may share an interest in betting on racing, but that's hardly a strong enough bond to induce the five of them to give each other alibis for the time of Sandra Websdell's death. Unless they were all in some way involved."

"We've no reason to suppose that more than one man was involved," said Hilary. "Where's the motive? Gang rapes happen, of course, but Sandra hadn't been raped by one man, let alone five. No violence was used against her until moments before her death, and afterwards her body was handled with remorse. I still think we're looking for one man who loved her."

"You may be right," said Quantrill. Sergeant Lloyd often was; but not always. "Supposing the group used a front man, though, to keep her captive while he tried to persuade her to go along with whatever they wanted."

"Such as?"

"Possibly nothing more than a bit of sport. Something they were betting on, perhaps. Did you see that very old book Braithwaite had on his desk among this year's form books? It was an illustrated volume called *Sporting Life in Old England*. There was a chapter on racing, but it seemed to deal chiefly with various kinds of hunting and shooting that are still legal, and things like bird-trapping and badger-baiting that aren't."

"All hunting should be made illegal," said Hilary. "It's uncivilized to gallop after a pack of hounds in pursuit of one defenceless wild animal."

"I don't mind about foxes," said Quantrill. "Foxes are killers themselves—they're cunning too, and good runners. They have a reasonable chance. But this isn't fox or foxhound country. Near Breckham Market there's a pack of harriers—they're a bit smaller than foxhounds, but fast—and what they hunt is the hare."

"That's barbaric."

"I didn't think so, when I was a boy. When the local harriers held a meet near our village, a gang of us would play hookey from school to follow them. We'd run about with sticks, hoping to flush a hare out of cover. Not that we ever did, but we thought it was great sport. We were so excited that if we'd managed to catch a living thing—anything that couldn't defend itself, a rabbit, a mouse, a frog—we'd have egged each other on to beat it to death."

"Little brutes," said Hilary.

"Yes, we were. But that's how I found out how exciting it is to gang up in mindless pursuit of something—or someone—completely inoffensive. In that situation, people behave entirely out of character. They'll do things that they'd never dream of doing as individuals."

"And you think that might apply to the regulars of the Flintknappers Arms, and Sandra Websdell?"

"I'm wondering about it. Braithwaite's book made me remember hare-hunting, you see. As I said, I loved the thrill of it when I was a boy, though I never got near a hare. But my grandfather did, when he was young, and he liked to tell a story about it.

"He had to start work on a farm when he was twelve, so there wasn't much opportunity for him to follow the harriers.

But one frosty winter day he heard the hounds approaching the turnip field where he was working. They were in full cry. Then they stopped, a field away, and began casting round for the scent. They'd temporarily lost the hare.

"That was when my grandfather saw it. The hare was moving up a frozen ditch towards him with a kind of zig-zagging crawl, and its long ears were drooping over its head. It had been chased to exhaustion.

"It tried to find some cover, but there wasn't any. The ditch was wide and open, and came to a dead end not far from where my grandfather was standing. The hare crawled to the end and tried to spring out, but its hind feet kept skidding on the ice and it fell back. The hounds began baying again in the next field, and Grandad could see that the hare had given up hope of escape. He used to tell us how he watched it give up. It crouched where it was, trembling, ears down, and hid its face in its paws. And he could hear it making a thin, despairing, wailing noise, like a terrified child."

Hilary looked sickened. "What did your grandfather do?"

"Jumped the ditch, ran to the nearest huntsmen and pointed them in another direction. When they'd streamed away, taking the hounds with them, he went back and picked the hare up. It struggled and cried as he lifted it, and then suddenly went limp. It simply died in his hands, without any violence on his part, and without a mark on it."

"I see . . . And Sandra Websdell also died with hardly a mark on her—but as a direct result of God knows what ordeal. Do you think that she was in some way harried to death?"

"It's possible, isn't it? I don't mean physically; but during the three weeks of her captivity she must have been under extreme mental and emotional pressure. And then she had that infection, which would have lowered her resistance. By the time she died, she must have been totally exhausted. You may be right that only one man was directly involved, but if the landlord and the regulars of the Flintknappers Arms persist in covering up their whereabouts on Tuesday evening, we're bound to suspect that the whole gang contributed in some callous way to the girl's death."

"What had your grandfather intended to do with the hare, when he tried to rescue it?" asked Hilary as they approached Fodderstone.

Quantrill, a down-to-earth countryman, gave her a grin. He was glad to know that she had a heart, but he didn't propose to encourage her inclination to be sentimental about animals.

"The same as he did when it died in his hands. They were a large family, poor and always hungry, and the hare was a prize. He took it home to his mother, and they ate it next day for their dinner."

27

Charley Horrocks lived in what had once been a gatekeeper's lodge at one of the entrances to the park surrounding Fodderstone Hall. The ornamental iron gates, chained and padlocked, still hung between two imposing stone pillars. But the metalled road that had once led from Fodderstone village past the Green and on through the gates and the park to the Hall, now came to a dusty end at the lodge. All that could be seen through the rusting gates was one great harvested field, blackened by the firing of surplus straw, that extended northwards in the direction of Stoneyhill wood.

The boundaries of the former park were still marked in places—as here, on either side of the lodge—by a straggle of trees. From the lodge a dirt lane led off to the right, parallel with the boundary. This was the lane that gave Howard Braithwaite access to his private office in the old boathouse. It also led on to the conifer plantation where Sandra Websdell's car had been found.

The former gatekeeper's lodge had been built in the same Regency *cottage orné* style as the houses on Fodderstone Green. But whereas they were all carefully maintained, the lodge was in decay. Thatch had crumbled and slipped from the roof, the rustic poles that supported the porch looked about to collapse, the Gothic front door sagged open, partly off its hinges. Rampant bindweed half-smothered the fruit trees in the garden and pulled the roses away from the walls, leaving the knapped flints bare and black.

Despite the evidence of neglect, an electricity power line led to the lodge and its twisted brick chimneystack sprouted a television aerial. As the detectives approached the open door they could hear that the set was on full blast. Like Howard Braithwaite, Charley Horrocks was spending the hot afternoon at the races.

But his method of following the sport—his interest in racing—was very different from Braithwaite's. Above the noise of the commentary the detectives could hear a rhythmic whacking sound and a voice raised in hoarse excitement: "COME ON! *Come on come on—*"

Hilary Lloyd gestured the Chief Inspector ahead of her, in acknowledgement of the fact that masculine fantasy was better dealt with by a policeman than a policewoman. Quantrill took a look through the door that opened straight on the squalid living-room of the lodge.

Charley Horrocks, oblivious of everything except the 26-inch colour television screen, was riding the winner. He sat, hugely hunched, astride the sagging back of an old sofa, one bare foot on the seat, one on a wooden box of approximately the same height. He had stripped in the heat to a grimy singlet and a pair of underpants that were not quite long enough to cover his massive knees. On his grey head was a jockey cap in racing colours, and in his right hand was a riding whip with which he was belabouring the sofa. "Come on!" he urged as the tiring horses approached the final furlong. "*Come on come on comeoncomeoncomeon . . .*"

Quantrill withdrew from the doorway, grimaced at Hilary, and waited until the excitement of the race had subsided. Then he thundered on the iron knocker, steadying the insecure door with his other hand. "County police," he called. "Detective Chief Inspector Quantrill. Anyone at home?"

He walked into the room. Charley Horrocks dropped both his jaw and his whip. He scrambled off the sofa and stood behind it, his scarlet cap making a wincing colour-clash with his sweating purple face.

"Just watchin' the racin'," he mumbled. "Turn it off, if you like . . ."

Quantrill did so. "I was told that you were interested in racing," he said. "It's something you have in common with Mr. Braithwaite, I believe?"

Horrocks looked uneasy. He seemed about to deny it, then changed his mind. "You've been talkin' to Braithwaite?" he asked.

"About half an hour ago." Quantrill gingerly lifted a shirt

and a vast pair of khaki trousers, army tropical issue circa 1952, from the floor. "Make yourself decent, Mr. Horrocks, there's a lady detective with me. No, not in these—" he dropped the clothes again. "You must have been wearing them for weeks. Can't you find yourself something cleaner?"

Horrocks rumbled off up the stairs. The Chief Inspector took the opportunity to make a quick inspection of the dirty living-room and the dirtier kitchen that led off it. "Ah, that's better," he approved as the man reappeared, still shirtless but wearing a heavy tweed suit. "If I were you," Quantrill added, "I'd ease off the racing, especially in this hot weather. If you go on like that you'll give yourself a heart attack."

Horrocks shrugged away the risk. Something else was on his mind. "You said you were talkin' to Braithwaite. What else did he tell you?"

"He talked about what he was doing last Tuesday, in the afternoon and early evening. And now Sergeant Lloyd and I have come to hear exactly what you were doing at that time."

Hilary took a final breath of fresh air, then walked into the room. The reek of unwashed clothes and an unwashed body assaulted her nostrils, but she kept her face professionally straight. Horrocks's eyes—pale-blue irises, yellowed whites—swivelled towards her and away again, his expression mingling embarrassment, resentment and suspicion. Sweating in his tweeds, he addressed himself exclusively to Quantrill.

"Tuesday? Damned if I know. Shockin' memory . . . S'pose I did the same as usual—a drink at the Knappers before lunch, afternoon here watchin' the racin', back to the Knappers in the evenin'."

"And what time in the evening did you get there?"

"Damned if I know . . ."

"You said in your statement, Mr. Horrocks, that you got there at five minutes past six. But we know you weren't there before seven-thirty at the earliest. Where were you between six and seven-thirty? With Braithwaite?"

Charley Horrocks wiped his hot face on his hairy sleeve. "No, I definitely wasn't with Braithwaite. Absolutely not. I was here on my own until I went to the Knappers. Can't be sure about the time—somethin' wrong with m'watch." He looked unhopefully about the room. "It's here somewhere . . . Gold hunter and chain, bequeathed to me by m'grandfather the third Earl. Bloody good watch, but no use for tellin' the time."

Quantrill gave him a hard look. "You know why we're enquiring about Tuesday?" he demanded.

Horrocks shrugged his great shoulders. "The Websdell girl, I s'pose. The one who was killed by the feller she'd promised to marry. Promised herself to him and led him on, then tried to back orf. She was arskin' for trouble."

"Was she?" said Sergeant Lloyd. "How do you know that? How well did you know Sandra Websdell?"

Horrocks floundered: he knew her only by sight, hadn't seen her for months. He'd heard talk about her in the Flintknappers Arms, that was all.

Hilary Lloyd bent to pick up a newspaper that had fallen to the floor. "Were you ever married, Mr. Horrocks?" she asked.

"Good God, no!" he said promptly. "I've never had any time for young women. They're too selfish and demandin'."

Hilary gave him a cool smile. "I'll go and wait for you by your car, sir," she said to Quantrill, handing him the copy of the *Sun* and walking out. She thought that in her absence Horrocks might be persuaded to say more; she also wanted to take a good look round the outside of the lodge.

The newspaper was folded open at the racing page, but Quantrill knew why his sergeant had handed it to him. He turned to page 3 of the tabloid and studied the photograph that occupied the full length and half the width of the page; the model was bare, blonde and buoyant.

"A big girl," he commented, impressed. "You like them big, do you?"

"I dunno what you mean."

"Of course you know. There isn't a man alive who would choose to buy the *Sun* and not take a good look at page 3."

Horrocks protested that he didn't buy the paper for himself. He took it with him to the pub because it was the only way he could communicate with the peasants. "I told you," he said, "I've got no use for young women."

"Not sexually, perhaps," conceded Quantrill. "But you could certainly do with someone to clean this place up." He gestured disapprovingly at the dirt, the disorder, the disrepair, and at the cans of schoolboy grub—baked beans, sausages, custard, rice pudding—that stood opened, with spoons in them, on the table. "Look at it! How can you live like this? What would your grandfather the Earl say if he could see you now?"

Charley Horrocks sat down heavily on the sofa. He looked

desolate. With a quivering chin he explained that when the
rest of his family moved away, his nanny had continued to
look after him. She had married a Horkey shopkeeper, but
she came over to the lodge once a week to bring Charley's
laundry and supplies, and to do the cleaning for him.

"But she gave up comin' last winter. Said she was too old
. . . Her son still brings the groceries, but I do miss Nanny."
Charley fumbled in his pocket, found something that might
have begun life as a handkerchief, and used it noisily. "She's
eighty-four next birthday," he gulped. "I don't know what I'll
do when she dies."

Quantrill shelved his theory of group involvement; this line
seemed much more promising. He sat on the edge of the sofa
so that he could look into the man's face.

"You need someone here, then, don't you, Charley?" he
said sympathetically. "A healthy young woman—not to go to
bed with, but to look after you. That's what you want, isn't it?
And preferably a local woman, someone you've known all her
life. Sandra Websdell would have suited you ideally.

"But the problem was that Sandra didn't want to come, did
she? The only way you could get her here was by abducting
her. And the only way you could keep her here was by tying
her up. You didn't mean to hurt her, I know that. But that
was what happened, wasn't it?"

Charley Horrocks wiped his purple cheeks and shook his
great grey head. "No no no," he mourned, rocking himself
backwards and forwards on the sagging springs. "I don't want
any other women here. I don't like other women. It wouldn't
be the same as havin' Nanny to look after me."

The Chief Inspector returned to his car carrying a large
plastic evidence bag. It contained Charley Horrocks's tropical
trousers and shirt.

"How did you persuade him to let you take them away?"
asked Sergeant Lloyd. She had just emerged, stung, from the
nettle patch that had once been a garden; having learned to
come prepared for such rural hazards she was now treating
her tingling skin with antihistamine cream.

"No problem," said Quantrill. "I offered to have the clothes
washed for him. Send them to the lab, will you, Hilary?
There may be something on them that will provide a direct
link with Sandra Websdell."

"Do you think it's likely?"

"I did when he started to talk about himself. I thought you were right that it was a one-man job, because he certainly had a motive for abducting the girl." Quantrill related what Horrocks had said about his nanny. "On the other hand, when we first arrived he told us without hesitation that he was here at the time of Sandra's death. His chief anxiety was to convince us that he was alone, and not with Braithwaite—and that seems to rule out any possibility that Sandra's abduction was all his own work.

"He couldn't have hidden the girl anywhere in the house, either. I asked to look round, and he made no objection at all. I rather think he hoped that I'd offer to have that cleaned for him too. It was full of muck, but I couldn't find anything of any significance. What about the outbuildings?"

"One's an earth closet, in current use," said Hilary with wry recollection. "There's also an old wash-house that hasn't been used in years. But next door to the loo is a large shed with a strong door, and it's piled high with sawn logs. The area between the back door of the lodge and the outbuildings is well-trodden, dusty grass. The rest of the garden's waist-high with vegetation, and a new path has been beaten through it during the past day or two, leading direct from the garden gate to the shed. There are the marks of a wheelbarrow along the path, and pieces of bark and dribbles of sawdust. So Charley Horrocks has just taken delivery of a load of firewood. And what I'm wondering is whether he acquired it in a deliberate attempt to prevent us from searching the shed."

"That's an interesting thought," said Quantrill. "Yes, the man could have held Sandra there . . . either on his own account, or on behalf of the group. The whole place is isolated enough, and it might have suited their purpose very well."

"Before we get too hopeful, though," said Hilary, "I'd better find out exactly when the logs were ordered and delivered. There's a local woodman, Christopher Thorold, who's making deliveries in the village this week. I'll go and talk to him."

"Better make that your next job," Quantrill agreed. "As soon as we've had a cup of tea." He mopped his forehead with one of the large white handkerchiefs that his wife always laundered so immaculately. Hilary, he observed, still managed to look admirably cool; he hoped that she wasn't of-

fended by the increasing dampness of his shirt. "And while
you're with the woodman, I want to talk to the remaining two
members of the Flintknappers Arms mob. What do we know
about them?"

"Stan Bolderow and Reg Osler—they're local men, and on
the face of it they haven't much in common with Goodwin
and Braithwaite and Horrocks. They call themselves agricultural contractors, but that sounds like a delusion of grandeur.
They seem to be spending most of their time in the harvested
fields, burning straw."

"Hmm. They call themselves contractors because they're
self-employed," said Quantrill. "And that's probably what
they have in common with the other three. They're all either
self-employed or not employed at all, so they can organize
their time as they like. And they can spend far longer in the
pub than ordinary mortals. The five of them have probably
been looking for ways to pass the time, and taking bets on
some enterprise or other."

"Such as abducting Sandra Websdell? Yes, I can see that's
how it might have happened. Any one of them would have
been able to keep her supplied with food and water . . .
Though with what ultimate purpose—"

"God knows," Quantrill agreed. "Look, Hilary, the Flintknappers Arms seems to be central to this enquiry, doesn't
it? We need to know what's been going on there—or what's
still going on, come to that. Trouble is, the pub's so small and
Fodderstone's so isolated that I can't send a plainclothes man
in for a drink without arousing immediate suspicion."

"No need for that," said Sergeant Lloyd. "The landlord's
wife is worried sick, and longing for someone to talk to. I
thought I'd leave her to agonize over the situation tonight,
and then call on her for a heart-to-heart tomorrow morning.
She'll probably go on trying to protect her husband, but I
shouldn't be surprised if she's only too glad to shop the other
four."

28

Martin Tait had had enough of Fodderstone.

Ordinarily, with his aeroplane to fly and with a local murder to investigate—with or without the permission of the detective in charge—he would have been in his element. But his leave had turned sour. First there had been the row with Alison; then there had been the row with his aunt. Now Alison's father, the Chief Inspector, was being pig-headed and obstructive every time Martin made a suggestion about the murder enquiry. And although flying was as stimulating as ever, it was cripplingly expensive.

And that—the problem of having too little money, while his aunt was proposing to deny him his rightful share of her estate—was what had ruined his leave. But it wasn't going to ruin his whole life, not if he could help it.

There was nothing more to be gained, though, by hanging about Fodderstone Green. Being forgiving and gentle and affectionate didn't come naturally to Martin Tait, and he was afraid that if he stayed much longer he might spoil the act. Better to make some excuse for returning to Yarchester immediately, so that he could leave Aunt Con with an indelible impression of his niceness . . .

He still had one unfinished piece of business to attend to, however. He had reluctantly promised the Chief Inspector that he would call on Annabel Yardley to find out whether her Hooray Henry friends had made any mention of kidnapping a garden gnome. Having been seen off by Annabel yesterday with a flea in his ear, his inclination had been to send someone else to make the enquiry—DC Bedford, for example, a keen and innocent lad to whom it wouldn't occur that an inspector of the regional crime squad, currently on leave, had no authority to send him anywhere.

But on reflection Martin Tait had decided that he would make the enquiry himself. Now that he knew better than to lust after Annabel Yardley, it would be no bad thing to meet her again in his official capacity, and then re-establish his pride by walking out of her life in his own good time.

He had already been to Beech House that morning in the hope of seeing her, but she was not at home. He would try again this afternoon, on his way back to Yarchester.

"Must you really go so soon, Martin?" His aunt, returning from a conversation over the garden fence with Geoff Websdell to find her nephew already packed, took the news like a blow. She sat down abruptly, her long narrow face drawn as though with shock. "But your leave isn't half over."

"That's what I told the regional crime squad co-ordinator when he rang to recall me. But as he pointed out, the job always takes priority. I'm really sorry that I can't stay—it's been extremely kind of you to put up with me, Aunt Con, and I've enjoyed my visit."

"I'm sorry you're going, too," she said, moving her lips as though with difficulty. Her eyes had a distant, bleak focus. "I'd expected just a few more days . . ."

"Is there something you wanted me to do?" he asked, puzzled. His aunt had been so preoccupied with the Websdells' bereavement that he'd sometimes wondered whether she knew he was there.

"No, no." Con stood up, resuming her bright voice, and gave him her lop-sided smile. "You've already helped me tremendously, and I'm jolly grateful to you. Of course your work must come first." She paused, and then burst out, embarrassed, "I'm so pleased that you're doing so well in your career. Your father would have been very proud of you. *I'm* awfully proud of you, too. I want you to know that."

She had a fine way of showing it, he thought bitterly. But he gave her a charming smile, thanked her, and changed the subject by enquiring after her neighbour.

Beryl, Con reported—half wry, half envious—was so high on religious faith that she was practically floating. Her relatives, coming to give her their support, had found themselves superfluous; particularly as Marjorie Braithwaite had taken it upon herself to organize everything and everyone.

"It's Geoff I feel saddest for. He doesn't say much, but he feels Sandra's death deeply. It'll hit Beryl later . . . but she'll cope, I'm sure."

Con paused, frowning. "I think I was able to help her through yesterday evening, though." She spoke with a wistful uncertainty, as though she wanted some reassurance. "Beryl's been a very good, kind neighbour, and I'd like to think that I did the right thing."

"I'm sure you did, Aunt Con. Look, I hate to rush off, but—"

"I know. I won't keep you, old chap. Oh—you've taken the loot, I hope? The family silver, and the other things I gave you? I left them in your room, boxed for the journey."

"Of course I haven't taken them!" Martin protested warmly. It was part of his plan, to leave her gifts behind—temporarily —as evidence that he was not a grasper. "I wouldn't dream of removing them without your permission. I can pick them up next time I come."

"But don't you *see*," Con burst out, "that's the whole *point*." She sounded tired and irritated. "I don't expect to be here much longer, and if you're going now you must take them with you. I want to be absolutely sure you've got them."

Martin soothed her, took possession of the valuables without reluctance, and loaded them into his Alfa.

"And don't forget the sampler," said Con, her irritation forgotten. She had wrapped it, in its rosewood frame, in a dust sheet, and now she carried it out to her nephew's car. Placing it carefully beside her other gifts, she moved aside the protective cloth for a final look at ten-year-old Maria Bethell's stitchwork: the blossoming boughs, the cats, the dogs, the birds, the hearts, the cupids.

"I'm so glad you're having all the family treasures, Martin," she said. "I know you'll look after them—and in time, I hope, hand them on to your own children."

He nodded his agreement as the image of Alison Quantrill— the dark-haired, green-eyed girl who would so love the sampler—filled his mind's eye. As his young ancestress's verse reminded him, *Now in the heat of youthful blood*—

But Alison was no longer his girl-friend. In fact—dismissing her image and visualizing instead Annabel Yardley, with her air of superiority and her questionable cold sore—he'd temporarily gone off women altogether. As for Aunt Constance Schultz and the "family treasures" that she was bestowing on him so munificently, all they amounted to were a few scratched pieces of silver and a faded bit of needlework. Total value no more than £2,000 . . . while the real family treasure, the money that should have been his, was being given away.

But not if he could help it.

"Aunt Con," he began, embarking formally on his major,

carefully prepared speech, "you've always been extremely good to me—"

But she wasn't listening. To his confusion she suddenly lurched forward and gripped his shoulders in a strong embrace, pressing her soft-skinned old cheek for a moment against his.

"Bless you, dear boy," she muttered in his ear, her voice strangely hoarse. Then she turned and galloped away, up the long garden path and under the arching sprays of the fragrant pink Zephirine Drouhin rose that climbed over the knapped-flint walls of number 9 Fodderstone Green. And shut the door on him.

29

The mobile police incident room had stood in the centre of Fodderstone village all day. Noticeboards with blown-up photographs of the dead girl and the message *When did you last see Sandra Websdell?* had been placed conspicuously in the single main street, and also on Fodderstone Green. Shirt-sleeved policemen trod through the village trying to look friendly and approachable under their helmets; but all to no effect. Passers-by passed resolutely by and not one person offered any scrap of new information. As the Chief Inspector had predicted, the inhabitants of the isolated village had closed ranks.

Refreshed by longed-for cups of tea (provided by the balding constable with the unsociable socks, who observed with tolerant amusement that beer no longer seemed to be the DCI's favourite thirst-quencher, now that Sergeant Lloyd was working with him) the two detectives sat in the incident room under Hilary's electric fan and read the latest reports.

Desmond Flood had been eliminated. His prematurely white-haired good looks were memorable, and a Saintsbury woman who travelled regularly to London had recalled that he was a fellow-passenger on the Tuesday afternoon coach. At the time of Sandra's death he would have been passing through East London, somewhere between Whitechapel and Aldgate.

No fingerprints had been found on the Websdells' itinerant

garden gnome. This was not surprising, as the wife of the landlord of the Flintknappers Arms had admitted to scrubbing the gnome clean after it had been found in a ditch beside the Horkey road. Mrs. Goodwin had asserted that she had done the scrubbing entirely for the benefit of Beryl Websdell. The detectives, remembering the way Lois Goodwin had lied in support of her husband, put another question-mark against her name. They also, in view of the fact that Inspector Tait had just rung in to report that Annabel Yardley knew nothing about any gnome-napping expeditions by her weekend guests, put another question-mark against the gnome.

The forensic lab had reported that the fragment of twig found on the dead girl originated from an apple tree. There was an apple tree, Hilary recalled, in Charley Horrocks's overgrown garden. But then, as Quantrill tetchily pointed out, there were apple trees in almost every garden in the village; and an orchard of them at the back of the Flintknappers Arms.

Another report concerned Sandra Websdell's car. The only usable fingerprints on it were her own. But what had been found inside the vehicle was a scattering of sawdust, most of it on and immediately in front of the driver's seat, but some on the back seat as well. The sawdust was similar to that found on the girl's clothing: hardwood sawdust, coarsely cut, of the kind produced by a hand-held chainsaw.

"Now this is interesting," said Quantrill. "When we first heard about the sawdust on her clothes we assumed that she must have been lying on the ground, either immediately before or just after her death, at a spot where tree-felling had taken place. But the car has been hidden in the forest, untouched, ever since the girl was abducted. And from the distribution of the sawdust, it looks as though whoever abducted her could have been carrying it on his own clothes."

"As a kind of occupational accumulation, do you mean?" asked Hilary. "That suggests a forester. When I first went to the Websdells', the husband got a scolding from his wife for coming home from work and dripping sawdust over the floor."

Sawdust on Websdell's clothes, sawdust in Sandra's car; and Websdell had disapproved of his daughter's proposed marriage. The facts fitted in the Chief Inspector's mind with a jig-saw puzzle click. "The girl's *father?* Didn't you—"

But then he saw an unfriendly chill in Sergeant Lloyd's expression. Oh hell . . . women were so touchy. He might have known that she'd take exception to any hint of doubt about her competence, and the last thing he wanted was to antagonize her. "Sorry, Hilary. Yes, of course you checked. Geoff Websdell was a natural suspect as soon as his daughter disappeared."

"Yes," agreed Hilary coolly, "I checked his movements that day, and on the evening she died, and I'm satisfied that he wasn't involved. But he's not the only forester in the village."

"That's true. But foresters always work in gangs, so it would have been almost impossible for any one of them to have got away on the day of her disappearance. Unless of course he was on holiday, or off sick . . . It's certainly worth running a check on absentees. Another snag, though, is that timber from the plantations is softwood, and the lab says that the sawdust in the car is hardwood . . . Ah, wait a minute! The logs you saw piled in Charley Horrocks's shed—which were they?"

Hilary was floored. "Sorry, sir. I've no idea."

"That's all right," said Quantrill, glad that she was both fallible and prepared to admit it. "Doesn't matter—the chances are that the logs are a mixture. What we really need to know is whether they were cut by a chainsaw or an axe."

"It must have been a chainsaw," said Hilary. "The cut ends of the logs were smooth, I remember that. And there were dribbles of sawdust where they'd been barrowed from the garden gate to the shed."

"Right," said the Chief Inspector, draining his tea mug. "You were going to find out from the woodman when he made that delivery, weren't you? I'll come with you. If there's a conspiracy over Sandra's abduction and death, it begins to look as though he might be a part of it."

The cottage where Christopher Thorold lived was as isolated as Howard Braithwaite's boathouse and Charley Horrocks's lodge. It was situated somewhere between the two, just off the dirt lane that led from Fodderstone Green by way of Stoneyhill wood to the plantation where Sandra's car had been found.

The woodman's cottage, once part of the Fodderstone Hall estate, was built of the same grey brick as the fire-ruined house in the middle of Stoneyhill wood. It too stood in a large clearing, ringed by mature oaks and beeches. But the whole of this clearing was in current use, partly as woodyard, partly as vegetable garden and orchard, and partly as barnyard for free-ranging poultry.

Of the original one-storey cottage itself, not much was visible from the dirt road except the blue-grey pantiles of the roof. Successive occupants had, over the years, enlarged the accommodation by tacking on makeshift extensions and porches, so that the detectives' first impression was of a huddle of tarred planks, cucumber-frame windows and corrugated-iron roofs. Elsewhere in the clearing were various sheds of similar construction, though with chicken-wire rather than glass in their windows.

Quantrill left his car in the shade of the trees. He and Hilary approached the cottage across grass worn so bare by the poultry that only well-pecked tussocks of it remained. In craters between the tussocks, basking hens shifted in their dust baths and made querulous complaint about the intruders; but apart from the grumbling of the hens and the persistent hum of insects, the whole of the forest clearing was heavy with heat and silence.

And then the still air was ripped by a high, nerve-grating scream, agonizingly prolonged. Hilary started: "God, whatever—?"

"Chainsaw," Quantrill reassured her. He made off in the direction of the woodyard, following the scream that rose to a metallic crescendo and then stopped as abruptly as it had begun.

The woodyard looked rather like a deserted Red Indian encampment, with the trimmed trunks of larch trees set up in teepee form so that the resinous wood could dry. Between the teepees, rosebay willow herb grew tall, its pink blossoms lively with butterflies. Heavy logs of deciduous wood lay in a great pile, behind which was parked an old pick-up truck. Christopher Thorold was there at work, methodically reducing a tree-trunk to chumps of manageable size.

When he saw that he had visitors he stood disconcerted, open-mouthed, nervously changing his grip on his heavy-duty chainsaw. His shock of grey-fair hair was dark at the roots with sweat, but his only concession to the heat had been to undo the top button of his flannel shirt and roll up his sleeves.

The Chief Inspector introduced himself and his sergeant.

Christopher Thorold glanced with embarrassment at Hilary, placed his chainsaw on the ground and buttoned his shirt to the neck in a gesture of deference and courtesy.

"Y-you'll want to see Pa," he burst out, blinking his thick pale eyelashes. "He's indoors. He can't get about any more."

Quantrill explained that they had come to enquire whether he had recently delivered a load of logs to Mr. Horrocks at the lodge. Christopher Thorold said that he had done so on Monday. Yes, he was sure it was Monday. It would be in the account book, which his father kept. No, Mr. Horrocks hadn't exactly ordered the wood: he always had a load at that time of year, and Christopher delivered it when he had it ready.

"Is Charley Horrocks a friend of yours?" said Sergeant Lloyd.

It was a question that Quantrill, knowing the rural social structure, would have had no need to put. Christopher Thorold looked shocked. "Why no! Mr. Horrocks's Grandpa was the third Earl. My Pa worked for the family at the Hall, and his Pa afore him. I couldn't be a friend to Mr. Horrocks. 'Twouldn't do."

"Who are your friends, Mr. Thorold?" asked Quantrill. "Where do you spend your evenings? Do you go to the Flintknappers Arms?"

Flustered, Christopher said that he always spent his evenings at home. He didn't drink, didn't go to the Knappers, had no need of any company except his Pa's.

Yes, they sometimes had callers. People came from the village to buy eggs, or to order wood. Yes, he knew Stan Bolderow and Reg Osler—had known them all his life. But they'd always tormented him at school, so he didn't seek their company. Yes, he knew by sight Mr. Braithwaite from Fodderstone Green and Mr. Goodwin from the Flintknappers Arms, and their wives to deliver wood to; but that was all.

"Do you know any young women?" asked Quantrill.

"No," he said simply. Then he added with dignified reproach, as though his status were as much a calling as the priesthood, "I'm a bachelor."

"But you knew Sandra Websdell, didn't you?"

Christopher's eyelashes went on the blink again. Sandra was a relation, he said. That was different. He hesitated; then added, "She's dead."

"Yes," said Quantrill. "But how did she die?"

"I don't know." A single large tear rolled out of one of

Christopher's pale-blue eyes, broke against the first outcrop of stubble it encountered, and spread a patch of damp over his rough cheek. "We're wholly upset about it, me and Pa."

"When did you last see Sandra, Mr. Thorold?"

"I don't know." He wiped his cheek with the back of his fist, and picked up his chainsaw. "I can't rightly say. Pa will tell you."

"Did you bring her here, three weeks ago? Did you keep her here, somewhere in the house or in one of your sheds?"

Christopher Thorold seemed not to hear the question. He had lifted his head, listening to something else. His eyes searched the apple trees that grew just beyond the woodyard, and suddenly he pointed, his solemn face alive with pleasure.

"Look," he whispered hoarsely. "See there, on the trunk of that ol' Bramley? Hear it drumming for insects? That's a lesser spotted woodpecker—see, red on its head, black an' white splodges on its back. They're shy birds, you hardly ever see 'em. Wait 'til I tell Pa!"

"I asked you a question, Mr. Thorold," said the Chief Inspector sharply. "Have you been keeping Sandra Websdell here?"

"I heard you, Mister," said Christopher, his eyes still on the bird. "No, I haven't. I couldn't do a thing like that without Pa knowing, and he'll tell you I haven't. If only he could come out and see this woodpecker! Look, there it goes—"

Countryman that he was, Quantrill was no birdwatcher, either on or off duty. He snorted, and marched off to the house. But Hilary Lloyd, interested in the change that had come over Christopher Thorold as soon as he was on his own territory, lingered for another word with him.

"I've never seen a woodpecker before," she said. "Thank you for showing it to me."

Embarrassed again, Christopher hung his head and shuffled his heavy boots.

"You're very lucky to live in a place like this, on the edge of the forest," she went on. "All the birds, and the butterflies . . . I can understand why you spend all your spare time at home. You've got everything that you could want here, haven't you?"

Christopher raised his head and gave her a shy smile. "It's beautiful," he said simply. "There's deer, too, roe an' fallow . . . I don't want to leave here, ever. I wouldn't leave here. I—I'd rather die."

30

Christopher Thorold set to work again, splitting the still air with the scream of his chainsaw and emitting a jet-stream of sawdust. Hilary crossed the dusty grass of the barnyard, avoiding the most recent poultry droppings, and joined the Chief Inspector. As they approached the wide open porch door of the woodman's cottage, a hen that had been pottering about inside took fright at their intrusion and came out flapping and squawking.

The doorway led into a corrugated-iron porch that housed the essentials of serious country living: heavy rubber boots, old greatcoats, a hurricane lantern, a spade, sacking, spare rat traps. Through the porch, another open door led into a lean-to scullery that sheltered both the original cottage door and the cast-iron water pump. On a bench by the pump stood an enamel bowl with cut-throat shaving tackle beside it, and also a paraffin-fuelled cooking-stove. The scullery smelled of paraffin, and of the ancient Border collie, too deaf to lift its head, that lay panting and twitching on the doormat.

The original door was also open. Through it, the detectives could see an old man, his flat cap on his head, his eyes closed, sitting upright in a wooden armchair beside a large square pinewood table. A house fly had settled on his chin, and others were walking over his hands, but he remained completely immobile. The only sounds from the room were the tick of a long-case clock and the worried cluck of a white hen that was standing on the table facing the visitors, its head on one side, observing them with a single beady eye.

Quantrill and Hilary exchanged glances, speculating on whether the old man was deeply asleep or dead. They retreated to the porch, and Quantrill rapped loudly on the outer door. The hen's clucking increased in frequency and anxiety; it trod up and down the table, jerking its raised claw at every step, working itself into a state of hysteria. The detectives, expecting it to fly in panic for the door, prepared to duck.

But then the old man spoke. "All right, my beauty, all

right," he murmured, his voice still thick with sleep. "I can hear y'. Quieten down, now." He lifted the hen on to his knee and stroked its scaly feathers, soothing it into stillness, though it continued to make quirking sounds of unease. "Come you in," he called drowsily, catching sight of his visitors in the doorway. "You'll be wanting eggs, I daresay?"

Albert Thorold had the same heavy, solemn features as his son, the same innocent pale-blue eyes. Age had put tremors in his voice, his lips and his hands, but he had none of Christopher's shyness or nervous mannerisms. He was dignified, calm, as independent as his infirmities would allow him to be.

The detectives stepped over the dog and into the airless living-room. "You must help yourselves," said the old man, pointing to a big mixing bowl, brimful of brown eggs, that stood on the table. Beside the bowl was an assortment of clean crockery and cutlery, the day-long requirements of two men, left ready to hand; also ready for use at the appropriate meal were jars of jam and pickled onions, and the makings for tea. Above the table dangled a flypaper, already too black with captives to trap any more, though a score of them hovered round it.

Apart from the flies, and some evidence that the pet hen was not completely housetrained, the room was moderately clean; not dusted, but kept tidy and given an occasional sweeping. Unlike Charley Horrocks, the Thorolds seemed capable of looking after themselves.

Albert Thorold heard who his visitors were, and the subject of their enquiries, without any trace of unease. He spoke about his late wife's cousin's daughter with composure, although his lips trembled rather more than usual. "That feller from London," he asserted. "He must ha' carried her off."

"When did you last see Sandra?" Quantrill asked him.

The old man paused for thought, caressing the hen's white ruff. It closed its fleshy eyelids and settled on his knee, half-asleep. "Why, it 'ud be two months or more ago. She came to tell us that she was getting wed."

"Did your son mind about that?" asked Hilary.

"Mind, Miss?" Albert Thorold turned his head and neck in one stiff movement, so that he could look straight at her. "Why, no. Why should he?"

"Christopher seems to have been very fond of her."

"That he was. We both were."

"Yes. So I wondered whether perhaps he'd hoped to marry her himself?"

"Marry? Our Christopher? Oh no, Miss, he wouldn't think o' that. He's always been wholly shy wi' women."

"But you do need a woman here, don't you?" said Quantrill. "Two men, living on your own—you need someone to cook and clean for you."

"No, Mister." The old man's response was stern and proud. "We manage for ourselves, me an' the boy. We live as it suits us. My late wife's cousin Beryl was all for coming over once a week to clean for us, but I wouldn't have it. She's a terror for cleaning. She'd turn everything upside down, throw things away, make us uncomfortable. She wouldn't let us keep the ol' dog indoors, nor yet the hen . . ." His trembling hands clutched the white Leghorn so hard that it woke with a squawk of protest. "No, Mister. We want no women here!"

Quantrill verbally smoothed their ruffled feathers, and pointed out that Sandra Websdell had been kept under cover somewhere in the vicinity of Fodderstone. The Thorolds had a number of outbuildings on their property, which someone might have used without their knowledge; might he and Sergeant Lloyd take a look round?

Albert Thorold seemed exhausted after his outburst. He sat back in his chair, nursing the hen which was still chuntering with black-eyed, wattle-quivering indignation. "There's no need for you to do that, Mister," he said tremulously. "If anybody had been here, I'd ha' known. But you may look an' welcome." His eyes closed, then flicked open again. "Will you be wanting any eggs afore you go?"

Most of the buildings scattered about the clearing were hen-houses, their size and shape dictated by whatever construction material had been to hand. Although the Thorolds were woodmen, they were clearly not carpenters; without exception the sheds were too ramshackle to have contained a strong young woman for three weeks. Even so, the detectives made a point of looking into all the larger buildings.

The ensuing commotion from the resident hens brought Christopher Thorold hurrying from the woodyard. The Chief Inspector listened to his stammered protests, and explained that they had his father's permission to look round. Christopher shifted his boots uneasily, but he said, "That's all right, then."

Quantrill asked to see where the corn was kept. Christopher hesitated for a few moments, then plodded off towards the rear of the cottage. Quantrill followed him. Hilary stopped to wipe her shoes on a tussock of grass and then went after them, observing as she did so that there were no sheds of any kind behind the main building. There had once, perhaps, been a flower garden, but like the rest of the clearing—apart from the wired-off vegetable patch—it had been scratched and pecked to a dusty waste.

The back wall of the cottage was built not of grey brick but of rough flints; it looked as though it had once belonged to a much older building. It contained no windows, but a stable door, the upper half of which was open.

Christopher came to a halt some yards from the door. "That's the barn," he said. "That's where we keep the corn for the hens, an' the straw for their nests. An' suchlike."

"And you come here every day? No one else could use this barn without your knowledge?"

"Why, yes—no—" Confused, Christopher hung his head. Then he took one long pace forward, and shuffled his feet. "I—I feed the hens twice a day," he volunteered. "They lay well. W-would you like some eggs?"

Hilary gave him a half-smile and shook her head. Quantrill ignored the question and opened the lower half of the stable door.

Although it was housed under the cottage roof, the barn's only entrance was from the outside. A narrow, gloomy place, the width of the cottage and the height of the rafters, it contained—as far as they could see—exactly what Christopher Thorold had said: corn in sacks and in a large zinc bin, straw in bales and scattered loose on the floor.

"This looks a possibility," muttered Quantrill to Hilary, taking advantage of the fact that Christopher Thorold made no attempt to follow them inside. "It's even more isolated than Charley Horrocks's woodshed."

"Yes—but the cottage isn't unvisited. People come here for eggs. If Christopher had tried to keep Sandra in this barn, surely she'd have heard the callers and cried out. He couldn't have risked it."

"I doubt if she would have heard, shut in round the back here."

"I don't see Christopher abducting her, though. Or his father being a party to it. I don't think they're the kind of men who'd do that."

"You're not being sentimental about them, are you?" Quantrill asked.

"Possibly," she admitted. "But where's their motive? They're obviously very contented with the life they live here."

"That's true. But Christopher's afraid of bullies, isn't he? He might well have acted under pressure from the Flint-knappers Arms mob. I'd certainly like to have this barn thoroughly searched, as well as Horrocks's woodshed. I reckon—"

He was interrupted by a call, in a vigorous masculine Suffolk voice, coming from someone approaching from the front of the cottage. "Chris! Where are you, boy? Your Pa says the police are here upsetting you!"

"G-good-day, Stan . . ." they heard Christopher Thorold say. It was not an enthusiastic greeting.

"What are the coppers doing to upset you?" demanded the newcomer.

"No upset, Stan. They're jus' looking round. Pa told 'em they could."

"So he said. Looking round's one thing, though—poking about's another. They've got no right to poke about on your property, Chris, and you're a fool to let 'em. You tell 'em to clear off."

Quantrill stepped out of the barn door. Christopher Thorold stood exactly where they had left him, his head hanging. His visitor, bald and belligerent, stood with his hands on his hips, his greying chest hair thrusting through the sweat-damp lattice of his vest.

"Stanley Bolderow?" enquired the Chief Inspector. "I was going to come to talk to you, so you've saved my time." He glanced towards the man with the flourishing sidewhiskers who was sidling up behind Bolderow. "And are you Reginald Osler?"

"That's us," said Stan Bolderow. "An' we've come here to talk to *you*. They told us at the police caravan that this is where we'd find you. Me and Reg—"

"What it is, Chief Inspector and Miss," intervened Reg soapily, "is that when the police officer came round yesterday to ask us what we were doing on Tuesday evening, we told him that we'd spent the whole of opening time at the

Flintknappers Arms. We forgot to tell him that we went somewhere else first. We didn't remember until we were talking about it not an hour ago, and we knew we ought to put the record straight right away. Else you might ha' thought we'd been ly ng."

"Very probably," said the Chief Inspector. He swatted some flies away from his face, and then folded his arms. "All right, I'm listening. Where were you, between six and seven-thirty on Tuesday evening?"

"Why, here!" said Stan Bolderow. He clapped Christopher Thorold on the shoulder. "Here along o' young Chris—eh, boy? Me an' Reg were just setting off for the Knappers at six, when my missus said she wanted some eggs. She likes to get 'em fresh from Chris's Pa, but it's a long walk for her. So we got in my truck, the three of us—"

"His missus came too," explained Reg, "on account of her own Dad was an old pal o' Chris's Pa—"

"—an' we came here. Bought the eggs, had a mardle with the old boy in the house, came out to the woodyard to see young Chris—eh, boy?—and then drove the missus and her eggs back home. It must ha' been after half-past seven afore we got to the Knappers, and that's where we were for the rest o' the evening. An' that's the truth."

"Definitely," said Reg. "Chris's Pa remembers us being here early Tuesday evening, an' I bet Chris does too. You do, don't you, Chris boy?"

Christopher swung his head like a frightened bullock. The combination of nervous tension and humid air had brought a rash of sweat out on his forehead, and now the drops began to trickle down and soak his fair-grey eyebrows. "W-why yes. That's right . . ."

"An' you can ask my missus to prove it," Stan concluded triumphantly, announcing her name and their address. "She'll tell you we were here. She'll show you the very eggs!"

Quantrill didn't doubt it. Whatever had gone on in or near the village on Tuesday evening was evidently regarded as a private local matter. From where he stood, watching Stan Bolderow and Reg Osler move up on either side of the hapless Christopher Thorold, Fodderstone's closed ranks looked solid.

31

On the morning of Friday 11 August, Annabel Yardley disappeared.

As she was staying by herself at Beech House, and spending much of her time dashing about the countryside visiting friends and arranging flowers, her absence might not have been noticed for some days. It was her horse that gave an immediate alarm by clattering, saddled but riderless, through Fodderstone village soon after 8:30 a.m.

The sweating black gelding was caught outside the mobile incident room by two policemen. Several villagers identified it as belonging to Mrs. Seymour of Beech House, and knew that it had been ridden latterly by the woman who was staying there. Police visited the house and found no one at home. Mrs. Yardley was not in the stable yard nor in the grounds.

The natural presumption was that she had been thrown from her horse. Possibly she was lying injured somewhere. The Sandra Websdell enquiry was temporarily shelved, and all available police officers were sent out to search the lanes and bridleways.

Local people also helped. A farmer's wife who sometimes rode with Annabel Yardley toured their favourite forest tracks in a Land Rover, with friends as look-outs; with no result. But there was of course the possibility that the horse had taken fright and bolted among the trees, throwing its rider some distance from the bridleway. In that event, she might be lying anywhere.

"Looks as though we'll have to put out a public appeal for volunteers and mount a general search," said Chief Inspector Quantrill towards the end of the morning. "She must be out there somewhere. Unless . . ."

He and Sergeant Lloyd looked at each other, half-reluctant to voice the thought that had occurred to both of them.

"Do you think it's likely?" asked Hilary.

"It's possible, isn't it? We suspect that more than one man was involved in Sandra's abduction, but we still don't know what they wanted her *for*. Her death seems to have been unpremeditated, so it must have left them with their business unfinished. If one of them came across another woman this morning, on her own in the forest after having been thrown from her horse, he might have seen her as a replacement for Sandra."

"But the Flintknappers Arms lot know that we're on to them. Surely they wouldn't take that risk?"

"They might, if they're using some other building. Somewhere we haven't yet found. But we'll start with their own premises—I want a quick swoop made on Thorold's barn, Horrocks's woodshed, and Braithwaite's boathouse, just to make sure that Mrs. Yardley isn't there. We'd better have simultaneous visits made on Bolderow and Osler as well."

"I'm going to see Lois Goodwin today," said Hilary. "I'll persuade her to give me a tour of the Flintknappers Arms while I'm there. But even if this does turn out to be an abduction, mightn't it be personal to Mrs. Yardley? Perhaps someone completely unconnected with Fodderstone had a motive for abducting her. I can imagine that her private life is a bit complicated."

"Hmm. Well, yes, that's another angle to be considered." Quantrill scratched his chin and thought about it. "And as it happens, we know someone who's involved with her, don't we? What's more—not that I'm suggesting he'd abduct her—we know that he went to see her last night."

Though the weather was still hot and humid, visibility had improved sufficiently for Martin Tait to go flying. When he landed, he found the Chief Inspector waiting for him outside the hangar.

"I've had a devil of a job tracking you down," complained Quantrill. "What's this bull you gave your aunt about being recalled by the regional crime squad?"

Tait was in an icy mood. He hadn't been able to enjoy his flight, conscious all the time of the hideous cost of private flying: aircraft fuel, hangar space, engineering, insurance, airworthiness certification, club membership.

"What I told my aunt is no concern of anyone else," he snapped.

"I thought you were going to stay with her all week. Anything wrong between you?"

"Of course not. Aunt Con's not well, that's all. I thought I was imposing on her, so I made an excuse to leave. Though what it's got to do with you—"

"All right—sorry I asked. I've come to see you about Mrs. Yardley."

They were walking together across the hot concrete apron towards the flying-club premises. Quantrill had hoped to be offered a beer at the bar, but it began to seem unlikely. Tait had stopped in mid-stride and was staring at him with suspicion, even hostility.

"What about Mrs. Yardley?"

"You visited her yesterday evening, didn't you? You rang the incident room afterwards to say she knew nothing about the Websdells' garden gnome."

"Yes."

"Well, she's now missing." Quantrill explained the circumstances, and the possibility that Mrs. Yardley's disappearance might be linked with Sandra's. "On the other hand, the answer may be in her private life. And I thought you were the man to talk to about that."

"Me? Good God, you don't mean to say you suspect—?"

"Stop jumping down my throat, will you? I'm simply asking for information about the woman. You're obviously on intimate terms with her, so I thought you'd know."

"That's not true. I am not on intimate terms with her."

"No? Didn't you spend the night with her on Wednesday? It certainly looked as though that was what you'd planned. And then last night—"

Tait controlled his temper with an obvious effort. "For your information," he said, stiff-jawed, cold-eyed, "I have never had any kind of sexual relationship with the woman. I haven't even touched her. And I know nothing about her private life. My visit last night was official, at your request. I wasn't with her more than five minutes. And on Wednesday evening I didn't stay with her for more than a quarter of an hour after you'd gone."

The Chief Inspector said nothing. He folded his arms, and gave the younger man the same kind of quizzical look that he'd given the suspects in the Sandra Websdell enquiry. It was a look that Tait knew well, though this was the first time he'd been on the receiving end of it.

"What I told you is the truth," he persisted in a more conciliatory voice, remembering whose father Quantrill was.

"Yes, I know I lied to my aunt, but that was different. Whatever impression I might have given you about my relationship with Mrs. Yardley, it went no further than eye-contact and chat. I didn't intend it to go any further. I'm extremely fond of your daughter—sir—and I wouldn't do anything to jeopardize my relationship with her. I may well marry her, eventually."

"Not if I have anything to do with it, you won't," said Quantrill.

At the Flintknappers Arms, Lois Goodwin greeted Sergeant Lloyd with alarmed relief. She'd dreaded the detectives' return; but the sergeant alone was different. At the sight of her, smiling pleasantly, sympathetic, ready to listen, Lois suddenly realized that since she'd been in Fodderstone she had made no friends. She'd been so busy with the wretched pub—not to mention her exhausting family—that it hadn't until now occurred to her that she had no other woman to talk to. And she needed to talk.

Phil was in the bar doing the lunch-time serving. Sergeant Lloyd approached by way of their private backyard, commenting on the number of their outbuildings. Lois willingly showed her round, then shooed the children out of the kitchen and made a pot of coffee.

"I'm sorry I wasn't honest with you yesterday," she said, her hamster cheeks crimsoning. "About Phil being here asleep on Tuesday evening, I mean. He wasn't. He didn't come in until just after eight o'clock. He didn't tell me what he'd been doing, but I can guess. He's often had affairs—nothing serious, he always comes back—and I expect he was in Breckham Market with some other woman. Keeping a pub doesn't really suit him, and that's his way of escape. He would never have harmed Sandra Websdell though, I'm absolutely convinced of that."

"Keeping a pub doesn't suit you either, does it?" said the Sergeant. "I can understand why. Having to serve the same small bunch of regulars, all of them saying the same old things, every single day of the week, must be deadly."

"Oh, it's worse than that! They're not just boring, they're cruel. You've no idea—I had no idea, or I'd never have agreed to take a pub in the first place."

Lois had tied a plastic apron over her frilled blouse, put on rubber gloves, and begun to tackle a sinkful of washing up. Her neatly rounded body quivered with activity and fury as she described the various humiliations she had to endure from the regulars. Clashing the dirty dishes together as she talked, she was too preoccupied to register the fact that her visitor had picked up a tea-towel and begun to do the drying. But she felt supported, and she gladly told everything she knew about Stan Bolderow and Reg Osler and Howard Braithwaite and Charley Horrocks.

"They'd been up to something on Tuesday, I know that. Stan and Reg and Charley always come in every evening, early, but on Tuesday they weren't back until after Phil returned from Breckham Market. Howard comes here only occasionally in the evenings, but he followed the others in."

"What made you think they'd been up to something?"

"They were so noisy—almost as noisy as Phil always is. Flushed and excited . . . even Howard. I'd have said they'd been drinking somewhere else, except that I couldn't smell it on them."

"What were they talking about?"

"I don't know. I didn't stay to listen. I was so angry with Phil for being late that I got out of the bar as soon as I could."

"But what was your general impression? Were they boasting, for example?"

"Not boasting, no . . . I think perhaps they were being careful about what they were actually saying. Secretive. They seemed very pleased with themselves, but at the same time—well, guilty."

Her visitor made no comment. "Which drawer does the clean cutlery live in?" she asked. "Ah, I've found it. You've heard about Mrs. Yardley, I expect?"

"That she's been thrown from her horse—yes, it's all round the village." Lois paused for a moment, with the greasy foam-flecked water almost over the top of her rubber gloves, remembering Annabel Yardley's infuriating attitude of superiority. "I don't really wish her any harm. I hope she's soon found, and that she hasn't been badly hurt. But quite honestly I've never liked the woman. She comes here when it suits her, but she either patronizes me or ignores me."

"Oh yes, the upper-class put-down. I get it in my job, too. Mrs. Yardley does look stunning, though, I'll give her that. She must turn quite a few heads when she comes into the bar."

Lois snorted. *"Men,"* she said, punishing a grease-baked casserole dish with a pan-scrubber. "Yes, they all ogle her and fancy their chances."

"And do any of them have a chance with her, do you think?"

"That's what's so annoying!" exclaimed Lois, pounding the finally emptied sink with a dishcloth and scouring powder. "Mrs. Yardley looks and sounds immaculate, but she doesn't seem to have any morals. After all, she *is* a married woman. But if a man attracts her, she'll go for him. And from what I've heard young Andrew Stagg saying—"

"Andrew Stagg—isn't he the farrier from Horkey? Dark curls, handsome face, good body?"

"That's him. Though he'll soon lose his figure if he goes on drinking so much. He's too fond of beer, and of what he calls wenching—he's been after every attractive female for miles around. He was determined to add Mrs. Yardley to his list as soon as he set eyes on her, and if you can believe what he's said since—"

"Do you believe it?"

A bellow of "Lois!" came down the long corridor, a summons from her husband in the bar. She raised her eyes, sighed, and pulled off her rubber gloves with a squelch and a plop.

"Thanks for your help," she said with wry gratitude as she took the damp tea-towel from her visitor. "I'm sure it isn't every woman you ask for information who gets her drying up done for her. Look, as far as Andrew Stagg's concerned, I really don't know what his relationship with Mrs. Yardley is. I don't know whether to believe what he says about her or not. I don't know what to believe about anybody—except that I'm sure my husband had nothing whatever to do with Sandra Websdell's death."

"I heard you the first time," said Sergeant Lloyd.

32

Later that afternoon, Chief Inspector Quantrill drove over to
Horkey to interview Andrew Stagg. He decided to go alone.
He didn't ask himself why, but he knew that he didn't want
Hilary Lloyd with him; still less did he want her to go by
herself.

As Quantrill arrived at the forge, Stagg was leading a
chestnut mare out into the yard. A girl of about eighteen
walked with the farrier, making up to him shamelessly. He
had good features, strong teeth, a column of a neck; and as
before he was shirtless, all tanned skin, pectoral muscles
lightly oiled with sweat, and curling dark hair. A public
menace where women were concerned, thought Quantrill,
who was not predisposed to like him.

Andrew Stagg bent, cupped his hands for the girl's knee,
and gave her a lift up into the saddle. They talked for a
minute longer. "Tomorrow, then?" asked the girl.

"Maybe," said Stagg lazily. He slapped the mare's flank in
farewell, and ambled over to the Chief Inspector. "Anything
I can do for you?" he asked, politely enough but with a
dismissive glance at his caller's unhorseman-like girth.

Quantrill told him sharply who he was and what he wanted.
Andrew Stagg agreed without hesitation that Mrs. Yardley
was one of his customers. Yes, he'd heard she'd been thrown.
Hadn't she been found yet? Well, as soon as he'd finished
work that afternoon he'd gladly come and help search for her.

"Is Mrs. Yardley a friend of yours?" asked Quantrill. "A
personal friend, I mean?"

Stagg laughed cheerfully. "Not with her expensive tastes!
No, I keep well away from women with her standard of
living."

"That's not what I heard. My information is that you boasted
in the Flintknappers Arms that she was one of your conquests."

"Ah, talking's different. When you've got a reputation, you
want your mates to believe you're living up to it." Stagg gave
the Chief Inspector an inoffensively cheeky grin. "You were
my age, once. You know how it is."

Quantrill did know, of course. He pulled in his stomach, recalling that he'd once had a bit of a reputation himself. He'd enjoyed exaggerating it, too—until he rashly went all the way with a pretty girl called Molly, in those far-off pre-pill days when you were expected either to be more careful or to pay for the mistake for the rest of your life. Modern young men like Andrew Stagg didn't know how lucky they were, blast them.

"Mrs. Yardley is a very attractive woman. I can well imagine that you fancied adding her to your list," said Quantrill censoriously. "But she's married, and socially she comes out of the top drawer. What I'm wondering is whether you pursued her, and then resented the fact that she turned you down."

Stagg's open face crumpled in protest. "Here, wait a minute! You're not suggesting that I knocked Annabel Yardley off her horse so that I could have my evil way with her, are you? That's squit. Look, there's no need for me to go to that trouble—I could have her any time I liked. Except that it wouldn't be me having her, it'd be her having me . . . When I go wenching I want to get straight on with the job and finish it, but that woman's got ideas of her own. She's insatiable. I went to bed with her just once, and I thought I'd never get out of it intact. I'm not risking that again!"

Quantrill grunted, somewhat appeased. Stagg sounded like a man in his own mould. "Do you know any of Mrs. Yardley's men friends?" he asked.

"I met some of them at a weekend house-party she gave in July. Noisy buggers—just like old Charley Horrocks, only younger. *Wah wah wah*—I've never come across so many toffee-nosed twits in my life."

"Hmm. And when did you last see Mrs. Yardley?"

"About ten days ago. I shoed her horses and chatted her up a bit—no harm in letting her think she's still in the running—but that was all. If she's not found before this evening, though, I'll certainly help look for her." Stagg shook his head, recollecting his close encounter with Annabel Yardley with reluctant admiration: "Phew! She's some woman . . ."

But the Chief Inspector had reverted to a previous preoccupation. "Can you remember the date of that house-party?" he asked, taking out his notebook. Stagg thought it had been the middle of the month: yes, probably 21—22 July.

Sandra Websdell, Quantrill meditated, had disappeared on

Wednesday 18 July. And it was on the following Friday night
that the Websdells' family gnome had gone missing. If there
was no connection between the two events—if the gnome
had, as Tait suggested, been lifted by some Hooray Henry
guests of Mrs. Yardley—Andrew Stagg might be just the man
to confirm it.

Stagg did confirm it. In fact he'd been with them at the
time. Some of the male guests, he explained, had persuaded
him to do the driving (and use his petrol) when they went out
on an evening pub crawl. On their way back to Beech House,
just before midnight, they'd been making such a racket in the
car that he'd taken the wrong road. He'd had a pint or two
himself, of course, and that might have had something to do
with it.

Anyway, finding himself by mistake in Fodderstone Green,
he'd turned the car. As he did so, his headlights had picked
up a garden gnome that was propped outside somebody's
front gate. The Henries had made a lot of hunting noises, and
insisted in kidnapping the gnome and leaving a ransome
note. They wanted to find somewhere original and witty to
park their capture, so they'd instructed Stagg to go on driving
while they cudgelled their brains.

But they hadn't gone far before the Henries realized that
the gnome was badly damaged. One of its legs had been
knocked off, and the broken plaster was crumbling. They
began to wonder whether the gnome had in fact been put
down by the gate for the next refuse collection. If so—if it
wasn't its owner's cherished possession—there was really no
fun in taking it. So they'd chucked it out of the car window.

"Whereabout would that have been?" asked Quantrill.

"Somewhere along the Horkey road, as far as I can
remember."

"And was this on the Friday night?"

"No, the Saturday. Definitely Saturday."

The Chief Inspector scratched his chin. So twenty-four
hours in the gnome's life were still unaccounted for. Where it
had been taken on the Friday, by whom, how it had got
damaged and why it had been returned to the garden gate,
was a mystery. There was no reason to connect its adventures
with Sandra Websdell's disappearance and death; but on the
other hand there could be a link. It was something he would
have to discuss with Hilary Lloyd.

*   *   *

By mid-afternoon, Annabel Yardley had still not been found.

While the search for her continued, detectives made return visits to the Thorolds, Charley Horrocks and Howard Braithwaite. They also sought out Stan Bolderow and Reg Osler. All the men had denied any knowledge of Mrs. Yardley's whereabouts, and some—the Thorolds, father and son—had denied any knowledge of Mrs. Yardley. She was certainly not to be found in any barn, hen-house, woodshed, boathouse or any other of their outbuildings.

"But I wouldn't trust the Flintknappers regulars any further than I could throw them," said Chief Inspector Quantrill. "And that includes the landlord, Phil Goodwin. If—for God knows what reason—they've got Annabel Yardley tucked away somewhere, it's likely to be a hidey-hole we don't yet know about. Possibly even on the other side of the forest."

"If she *is* being held captive," said Hilary practically, "someone will have to visit her regularly with food. Why don't we start keeping a watch on the lot of them?"

Quantrill shook his head. "That'd tie up too much manpower. Look at it like this: if the same people who held Sandra Websdell have now got Mrs. Yardley, we have reason to believe that they mean her no physical harm. In that case, we can afford to leave her with them for another twenty-four hours.

"But if she really was thrown from her horse and she's lying out there in the forest in this heat—with no water, and possibly badly injured—we must find her as soon as possible. For that, we need all our manpower, plus every volunteer we can raise, to make a concentrated search before nightfall."

33

Martin Tait was so annoyed by the words he'd had with Chief Inspector Quantrill that he made no offer to help in the search for Mrs. Yardley. *It's their problem, let them get on with it*, he thought. Besides, he had things of his own to do that evening.

Next day, Saturday 12 August, he went flying again. There was still no break in the weather. Heat haze, augmented by smoke from the last of the straw fires in the harvested fields, continued to obscure the horizon. But he decided to make a longer trip, as a navigational exercise: down to Ipswich for a touch-and-go landing, and then across country to Cambridge, where he stopped for a snack lunch.

As he returned to Horkey, approaching the airfield at 2,000 feet, he noticed some unusual activity five or six miles north of Fodderstone. The area—an uninhabited part of the forest—was a stretch of heath bounded on one side by a conifer plantation. On the other side of the heath was a large field of pale stubble that was flickering into orange blossoms as fire was put to heaps of straw. The open heath was crossed by a dirt road, and travelling along it were a number of vehicles; twenty or more of them, all heading northwards.

But Tait had no time to see where they were going, because he was flying south and the airfield was in sight. He called the control tower when he was overhead, and then began to descend to circuit height. He looked again for the vehicles when he was flying the crosswind leg, but the flames from the burning straw had turned to smoke that spread over the heathland and obscured his view.

After he had landed and parked his Cessna in the hangar, he found that Hilary Lloyd was waiting for him outside the clubhouse. Her face was grave and her tone unusually formal as she told him that Chief Inspector Quantrill wanted to see him in Fodderstone, as a matter of urgency.

"What's up?" said Tait. "Haven't you found Mrs. Yardley yet? Look, I had Doug Quantrill here yesterday, trying to grill me about her private life, and I'm damned if I'm going to put up with any more of it. I've already told him I know nothing at all about the woman. Believe it or not, Hilary, I took your advice and walked out on her."

"I'm glad to hear it," she said seriously. "We haven't found Mrs. Yardley yet, and of course we're still looking. But—"

"Was that convoy, going across the heath to the north of what used to be Fodderstone Hall, anything to do with your search?" asked Tait. "Because if not, it seems a bit odd that twenty private vehicles should all be heading purposefully towards nowhere in particular. It might be worth your while to investigate the area. I'll show you on my map."

They had reached his parked Alfa. He opened the door and bent to take out his Ordnance Survey map of the forest, but Hilary touched his arm to stop him.

"Martin," she said quietly. "This is nothing to do with Mrs. Yardley. It's bad news for you personally, I'm afraid."

He straightened very slowly, his hands on the hot metal of the car roof, and stared out over the exhausted grass of the airfield. The air was heavy, almost too thick to breathe. He felt sweat springing on his forehead, and wiped it away with the back of his hand.

He cleared his throat. Without looking at Hilary he asked, "Is it—my aunt?"

"Yes. I really am sorry, Martin. I'm afraid she's dead."

He gripped the edge of the car roof. "Aunt Con must have killed herself," he said. "It was suicide, wasn't it?"

34

"Tell me: what made you say that Mrs. Schultz must have taken her own life?"

Chief Inspector Quantrill stood with his arms folded, watching the younger man. Tait sat—uncharacteristically slumped —on his aunt's chintz-covered sofa, gazing blankly through the sitting-room window of number 9 Fodderstone Green. He looked grey-faced, shattered. Ordinarily Quantrill would have offered his condolences and left the man alone; but the circumstances of Constance Alice Schultz's death had given rise to suspicion.

She had last been seen by her neighbours, Mr. and Mrs. Braithwaite and Mr. and Mrs. Websdell, at approximately 6 p.m. the previous evening. A police car with a loudspeaker had driven through Fodderstone Green calling for further volunteers to help in the search for Mrs. Yardley, and all the able-bodied residents had gathered on the Green to receive their instructions. Both Marjorie Braithwaite and Beryl Websdell had thought that Mrs. Schultz was not looking well, and they had persuaded her to return home.

The following morning—that morning—Mrs. Braithwaite had made a neighbourly call on Mrs. Schultz at approximately 9:30 a.m. The back door was unlocked, but Mrs. Schultz was not in. Mrs. Braithwaite had then walked down the garden, expecting to find her neighbour there.

As she neared the garage, Mrs. Braithwaite heard the noise of an engine. The garage doors were closed but not locked. Opening them, Mrs. Braithwaite saw that the white Ford Escort was filled with fumes, and that a vacuum-cleaner hose led from the exhaust and through the partly open rear window of the car. The remainder of the window opening was blocked with a cloth.

Mrs. Braithwaite opened the driver's door and found Mrs. Schultz at the wheel, apparently unconscious. The key—one of a bunch—was in the ignition, and Mrs. Braithwaite switched off the engine. She tried to rouse Mrs. Schultz, but was unable to do so. She then ran to her own house and telephoned for the police.

A uniformed police officer from the Fodderstone incident room went immediately to the scene, together with a detective constable. They removed Mrs. Schultz's body from the car, and a police surgeon who arrived shortly afterwards confirmed their opinion that she was dead. Her body was taken to Breckham Market mortuary to await a post-mortem examination.

Inside the car, on the passenger seat, was found a bottle of brandy one-quarter empty. A glass that had held brandy was on top of the dashboard. Also on the passenger seat was a battery-operated tape-recorder, and in it a run-through tape of the St. John's College, Cambridge recording of Gabriel Fauré's *Messe de Requiem*. No note from the dead woman was found in the car.

Having heard from Mrs. Braithwaite the identity of Mrs. Schultz's next-of-kin, the detective constable tried to get in touch with her nephew, without immediate success. He and his uniformed colleague then carried out the necessary search of the house in an attempt to find the reason for Mrs. Schultz's death; again, no note was found. The detective subsequently took statements from the dead woman's neighbours, as a result of which he called in Detective Chief Inspector Quantrill.

"What was your reason for saying that your aunt must have killed herself?" repeated Quantrill. "Because that was your immediate reaction to what Sergeant Lloyd told you. If Miss

Lloyd had said that your aunt had been 'found dead', then suicide might have been a reasonable inference. But all you were told, on my instructions, was, 'She's dead.' For all you knew, the old lady might have had a heart attack, or a stroke, or a car accident. And yet you immediately jumped to the conclusion that it was suicide. Why?"

"Because Aunt Con told me what she was going to do," said Tait in a leaden voice. He stood up and began to walk about the room. "Oh, not in so many words. She never mentioned suicide. But everything she did and said while I was staying with her pointed to the fact that she was making her final arrangements."

He explained to the Chief Inspector about his aunt's expressed intention to leave Fodderstone Green, and her refusal to look for alternative accommodation; about her attempt to give him her furniture, and her insistence that he should take the family valuables with him; about the way she had disposed of her old clothing, and burned letters and diaries and photographs.

"Aunt Con even told me what kind of funeral she wanted. She asked me to take notes . . . God, what a fool I was not to realize what she was planning! I suppose I was too absorbed in my own affairs to think about her, at the time. But as soon as Hilary said she had bad news for me, everything clicked into place. I didn't need to be told anything else. I knew that my aunt had killed herself, and I knew how she'd done it."

Quantrill gave the younger man a hard green stare. "But she didn't leave a note. And you know as well as I do that the coroner will want to know *why* she did it."

"Aunt Con told me that, too, in a way. You see, she was growing old, and the garden was getting too much for her to manage, and her dog had died—"

"That doesn't add up to any reason for killing herself at the age of seventy. Not unless she was ill with depression, and neither of her women neighbours believes that of her. I understand that Mrs. Schultz was on friendly terms with both of them. She hadn't seemed to them to be depressed, she'd never mentioned suicide, and neither of them can believe it."

"Which just goes to show how little they really knew her," said Tait in the superior voice that never failed to irritate his colleagues. "My aunt liked to be friendly with her neighbours, yes. But she would never have discussed her private

affairs with them. She was independent, and she had her own
reasons for what she did. I respected her, and I can accept
that. If her neighbours can't, that's their problem."

"True . . . But that brings us back to the question why
Mrs. Schultz didn't leave a note. An elderly lady who plans
her own death in such detail is almost certain to leave notes
for relatives, and usually for the coroner too."

"That's easily explained," said Tait. "My aunt had told me
so much that she knew there was no need for her to put it in
writing. She'd even said good-bye to me, though of course I
didn't realize it was for the last time—" His voice wavered,
and for a moment he looked stricken again, rather than
superior. "Of course, there might have been a medical reason
for what she did. She didn't look well, I noticed that. Perhaps
she had a terminal disease."

"We've checked," said Quantrill. "The last time your aunt
saw her doctor was eighteen months ago, when she had
bronchitis."

"Aunt Con wasn't the kind of woman to keep running to
her doctor," said Tait, superior again. "But that doesn't mean
she wasn't ill."

"Possibly," Quantrill conceded. "We shall find that out for
sure from the post-mortem, shan't we?"

"Not necessarily. Even if no pathological evidence of disease is found, it doesn't mean that she didn't *feel* ill. Or
imagine it. And as I said, she was an independent woman.
She'd have hated the idea of having to be dependent on
anyone." Tait shook his head in self-reproach. "Poor Aunt
Con—it doesn't seem possible that I shall never see her again
. . . It doesn't seem possible, now, that I didn't realize what
she was planning. But I can understand her logic. And
when it comes to the inquest, I'm sure the coroner will
understand it too."

"Maybe," said the Chief Inspector heavily. "It sounds plausible. But that's the trouble with you, boy, you always were a
damn sight too plausible." He paused, angry with himself
that even after all these years as a detective, he was unable to
decide whether the young man standing in front of him was
an honest smoothie or a smooth liar.

"Look, Martin," he went on, "this isn't an official interview
because I've already reported the matter to the Assistant
Chief Constable. I had no option. Not in view of the circum-

stances the investigating detective uncovered. But we've worked together for a year or two, you and I, and the least I can do is to tell you what I know. You see, my information is that some days before she died, your aunt told you that she was a very rich woman. She also said that she was virtually cutting you out of her will."

Tait stood silent, his skin drawn tight over his cheekbones, his nose sharper than usual, as Chief Inspector Quantrill went through the details of his quarrel with his aunt.

"I can guess where your information came from," Tait said at last. "That bloody snooper from number 10, Marjorie Braithwaite! She must've been looking for an opportunity to get back at me ever since I told her to mind her own business."

"You don't deny the quarrel with your aunt, then?"

"No. I regret it, now that Aunt Con's dead. I regret the unkind things I said to her. But at least I did my best to make up for it. I went out of my way to be really nice to her for the rest of my stay."

Quantrill gave him a narrow-eyed look. "Why?" he said bluntly.

Tait shrugged. "Partly out of a sense of shame, I suppose. But I'll admit that it was mostly self-interest. I decided that Aunt Con had been so taken up with the idea of giving her money to charity that she hadn't looked at it from my point of view at all. I felt sure that when she'd had time to think it over, she'd realize the injustice of cutting me out—particularly if I showed her that I really was a deserving character, despite the row. The snag was that I didn't know whether she'd actually made a new will, or whether she was merely thinking of it."

He hesitated, and then said with an attempt at nonchalance, "Was a will found when this house was searched for a suicide note?"

"No. But there was the name of a Woodbridge firm of solicitors in her address book. Your family was connected with the firm at one time, I believe. They tell me they've had no recent communication from Mrs. Schultz—but they are holding her will." Quantrill paused, deliberately keeping the younger man in suspense. Tait's lips had parted, and his breathing was fast and shallow.

"The will was made some years ago," continued Quantrill. "I understand that apart from a few minor bequests, her nephew Martin Gregory Maitland Tait—that is you, isn't it?—will cop the lot."

Colour flooded back into Tait's face at such a speed that Quantrill almost expected it to extend into his fair hair. His eyes had a hard, bright shine. "Glory hallelujah!" he muttered fervently.

"You may well say so," agreed Quantrill. "Lucky for you that your aunt didn't do as she intended, wasn't it? Lucky for you that she didn't make another will after all. Perhaps she did, of course, and we haven't been able to find it . . ."

Tait's colour began to ebb. He said nothing.

"My information," the Chief Inspector went on, "is that you were seen in this garden on Wednesday evening burning some of your aunt's private papers. You admitted at the time that you were doing so without her knowledge or consent."

"Oh, I see." Tait sounded almost relieved. "Someone's suggested to you that having quarrelled with my aunt, I waited until she went next door to the Websdells' and then burned her new will in public view on a bonfire! I know where *that* idea came from—Mrs. Bloody Braithwaite again. I wouldn't have thought you'd take such an allegation seriously."

"We don't dismiss any allegations where an unexplained death has occurred," Quantrill reproved him. "You know that perfectly well. But it isn't just your aunt's will that's in question. It's her actual death."

Tait stared, his face white again. "You don't mean—? Good God, surely you don't suspect me of having *killed* her? But that's crazy—I loved her. I would never, ever—for God's sake—"

The Chief Inspector let him talk himself into silence. Much as Tait had annoyed him over the years, often as he'd longed to slap the blasted boy down, he wasn't enjoying this. Odd, though, he thought in passing, that when it came to this crisis point, every suspect, villain or cop, used the same words of denial.

"We have to consider that possibility," Quantrill said. "Someone who knows the ropes could have sedated Mrs. Schultz or confused her with alcohol, and then arranged her in the car so that her death would look like suicide. The circumstance that all the neighbours were out yesterday evening looking for Mrs. Yardley would have made it that much easier. And the fact that you took your aunt's car to the local garage on Wednesday morning and asked for the engine to be adjusted to a reasonably fast tick-over—"

"At my aunt's *own* request! I didn't think it significant at the time, but she was obviously preparing for her death."

"And that your fingerprints appear on the bottle of brandy that was inside the car—"

"My prints? Oh, then I know who the investigating detective was," said Tait with disdain. "That malicious oaf, Ian Wigby! He was furious that I was in at the beginning of the Sandra Websdell enquiry, and he's probably been looking for an opportunity to get back at me. Well, his allegation's ridiculous. If a detective commits a crime, he's hardly likely to leave his own dabs at the scene."

"Not unless he's being extra clever," said Quantrill. "Doing a double bluff, perhaps? Your prints were also found on the tape-recorder in the car, by the way, and on the cassette."

"But I can explain that. There's a perfectly straightforward explanation for everything."

"I hope you're right. The ACC wants to see you at nine-thirty on Monday morning. Explain it all to him."

Tait looked anguished. "I didn't destroy my aunt's will," he said in a low voice. "And I most certainly didn't kill her. I realize that because the allegation's been made we have to go through the whole official procedure, and I'm prepared to put up with that. But you do believe me, sir, don't you?"

"You know better than to ask me that, Martin," said Quantrill wearily. "Oh, one thing. When you go before the ACC, you're entitled to have a solicitor present. Make sure you get yourself a good one."

35

"You look," said Sergeant Lloyd, "as though you could do with a beer."

"Chance 'ud be a fine thing," grumbled Quantrill, sitting down heavily in the caravan and mopping his forehead.

Hilary handed him a can of Carlsberg. She was in sole charge of the incident room, all the other police officers having gone out to search for Mrs. Yardley; it had been—was still being—a very difficult week, and she had decided to get in a supply of something stronger than tea.

"How did the interview with Martin go?" she asked, opening a Carlsberg for herself. Doug Quantrill was swigging straight from the can, but Hilary found it less messy to use a cardboard cup. "He had an explanation for everything, no doubt?"

"Of course." Quantrill told her what Tait had said. Had the two of them been civilians, they would have exchanged opinions on whether or not he had destroyed his aunt's latest will and caused her death. As they were police officers, what they discussed was whether or not the allegations were likely to stick.

"It'll all come out at the inquest on Mrs. Schultz," said Quantrill. "The coroner will call Mrs. Braithwaite as a witness because she found the body, and so she'll repeat her allegations in public. But an inquest isn't a trial, even if the coroner decides to sit with a jury. Mrs. Braithwaite can't be cross-examined. And unless the coroner decides to call him as a witness, Martin will have no opportunity to defend himself."

"I suppose a lot will depend on the pathologist's finding," said Hilary. "As long as Mrs. Schultz died of carbon monoxide poisoning, with no evidence of anything in her blood other than that and a small quantity of alcohol, the coroner may be satisfied that it was a straightforward suicide. If any traces of sedative are found as well, though, it could look suspicious."

"Let's face it," said Quantrill, "the boy's got himself into a hell of a mess. Even if things go well for him at the inquest, we all know that his future life in the force isn't going to be worth living."

"No sign of Annabel Yardley, I suppose?" asked Quantrill when he had drained his can.

"None. Though Martin did say something interesting," remembered Hilary, "before I mentioned his aunt's death. He told me that when he was bringing his aeroplane in to land this afternoon, he saw a number of private vehicles travelling across a stretch of heathland about six miles north of here. He wondered whether they were anything to do with our searches, but they're not. We haven't been out as far as that. He couldn't see where the vehicles were bound for because of smoke from burning straw, but it seems to me that they were on a road that no longer goes anywhere."

She pointed out the location on the incident-room map. The northern area of the forest had been appropriated for army battle training in the Second World War, and was still closed to the public. The heathland that Martin had referred to adjoined the battle area, and the road that had once crossed the heath was now a disused track that petered out at the Ministry of Defence boundary wire.

"I'd have driven over to take a look," said Hilary, "if I hadn't been stuck here. It certainly seems odd, as Martin suggested, that about twenty vehicles should all be heading for the remotest part of the forest in the middle of a Saturday afternoon."

"Perhaps that's the explanation," said Quantrill. "That it's Saturday afternoon, I mean. Some kind of sporting fixture, maybe—motor-bike scrambling, something like that."

The two detectives studied the map. The whole area had once belonged, at a time when it was useful for nothing but game shooting, to the Fodderstone Hall estate, and the old names on the map were evocative: Earl's Ride, Countess Covert, Brandon Heath, Prince Albert's Plantation; and Black-rabbit Warren, Fowlmere, Woodcock Hill, Curlew Lodge.

"This Curlew Lodge place," said Quantrill, pointing with a pencil to an isolated black dot on the map. It was just outside the battle area, on the northern edge of the heath that Tait had referred them to. "It can't be much of a dwelling, or its shape would be outlined on the map. Possibly it was built out there just as a place where the old shooting-parties could have a warm-up and eat their grub. It's probably in ruins now—but if those vehicles Martin saw were making for any-where, that must have been it."

He chewed the end of his pencil. "I wonder . . . how many vehicles, did you say? Hmm. Twenty isn't much of an attend-ance at any sporting fixture—unless of course it was by invita-tion only . . . Some form of indoor entertainment, perhaps?"

Sergeant Lloyd looked at him quickiy. "First Sandra Websdell, now Annabel Yardley?"

"It's worth investigating. Get someone in uniform to take over this incident room, Hilary. I'll call in a couple of cars to follow us, and we'll go and take a look at Curlew Lodge."

*   *   *

The un-signposted side road they turned on to, about five miles north of Fodderstone, had once been metalled. Grass was now growing along the middle of it. On the left was the heath, a relic of the original Breckland wastes, rusty with heather and thinly scattered with hawthorn bushes and birch trees. On the right was a harvested field, blackened by fires from which smoke was still drifting.

A belt of Scots pine at right angles to the road marked the boundary of the arable land. Once they were through the trees there was heath on either side of the road, which had now deteriorated into a dusty track. Half a mile ahead, a dark stand of conifers on Ministry of Defence land blocked the way completely.

But on this side of the conifers, with their windscreens setting up a dazzle as they caught the late afternoon sun, stood the vehicles the detectives had come to find. A piece of heathland had been levelled and hardcore had been put down to provide an all-weather parking area. It was completely full, with more than twice the number of vehicles Tait had seen.

Quantrill stopped his car across the track, blocking the escape route of everything except Land Rovers and motor-bikes. He got out. Hilary followed, carrying a clipboard, and they searched among the vehicles for the makes and registration numbers they wanted.

They were all there: Howard Braithwaite's nearly new Rover 2600, Phil Goodwin's rusting Cortina, the Japanese pick-up trucks owned by Stan Bolderow and Reg Osler. Of the Flintknappers Arms regulars, only Charley Horrocks was wheel-less; but that didn't mean he wasn't there too.

"They couldn't have chosen a more isolated place, if this is where they kept Sandra Websdell," said Hilary, looking at the building on the far side of the car park. It was an old single-storey barn, its flint walls solid, its pantiled roof showing signs of recent repair. The heavy wooden door, now wide open, looked brand new. "And perhaps it's where they're keeping Annabel Yardley now . . . but what in God's name are they *doing*?"

Curlew Lodge seemed to be throbbing with noise. The emanation was so powerful that Quantrill almost expected to see short straight lines radiating from the building, as in a cartoonist's sketch. The basic source of the throb, he decided, must be a diesel generator somewhere on the far side of the barn. But coming from the building itself was the roar of excited masculine voices, urging something or someone on.

"You'd better get back in the car, Hilary," said Quantrill. "Whatever it is, it's a stag event. I'll try to go in as a punter, and if they see you they'll immediately be suspicious. Call up the other cars, and—quick, get down, there's somebody coming out."

A heavily built man had just erupted unsteadily from the barn doorway. Quantrill hurried towards him. "Not too late, am I?" he called. "It's not over, is it?"

"No—got to go for a leak, I'm bursting!" The man was sweating copiously, his jowls dripping, his shirt saturated, whisky on his breath. His bloodshot eyes glistened with excitement, and there was a stupid grin on his face as he made his way round to the back of the barn.

The Chief Inspector kept him company. A young man was already there, crouched on the ground vomiting, but the two older men ignored him.

"Worth coming all this way, then?" said Quantrill.

"I'll say! I've come up from Essex—used to do business with Howard Braithwaite, and he gave me the word. God, the money that's flying about in there!"

"High stakes?"

"I'll say! But all properly organized, with a bookmaker Howard's roped in. The whole set-up's first class. Local pub landlord's got a bar going, pricey of course but well stocked. A tenner to get in, mind, but what the hell—it's only money."

Quantrill agreed, hoping that he had that much in his back pocket. He'd left his wallet in his coat in the car, and he didn't want to lose contact with his new acquaintance while he fetched it.

"First time you've been here?" he asked as they walked back round the building.

"No, I came on Tuesday evening for the trial run. I was in Breckham Market on business, so I thought I'd see whether it would be worth coming up again today. And it was! The wife thinks I'm playing golf, o'course . . ."

"Many people here on Tuesday?"

"Mainly Howard and the locals—Phil who runs the bar, and a few others."

"Can you remember who they were?"

The florid man lurched to a stop, putting a hand against the flints of the barn wall to support himself. He looked at

Quantrill with suspicion, squinting against the sun. "What's it to you?" he asked with slurred aggressiveness.

The Chief Inspector showed him his warrant card. The man peered at it, trying to focus. Then he slumped back against the wall. "Oh my God . . ."

"You're small fry," said Quantrill. "I'm not interested in you. Just tell me who was here on Tuesday—if you don't know their names, describe them."

The florid man mumbled brief descriptions. Two of the men Quantrill didn't recognize; but the others were unmistakably Charley Horrocks, Stan Bolderow and Reg Osler.

Quantrill handed over his informant to Sergeant Lloyd, went up to the barn and paid his money at the door to a swarthy man he didn't know.

"Who's your contact?" asked the doorman warily.

"Howard Braithwaite."

The doorman nodded him in. "You'll find Howard in his office behind the bar—he keeps his eyes on the money, not on the action! You've just missed the video, but the live action'll start again in a few minutes."

The Chief Inspector stepped inside the barn and immediately became engulfed in heat and noise. The place was heaving with men, all of them on some kind of high.

At first, Quantrill found it difficult to see through the gloom. Any natural light in the building had been blocked off. Electric fans whirred overhead, but all they were doing was stirring up smells of tobacco and sweat and alcohol. There were also other smells that he couldn't immediately identify, stomach-contracting whiffs of something degradingly earthy.

The interior of the barn was arranged like a three-sided boxing arena, with rows of seats facing a small, raised, spotlit ring. On the far wall was a large video screen, now blank. Below the screen, on a platform beside the ring, was a bookmaker's stand.

The bookie was hard at work, bawling the odds on the next piece of action. Shirt-sleeved punters milled about, placing bets, buying drinks, shouting to make themselves heard. Quantrill caught a glimpse of Phil Goodwin behind the bar, serving flat out and flushed with money-making success; and a more distant glimpse of Howard Braithwaite, aloof from the activity but showing signs of satisfaction at having master-minded it.

A buzzer sounded. Punters hurried for their seats. And there at the ringside, unshaven, red-faced, gleeful in antici-pation of the spectacle about to be presented, was Charley Horrocks; beside him, Bolderow and Osler.

Got them, thought Quantrill with grim satisfaction. *Whatever they've done to Sandra Websdell and Annabel Yardley, at least we've got the lot of 'em red-handed.*

A second spotlight illuminated the high, wired-in ring. The spectators hushed, tense with excitement. Bodies leaned for-ward, eyes gleamed, lips were compulsively licked.

In the hush, an unseen cockerel began to crow.

36

Chief Inspector Quantrill drove away from Curlew Lodge in a bad temper. He was disgusted by what he had seen, and furious because he felt that he had been conned; so furious that he had left it to his back-up team to sort out the punters. All he wanted to do at the moment was to get away from Howard Braithwaite—and from Goodwin and Osler and Bolderow and Charley Horrocks—as quickly as possible.

"I do believe you're disappointed," Hilary Lloyd accused him as, muttering crossly, he drove at a jolting speed over the rough track. "What did you expect to see? Bestiality? Gang rape? Women wrestling in mud?"

"Nothing of the sort," Quantrill growled. "I'd hoped to find Annabel Yardley, that's all. This whole episode, coming in the middle of our enquiry into Sandra Websdell's death, has been a complete waste of time."

"We weren't to know that. It was sheer bad luck that the Flintknappers Arms gang should have been holding their trial run on Tuesday evening, just at the time of Sandra's death. And that they couldn't admit what they'd been up to, because it's illegal and they'd intended to make a regular practice of it. Would it really have paid off for them, though, do you think? They must have made a big investment, and their running expenses would have been pretty high."

"Oh, Braithwaite would have costed it out, you can be sure of that. He's a businessman, he knew what he was doing. He must have calculated that the combination of gambling and blood-sport would bring enough big spenders to make the risk worth while."

"I still don't understand," said Hilary, who hadn't entered the barn until after the Chief Inspector had put a stop to the contest, "how the cocks can be persuaded to fight."

"These aren't ordinary domestic roosters," said Quantrill impatiently. "They belong to special breeds—I saw some illustrations in the cock-fighting chapter of the book Braithwaite had at his boathouse. Apparently they're bred for strength and aggressiveness."

"Who was handling them, then? I can't imagine—"

"No, it wasn't any of the Flintknappers Arms lot. The entertainment was arranged by an unsavoury pair of brothers from somewhere down in Essex, who breed the birds. It seems they've been hooked on cockfighting since they saw it in the Canary Islands, where it's legal. That's where they got the idea of using a ring rather than a cock-pit—it gives the punters a better view. They'd also brought some films of cockfights to pad out the live action.

"The whole thing was thoroughly organized. The brothers had a set of scales, and the birds were matched by weight, like boxers. I didn't stay to find out how many birds had been brought here this afternoon, but I can't imagine there'd have been many to take back. They fight to the death, and the winner I saw was so badly injured that I wouldn't give much for its chances of survival."

Hilary expressed her disgust on behalf of the birds, and Quantrill said no more. He was very glad that she hadn't been present at the fight. His own stomach had almost been turned, as much by the stench of the droppings that covered the ring as by the flying blood and feathers of the cocks themselves. The cruelty involved—the deliberate goading of the birds by their handlers at the start of the bout, the cutting and taping of their viciously sharp natural spurs so that the fights would be bloodily prolonged—was sickening.

But what disturbed Quantrill more than the suffering of the birds was the effect on the spectators themselves. Even though he could remember the excitement of being one of a hunting pack, the insidious lure of cruelty, he had been taken aback by the blood-lust of these punters. There they were—respectable businessmen for the most part, probably pet-lovers, kind fathers, decent husbands—howling instructions to the bird their money was on to savage its opponent, slash out its eyes, kill, kill, kill.

Cockfighting was bound to brutalize its spectators. And people who became brutalized—hooked on the excitement of seeing blood spilled, the spectacle of mutilation and pain— could in time become bored with the same old entertainment. Then, Quantrill feared, they might start to look for alternative victims, greater excitement, more blood, more obvious pain; and God knew where that kind of search might lead. Having learned, with difficulty, to control his own youthful propensity towards impulsive violence, he was angered at having witnessed a commercially engineered breakdown of civilized behaviour. Just as well, then, that this Fodderstone set-up had been discovered before it became established.

The penalties for illegal cockfighting, and for causing unnecessary suffering to animals, were regrettably minor: fines, that was all. But the case should attract a good deal of adverse publicity in the national as well as the local press, and Braithwaite would hate that. The Essex police would clamp down on the breeders, and none of the Fodderstone men would be likely to try it again. So perhaps, concluded the Chief Inspector, his ill-temper abating, this had been a useful week's work after all.

He must remember to make a point of letting the Assistant Chief Constable know that a good deal of the credit belonged to young Martin Tait.

"At least," said Quantrill as he turned on to the metalled road and drove more circumspectly towards civilization, "we know now that the Flintknappers Arms mob weren't involved in Sandra Websdell's death. We're back with the probability that she was abducted just before her wedding by someone who wanted her for himself. And we both know who *that's* most likely to be."

37

They found Albert Thorold exactly where they had left him on their previous visit.

Hilary followed Quantrill into the porch of the woodman's cottage with reluctance. It was always easiest to confront suspects who were, anyway, nasty pieces of work. Sadly, she had really liked Christopher and his Pa, who were so much nicer than the Flintknappers Arms lot.

But it was her own observation that led her to agree with the Chief Inspector about the Thorolds. She had remembered, when Quantrill had told her Andrew Stagg's story about the Hooray Henries and the garden gnome, that when she first saw the gnome there had been some loose fragments of plaster crumbling away from its damaged leg. The plaster was touched with green and red paint, and she had seen some similar fragments on her first visit to the woodyard.

She could recall that incident clearly. Christopher had taken them to his barn, and the three of them were talking outside when he had suddenly taken a long step forward and started shuffling his boots about. That was when she had caught a glimpse of the coloured fragments of plaster, before he had hidden them in the dust.

There was evidence, then, that the Websdells' gnome had been on the Thorolds' property. This had convinced her, in her own mind, that it was Christopher who had abducted Sandra. Only someone like Christopher would have imagined that he could abduct the girl and then talk her into staying with him. And when he couldn't persuade her to cooperate— when he found that he had to tether her to stop her from running away—he might well have decided to fetch something familiar for her from her home, in an attempt to keep her happy.

And this theory fitted in with the mysterious comings and goings of the gnome. It had been taken, in good condition, from the Websdells' garden on the Friday night after Sandra disappeared. But the Hooray Henries had found it, damaged, outside the Websdells' gate on the Saturday night. Whoever took it on Friday must have kept it for about 24 hours, during which time the damage was done. Hilary's guess was that Sandra, a girl of spirit, had probably thrown the gnome at Christopher when he offered it to her . . . and that he, a lop-sidedly conscientious man, had returned it to the Websdells' gate after dark on the Saturday, shortly before the Hooray Henries had arrived.

It was speculation, of course. What they needed was evidence—and as Quantrill had pointed out, testily, they'd have had the Thorolds' barn thoroughly searched long before, if they hadn't been mesmerised by the Flintknappers Arms mob. And if they hadn't then been obliged to tie up all their manpower in the search for Annabel Yardley.

Quantrill had come to the conclusion that if Christopher had abducted Sandra and lost her, the chances were that he had taken Mrs. Yardley as a replacement. They knew that she wasn't in his barn, because that had already been visited briefly in the search for her, but he might well have hidden her somewhere else. There was no need, though, in the Chief Inspector's opinion, to barge in with a new search party. If Annabel Yardley was there, the old man would know about it; and Quantrill didn't anticipate much difficulty in persuading him to give her up.

In the airless, fly-ridden living room, Albert Thorold sat exactly as before, cap on head, pet hen on knee. Both man and bird were dozing.

Quantrill rapped on the open door. The hen woke first, shooting up its head like an indignant periscope and making strangled warning noises. The old man soothed it and slowly opened his gummy eyes. "Come you in," he mumbled. "You'll be wanting eggs?"

The Chief Inspector stepped into the room over the smelly, recumbent dog, and reminded Albert Thorold who he was. "Sergeant Lloyd and I," he said, "are looking for a lady who's been thrown from her horse."

"Still looking for her?" the old man asked, his solemn face expressionless. "There were policemen here yesterday doing that. Seemed to think she might be in our barn . . ."

"But she wasn't," Quantrill acknowledged. "I thought you might know her, though, Mr. Thorold. Her name's Mrs. Yardley—Annabel Yardley."

"Can't say I ever heard of her, afore yesterday."

"No reason why you should've," agreed Quantrill. Then he added, "Her maiden name was Horrocks."

Albert Thorold's eyes opened wider. "That's a rum 'un," he commented, continuing to stroke the hen; it had quietened down, but it still kept a suspicious black eye on the visitors. "Same name as the family who used to live at the Hall—the Earls of Brandon."

He spoke the name with pride and respect. Hilary encouraged him to talk about his own family's long connection of service with the Horrockses. Then the Chief Inspector said, casually, "The lady who's missing—Mrs. Yardley, who was Annabel Horrocks—is in fact a member of the family. Didn't you know that, Mr. Thorold? Her uncle is the present Earl."

The news upset Albert Thorold. His eyes stared, his mouth trembled open, his dewlap shook. He clutched the hen so hard that it squawked in protest.

"I didn't know . . ." the old man quavered. "As God's my witness, Mister, I didn't know that! The boy found her, y'see, thrown off her horse, unconscious. He reckoned it was all right to bring her back here because she lived alone and she'd got no family. He thought there'd be nobody to miss her. I told her she'd be sought for, but once he gets an idea in his head there's no persuading him. If he'd known she was a Horrocks, though—granddaughter of the very Earl I was gamekeeper to—he'd never have brought her here. Never."

"Where is she, Mr. Thorold?" asked Hilary.

"Why, in his old den in the woodyard, like as not. Place he made for hisself when he was a boy. Couldn't keep her in the house, or she might have called out when somebody came for eggs. He'd have put her in the barn, I daresay, if he wasn't afeared you'd look there. She's alive and well, I know that. Christopher means her no harm, Miss. He just needs a woman here. I reckon he thought if he picked her up and tended her, she'd be grateful enough to stay."

"But you told us you didn't want to have a woman here, Mr. Thorold."

"No more I don't, Miss—no offence to you. But I can't get about like I used to. My old legs won't go. There's things as have to be done for me, and the boy's afeared he won't be able to manage. He feels the want of a wife."

"And that was why he took Sandra Websdell, wasn't it?" said Quantrill.

Albert Thorold's lips trembled. "The boy was right fond of her," he said. "He'd hoped for her ever since she was a little 'un, only he was too shy to speak for her. He meant her no harm. She never should ha' died . . ."

"Did you know at the time that your son had abducted Sandra?" Quantrill asked him.

There was a distant look in the old man's pale eyes. "Not at first, I didn't. Not 'til he started taking food out to the barn. I couldn't stop him doing what he wanted, not without the use of my legs. I told him he couldn't keep her, but he was sure she'd settle."

"You knew your son was doing wrong, Mr. Thorold," said Quantrill sternly. "You knew that it was a wicked thing to take a girl away from her family and friends, and keep her shut up against her will. I believe you're related by marriage to Sandra's mother, so you knew perfectly well how anguished she'd be. Why didn't you try to get a message to Mrs. Websdell? You could have done that easily enough, by way of someone who came here for eggs."

The old man shook his head. " 'Twouldn't have done. Christopher was too set on keeping Sandra. He wouldn't have given her up."

"All the more reason why you should have notified someone, Mr. Thorold. Your son can't be allowed to behave in that way. You know that."

Albert Thorold slowly straightened his back. The stiff old hands ceased their stroking of the pet hen. Looking directly at the Chief Inspector, he spoke with passionate, dignified reproach.

"Even an ol' rat will look after his own, Mister. Even an ol' *rat* will look after his own."

Somewhere in the woodyard, where swifts making the most of the evening light wheeled and swooped for insects, a chainsaw was screeching.

Following the sound past the piles of logs and the teepees of larch poles, Chief Inspector Quantrill and Sergeant Lloyd came upon Christopher Thorold. He was cutting up the trunk of a dead elm tree, his eyes protected by goggles from flying sawdust, his grip two-handed, his legs braced to control the weight and power of the petrol-driven saw.

Knowing that it would be dangerous to try to attract the

man's attention while he was using the chainsaw, Quantrill
waited. Christopher Thorold finished the cut he was making,
and allowed the machine to idle while he pushed the goggles
up on to his greying, tufted hair and wiped his sweating face
with his shirt-sleeve.

Wasting no time on preliminaries, the Chief Inspector
called to him, "Christopher! Where is she? Where is Mrs.
Yardley?"

Taken completely by surprise, Christopher gaped. Quantrill
said it again, and the man turned his head sharply away, as a
child does when it wants to pretend that it hasn't heard an
inconvenient question.

Hilary, moving up on his other side, tried to coax him.
"We do know that Mrs. Yardley's here, Christopher. You
can't keep her, you know. It would never do—she's one of
the Horrockses. Her uncle's the Earl of Brandon, and he
wants her back."

Christopher stammered with astonishment, "I—I didn't
know that . . ."

"I'm sure you didn't. Where is she?"

Still holding his chainsaw, the man frowned and hung his
head and shifted his boots. Hilary talked to him kindly, and
eventually Christopher nodded with reluctance towards a
distant pile of tree-trunks, in form not unlike a windowless
log cabin. "She's all right," he assured them. "Only she won't
settle . . ."

Hilary used her personal radio to call up the uniformed
men who were waiting out of sight in the lane. They hurried
into the woodyard and released Annabel Yardley. She emerged
from her prison dazed, dirty, but still elegant and extremely
vocal, and was helped away to the police car. Christopher
watched her go. "I—I meant her no harm," he protested.

"Probably not," said Quantrill heavily. "I don't suppose
you meant any harm to Sandra Websdell, either. But that
poor girl's dead, and we need to know how and why. You'd
better switch that chainsaw off, and go and tell your Pa you're
coming with us."

It seemed to take a few minutes for his words to sink in.
Christopher Thorold turned his unshaven face from one detective to the other, at first uncomprehending, then with
growing anguish. Finally he gave his head a stubborn shake,
and pulled down his goggles. Turning his back on them—

childishly, Quantrill thought—he put the engine up to full speed and raised the chainsaw shoulder-high over the tree-trunk.

It was only then that Hilary remembered the previous conversation she'd had with Christopher Thorold: how he'd told her that he loved his home in the forest, and that he would rather die than leave it.

Whether or not that remark was significant, neither she nor Quantrill would ever know. With Christopher's burly back to them, it was impossible for them to see what he was doing.

It could have been an accident. Chainsaws are notoriously dangerous. A moment's inattention, an unbalanced stance, an encounter with a nail embedded in the wood, and the saw can leap out of the user's control with the chain blades still whizzing round at a speed designed to cut through a hardwood tree in a matter of seconds.

All the detectives could see, as Christopher's chainsaw began to scream through a solid object, was that the jet-stream flying from it was composed of his life's blood.

38

On the day of Constance Schultz's funeral, it poured with rain.

Martin Tait drove to the Saintsbury crematorium alone. His mother—Con's sister-in-law—had pulled a calf muscle while overdoing her exercises, and was unable to attend. Apart from two old cousins in Eastbourne who were too frail to travel, Con had no other relatives.

Tait had tried to get in touch with his aunt's best friend, an old school chum, Eileen Farleigh. He knew that the two women had often taken holidays together and usually visited each other at least once a year. Mrs. Farleigh, a widow, lived in Shropshire. Martin wrote to tell her of her friend's death but received no reply. Expecting that she would want to be present at the funeral service—and hoping that he would not have to be the sole immediate mourner—he tried on two occasions to telephone her, without success.

It seemed, though, that there would be no lack of other

mourners. The newspaper notices of Constance Schultz's death had brought messages that a number of her friends and former colleagues from Woodbridge and Ipswich intended to be present. She had evidently been well regarded, and Tait was surprised, touched and ultimately ashamed to receive so many letters of condolence.

He had decided, after all, to put *"dear aunt of Martin"* in the notices. Not to do so might, he thought, be interpreted in some quarters as an admission of guilt.

From the residents of Fodderstone he had heard nothing but an accusatory silence. Despite the fact that the coroner had returned a verdict of suicide on his aunt, as far as the local community was concerned Marjorie Braithwaite's allegations had stuck.

Thank God he didn't live in the village. At least he need never see any of them again.

But what he hadn't taken into consideration was that, whatever they might feel about him, her Fodderstone friends would want to pay their last respects to Constance Schultz. The first thing he noticed, as he paced into the crematorium chapel behind her coffin, was the complete emptiness of the immediate mourners' pews on the right-hand side, where he would have to sit. The second thing was that the left-hand pews, almost full, contained many of the villagers he had hoped not to see; among them Mrs. Braithwaite, looking at her most formidable.

Martin Tait went to his conspicuous place in the front row. Most of the Fodderstone people had turned their heads away from him as he walked past, but he had seen nudges, and heard sharp inhalations of breath. Perhaps they'd thought he wouldn't have the nerve to come? Standing exposed, with his back to them, he sensed that they were watching him with undisguised hostility.

And then, just as the service was about to start, three late-comers hurried in and chose to stand behind him; two rows back, in acknowledgement of the fact that they were not family mourners, but at least on his side of the chapel. It would have been impolite for him to turn and look, but he recognized two sets of footsteps as women's. Moving his head slightly, he saw out of the corner of his eye that the third newcomer was Douglas Quantrill.

How very decent of the old man to come and give him such public support! Surprised and gratified, Tait sensed some of the tension of the past few weeks draining away. He hardly heard the opening prayers as he recalled what a hell of a time it had been: the row with Aunt Con, her death, the sticky interview with the Assistant Chief Constable, the ordeal of the inquest—and now this final ordeal of the funeral service.

But it was a great help to feel that his back was covered. Tait held his head high, and opened the hymn book. Having realized that there would be a sizeable congregation he had arranged for the inclusion in the service of all the music Aunt Con had wanted: not only part of the Fauré *Requiem*, but also the favourite hymn that, with characteristic diffidence, she had thought there would be too few people to sing.

The Taits had always been a musical family, and Martin knew that he had a pleasant light baritone voice. Thinking of nothing but the impression he wanted to make on the rest of the congregation, he opened his lungs and sang.

> Dear Lord and Father of mankind
> Forgive our foolish ways:
> Reclothe us in our rightful mind;
> In purer lives Thy service find,
> In deeper reverence, praise.

It was not until somewhere in the third verse that he found his thoughts dwelling on his aunt. There had been so many other things for him to think about that he had not taken into account the fact that he might be moved by her funeral service. But now, unexpectedly, the lines

> The silence of eternity
> Interpreted by love

caught him by the throat.

Too choked to continue, he stared dumbly at Aunt Con's plain coffin, with his wreath of her favourite pink Zephirine Drouhin roses on it. He remembered the lifetime of kindness he had had from her, her funny awkwardnesses, the final embrace she had given him. He thought with remorse of their quarrel, and with guilt of the way she had died.

> Drop Thy still dews of quietness,
> Till all our strivings cease;
> Take from our souls the strain and stress—

Her friends—more of them than he or she had imagined—
sang on, subdued. Martin was beyond singing. He stood stiff,
his eyes tightly closed, his tongue pressed hard against the
roof of his mouth, trying to hold back the seeping tears.
Ashamed to be seen to pull out his handkerchief, he wiped
his cheeks furtively with his fingers.

It was then that he became aware that someone had moved
out from the pew behind and was coming to stand beside
him. He glanced sideways, and his heart lifted as he glimpsed
Alison Quantrill's sweet grave face, and the beautiful eyes
that were damp with sympathetic tears.

Neither of them managed to sing the final verse, but they
gave each other silent support by sharing the same hymn
book.

"It's been a long time . . ."

They were at last alone together, having tea in the lounge
of the Angel hotel at Saintsbury. Realizing that he ought to
have made some provision of refreshment after the funeral
service, Martin had felt obliged to ask Hilary Lloyd and
Douglas Quantrill as well; but they both said they had to get
back to work.

Even so, there had been a delay while Martin stood at the
chapel doors during the Fauré *In Paradisum* to thank his
aunt's friends for coming. The attitude of the Fodderstone
contingent varied. Some, like Marjorie Braithwaite, swept
out into the rain pretending not to see him. Others, like
Geoff Websdell and Lois Goodwin, gave him a non-committal
nod. Only Beryl Websdell pressed his hand warmly and said,
"God bless you"; but then she would have done the same to
any sinner.

And now he faced Alison Quantrill over the teacups, talking to her for the first time since their stupid quarrel. That,
he remembered, had been about his aunt . . . "It's no use
avoiding the subject," he said. "A lot of people still think I
killed Aunt Con for her money."

"*I* don't," protested Alison. "Neither does Dad, nor Hilary.
Besides, you've been officially cleared—the coroner said he
was satisfied that your aunt had taken her own life."

"That's not the point," said Tait. "There is such a thing as
getting away with murder, if you're clever enough to destroy
all the evidence against you. You may be officially innocent,

but some people will go on thinking—and saying—you did it for the rest of your life."

"Oh, who cares about a pack of busybodies," said Alison.

"It's not the Marjorie Braithwaites of this world I'm worried about. It's my colleagues in the police force. Not all of them are as fair-minded as your father and Hilary Lloyd. Being selected for accelerated promotion has never made me popular with the PC Plods of this division, and you can bet they'll make sure the whole county force hears of this allegation against me."

Alison looked at him with sympathy. She had never seen Martin so vulnerable as he had been at his aunt's funeral, or so savagely depressed as he was now. But she couldn't help thinking how pale and handsome he looked in a black tie and a new, obviously expensive, dark-grey worsted suit.

"Couldn't you transfer to another county force?" she asked.

"Hell, no! That is, I *could*, but I'd be crazy to do it. For one thing, it would look like an admission of guilt. For another, however far I tried to run, somebody would make sure that the allegation went with me. No, I'm staying here."

He summoned a waiter and ordered a fresh pot of tea. There were plates of sandwiches and cakes on the table, but neither of them was hungry.

"I know you well enough not to suggest that you could leave the police force altogether," said Alison. "Dad says that your career is more important to you than anything else."

"It's a lot more important than lousy money, I'll tell you," he said. "That's something I've realized in these last few weeks. I love my job, and I want to make high rank—but in this atmosphere of suspicion, my file's certain to be marked. Even though there's nothing official against me, there'll always be a question-mark beside my name."

"But what about your promotion?"

"Oh, I don't suppose it will be blocked completely. I might even make Superintendent. But they'll certainly stop me from going any higher. It would never do, would it, to make a Chief Superintendent—let alone an Assistant Chief Constable —of a man who's suspected of murdering his aunt."

Hating to see him so bitter, she put a hand on his. "It'll be a nine-day wonder, Martin. Your colleagues may be talking about it now, but they'll forget it sooner than you imagine."

"With the fortune Aunt Con's left me? Not a chance! Not that I've got any of the money yet, my solicitor says it'll be

months before everything's sorted out. But it's a lot, Alison—
well over a quarter of a million."

She moved her hand away immediately, embarrassed lest
he should think she had designs on him.

"And *that*," he went on, "is why the suspicion will never go
away. Don't you see? The money will give me the kind of
lifestyle I've always wanted. I can have my own aeroplane,
more than one car, a big house. I'll be the envy of every
copper in the force. As a result, they'll make me pay for
being rich by keeping the story alive: *There's Tait, throwing
his poor old aunt's money about again. And we all know how
he got it from her, don't we?* Let's face it, I'm going to be a
social outcast. And the same will go for my wife, too."

The waiter approached with fresh tea. While he was busy
at their table, changing the teapots, Alison and Martin glanced
at each other. Their eyes met, sparked and locked.

The waiter went. Without premeditation, Martin heard
himself say: "Taking account of all that . . . and bearing in
mind that I've missed you, and I love you and I need you . . .
would you consider marrying me?"

Alison found that she was breathing more quickly than
usual. "If—if I answered you now," she said nervously, "when
I'm feeling very sympathetic towards you, it would probably
be 'Yes'. But you wouldn't want me to accept you out of
sympathy, would you? Let me think about it, please. I'm
going on holiday tomorrow, to stay with some friends in
Wales for a couple of weeks. I'll answer you for sure when I
come back."

39

Three days after his aunt's funeral, Martin Tait received a
telephone call from her old school friend, Eileen Farleigh.

Mrs. Farleigh had just returned from a visit to a daughter
in Canada. She had originally expected to come back in early
August, but her visit had been prolonged by an injury she
had received in a car accident.

She was now telephoning to thank Martin for his letter
telling her of Con's death, and to express her sympathy and

her own sorrow. There was also something she had to tell
him . . . but it was much too difficult to discuss over the
telephone. In fact, it ought to be done officially, through
their respective lawyers. Would Martin please be good enough
to give her the name and address of his solicitor?

Within forty-eight hours, Martin was asked to call on his
solicitor as a matter of urgency.

When he had needed a lawyer to accompany him at his
interview with the Assistant Chief Constable, he had chosen
an acquaintance, an up-and-coming young solicitor who was a
partner in an old-established firm with offices in the cathedral
close at Yarchester. William Carrow had as sharp an eye as
Tait's own, but he chose to camouflage it by wearing a flow-
ing late-Victorian beard in a rich shade of chestnut brown.

"Good news, and bad," he said. "First the good—"

He handed Martin a photocopy of a letter written by
Constance Schultz on the day before her death. It was addressed to her friend Eileen Farleigh, and it told of Con's
intention to take her own life, in her car.

"A note for the coroner was also enclosed with this letter.
I've sent it on to him to confirm his finding," said William
Carrow. "Had Mrs. Farleigh been at home when the letter
arrived, as Mrs. Schultz expected, there would of course
have been no question about your aunt's death."

Tait felt shaken by the sight of Con's handwriting, the sad
matter-of-factness of her letter, the affectionate farewell para-
graph. "You call this good?" he said. "I don't. Nothing can
undo the fact that I quarrelled with my aunt, and said unfor-
givable things to her that were overheard by a busybody of a
neighbour. I know that I didn't kill Aunt Con, but I do feel in
some way responsible for her death. I put so much pressure
on her, because I wanted her money, that I probably drove
her to kill herself. That's what the whole county police force
is going to believe and say about me."

"Relax," advised his solicitor, leaning back in his chair and
fitting his thumbs into the pockets of his waistcoat. His lean
stomach was ornamented with a watch and chain not unlike
the one Tait was wearing, except that his was only silver.

"Mrs. Schultz's death had nothing to do with you," William
Carrow went on. "Mrs. Farleigh has told her own solicitor
that she and your aunt discussed the subject of death on

several occasions. Mrs. Schultz was extremely anxious not to
go the same way as her mother—your grandmother. I understand that the old lady kept her health well into her nineties,
but lost her wits long before she died."

"I didn't know that," said Tait. "Granny was in a nursing
home for about five years, but—"

"Not a nursing home, according to Mrs. Farleigh. Your
aunt looked after her mother for as long as she could, and
then had to put her—for the sake of her own sanity—in a
private psychiatric hospital. It wasn't a fate that appealed to
Mrs. Schultz herself. She told Mrs. Farleigh some years ago
that she found the Almighty's arrangements for dying unsatisfactory, and that she intended to make her own."

Tait looked up, surprised and slightly shocked. "Some years
ago? Good grief, I had no idea . . ."

"And then in May of this year, when she was staying with
Mrs. Farleigh in Shropshire, Mrs. Schultz said she was beginning to feel that she'd had enough. She was forgetting, mislaying things, becoming easily confused, and so on. She told
Mrs. Farleigh that she might well end her life before long,
and that she'd write and tell her when she made the decision.
It was extremely unfortunate for you that we've only just
heard about your aunt's letter, but I'll pass it on to your
Assistant Chief Constable and that should finally clear your
name."

"Thanks, William," said Tait, dazed. Poor old Aunt Con . . .
what a hell of a life she must have had with Granny. How
grim it must have been for her to imagine that she was going
the same way . . .

He got up to leave, but William Carrow was already on his
feet and opening a corner cabinet. "What about a drink,
Martin? I should have one, if I were you. I haven't told you
the bad news yet."

Half-suspecting what was coming, Tait clutched at a glass
of single malt whisky. "Is it—my aunt's will?"

" 'Fraid so. She decided to make a new one, on her last
visit to her friend. Apparently Mrs. Schultz wasn't too keen
on using the Woodbridge firm, once the family connection
had been severed. Mrs. Farleigh recommended her own
solicitor in Shrewsbury, and that's where your aunt went.
She decided against taking a copy of the will home with her
to Fodderstone, because she was getting so absent-minded
that she thought she'd only lose it."

Tait swallowed some whisky to lubricate his throat. "The new will's valid, I suppose?"

"Perfectly. And of course it invalidates the previous will made in your favour. I believe you said your aunt told you the terms of her new will?"

"Ten thousand?" Tait mumbled queasily.

William Carrow nodded his patriarchal head. "Tough, I know. All the same, you're a lucky devil, Martin. You're not even married . . . I've got a wife, three children and a hefty mortgage. I'd be overjoyed if I had an aunt who was leaving ten thousand to me."

Martin made his way out into the damp cathedral close. A few days of rain, and the heat of the summer was over.

He felt numbed. Pacing across the close towards the cloister car-park where he had left his ageing Alfa, he sought to come to terms with his changed circumstances.

At least his career in the police force was no longer blighted.

At least he was no longer suspected of having killed Aunt Con.

At least his own conscience was more or less clear.

But he knew now that he would never get the money he so badly wanted; the money he'd been counting on getting, ever since his mother had told him about his aunt's will on his eighteenth birthday.

He'd assured Alison that his career mattered more to him than money, and that was true. But now he actually *needed* the money. After all, he'd proposed to her on the strength of it.

If Alison should accept him—and he couldn't imagine that she would refuse—how could he possibly afford to marry her on nothing but his police pay? It wasn't practicable, unless he completely gave up his hobby of flying. He loved her very much, and he was prepared to give up his freedom for her; but not his share in the aeroplane, not yet.

He was still waiting for her answer. If she accepted him, what the hell was he going to do?

On holiday in Wales, and unaware that Martin wasn't in possession of a fortune after all, Alison made up her mind how to answer him when she returned in a week's time.

She acknowledged now what she had known all along, but had refused to admit to herself: that she and Martin were not really suited. It was his attitude towards his newly acquired wealth that had finally convinced her. *The money will give me the kind of lifestyle I've always wanted,* he'd said. *I can have my own aeroplane, more than one car, a big house . . .*

But that high-flying lifestyle wasn't what Alison herself wanted. Marriage to an ostentatiously rich Martin would, she knew, distance her from all her friends and relations; and the prospect depressed her. Regretfully, because she had been very much in love with him throughout that long hot August, she knew that the only answer she could give him would be a sympathetic "No".

ABOUT THE AUTHOR

SHEILA RADLEY worked in a variety of professional jobs until the 1960s when she left London to help run a village store and post office. She is the author of *Death in the Morning, The Chief Inspector's Daughter, A Talent for Destruction,* and *The Quiet Road to Death.*

50 YEARS OF GREAT AMERICAN MYSTERIES
FROM BANTAM BOOKS

Stuart Palmer

"Those who have not already made the acquaintance of Hildegarde Withers should make haste to do so, for she is one of the world's shrewdest and most amusing detectives."
—*New York Times*
May 6, 1934

☐ 25934-2 THE PUZZLE OF THE SILVER PERSIAN (1934) $2.95
☐ 26024-3 THE PUZZLE OF THE HAPPY HOOLIGAN
(1941) $2.95
Featuring spinster detective Hildegarde Withers

Craig Rice

"Why can't all murders be as funny as those concocted by Craig Rice?   —*New York Times*
☐ 26345-5 HAVING WONDERFUL CRIME $2.95
"Miss Rice at her best, writing about her 3 favorite characters against a delirious New York background."
—*New Yorker*
☐ 26222-X MY KINGDOM FOR A HEARSE $2.95
"Pretty damn wonderful!"   —*New York Times*

Barbara Paul

☐ 26234-3 RENEWABLE VIRGIN (1985) $2.95
"The talk crackles, the characters are bouncy, and New York's media world is caught with all its vitality and vulgarity."   —*Washington Post Book World*
☐ 26225-4 KILL FEE (1985) $2.95
"A desperately treacherous game of cat-and-mouse whose well-wrought tension is heightened by a freakish twist that culminates in a particularly chilling conclusion." —*Booklist*

For your ordering convenience, use the handy coupon below: